It all seems simple enough—Ukrainian immigrant Nadja Petrov is determined to hold on to her thriving new coffee shop, Nadja's Literary Cappuccino, and Java Beans District Rep Kevin Langley is equally determined to move into her North Iowa town with a franchise and run her out of business.

He scopes her out, she keeps a watchful eye on him, and the sparring begins. But there are other players involved, and the web of intrigue soon threatens Nadja, her shop, and her aunt as well as Kevin, his potential franchise, and his son. Within this cauldron simmers a sexual attraction between Nadja and Kevin that catapults them to overcome their fears of intimacy and commitment. Their lovemaking is tender and raw. Their love is nearly lost in tragedy—can it survive doubts, fire, and even a death?

I am Not for Sale
Copyright © 2021 Adriana Kraft
ISBN: 978-1-4874-3458-8
Cover art by Martine Jardin

Published by eXtasy Books Inc

Look for us online at:
www.eXtasybooks.com

I am Not for Sale

By

Adriana Kraft

CHAPTER ONE

Glancing quickly at the clock on the far wall of her small coffee shop, Nadja fought back annoyance at customers who arrived when she was ready to close and go home. But in America, she reminded herself, the customer was always right.

She managed a small smile for the tall dark-haired man wearing a classic blue sport coat with a red tie knotted loosely about his neck. It was the end of the workday. He was probably grabbing a coffee for the drive home. "How may I help you?"

"Am I too late?"

He must've noticed her peeking at the clock.

"I'm sorry, I'm behind schedule. It's been a grueling day."

"It's okay," she murmured, not wanting to prolong her day by getting into a protracted conversation with a stranger. "What would you like?"

He studied the menu of drinks printed neatly on a chalkboard over her shoulder.

She didn't have to look at it. She'd printed the block letters herself and knew the menu and the ingredients of each specialty coffee by heart.

She tried to wait patiently for the man to make up his mind. She took pride in being decisive. The man in front of her — the man with the square jaw and deep-set brown eyes — looked like a take-charge sort of guy, but he couldn't seem to decide what he wanted. She cleared her throat.

The stranger flinched and glanced at her. "I'm sorry again.

And you're probably in a rush. It's just that you have so many choices. I'll have a grande vanilla latte."

"Caffeinated or decaf?"

"Caf, please. I don't know how far I'll drive yet tonight."

She nodded and turned to prepare his drink.

He followed her to the end of the counter and watched.

Steam gushed out of the machine. She narrowed her eyes. If she wasn't careful, steam would be pouring out of her ears. Many customers watched her work, but this one did so more deliberately than most.

It was a comfort knowing that since it was Tuesday, her aunt would keep the shop next door open another two hours. The door connecting their shops stood open, so it wasn't quite like she was alone with this intense guy.

She stirred the latte and set it on the counter. He paid her and she made change. She fully expected the gentleman to take his latte and leave, since he had miles to go.

She scowled when he turned his back on her and strolled to a corner table.

He looked back at her and grinned crookedly. "I hope it's okay if I drink this here. It's too big to set in my little car. Spilling hot coffee can be dangerous."

She nodded. "I've got to clean up anyway. No hurry." She grabbed a rag and began scrubbing down the counters. With any luck, the stranger was a fast drinker, or maybe he'd spill it.

She peeked at him out of the corner of her eye. He didn't seem to be hurrying at all—he seemed more interested in studying her shop, and her. Unless he was an avid reader, there wasn't a lot that should catch his eye.

Relief swept over her when the man stood. Just as quickly, her stomach knotted. He wasn't leaving. He walked over to one of several bookcases lining the walls.

What had gotten into her? She was a twenty-nine-year-old

woman capable of handling nearly any man. If nothing else, she knew her five-foot-ten size intimidated most men — though the fellow in the sport coat gave no clue he'd noticed. And her aunt was only a few steps away. It wasn't as if the guy intended to accost her. If he'd planned to rob her, would he have bought a drink first?

Still, he made her uncomfortable. She didn't like being uncomfortable.

He stared across the empty room at her. She couldn't escape his scrutiny. "This is a beautiful setting for taking one's time with a cup of coffee. I hope I'm not keeping you."

"No," she lied easily.

"You have a fine book collection." He drew one out from the shelves and leafed through it absently. "Do you sell books as well as coffee? Or do people borrow them?"

"I lend them out. It seems a shame to keep books stored away when others might find them useful."

"What's the penalty for people who fail to return them?"

She folded her arms across her abs. "I don't know. I use the honor system. So far each book has come back."

He carried her book and his half-full cup over and set them on the counter before her. "All of these books . . . Is that why this place is called Nadja's Literary Cappuccino?"

She grinned softly. She couldn't help it. The shop was her pride and joy — it was her child. And the man clearly approved of her establishment, of her work. "That, and because on most Friday evenings, we have readings by local writers. Some nights it might be live music. And occasionally we even feature graphic artists and their work."

"A cultural mecca, of sorts."

"This town is a cultural mecca," Nadja responded with pride.

"I'll have to take your word for that. I haven't had time to look around."

"Too many people hurry through on the way to the big cities."

"So are you Nadja?"

"I am. This is my shop."

"You've done a tasteful job with it."

"Thank you. It has been a joy to do."

"You surely don't run this place by yourself?"

"Not anymore. I have two full-time employees and a few part-timers who come in for our busy nights." She glanced at the clock, whose hands now showed five minutes after six. She blushed. "I close on Tuesday, Wednesday and Thursday at six o'clock," she said, in case he wondered why he was the only customer remaining. "On Friday and Saturday we are open until ten o'clock."

He eyed her levelly, with a hint of danger. "So how much would it take to buy this place?"

Stunned, she stepped backward and caught her breath. "I am not for sale!"

The stranger chuckled and looked curiously at her from head to toe. He blinked. "I didn't mean *you're* for sale." He shook his head. "I meant this place, the shop. How much?"

"You don't understand." She tried to smile but couldn't. "I *am* this place. I am not for sale. Perhaps you should finish your drink elsewhere. I have to close now. I have things to do."

"Of course." His brow knitted. "And I do apologize—I didn't mean to offend. I'd really like to talk with you more."

She tilted her head and glared at him.

"Some other time," he responded quickly. "May I borrow this book? I will bring it back. Scout's honor."

She didn't know about scout's honor, but she could hardly tell him no. He had paid for his coffee and was like any other customer. And she didn't want to have to debate with him about the wisdom of borrowing the book—though he might be a little surprised to discover it was written in Ukrainian.

She nodded, turned her back on him, and grabbed her mop. She didn't look up from her work for a full two minutes. When she did, he was gone.

Good riddance. The nerve of the man. Wanting to buy her — her place. If he knew her, he wouldn't so easily separate the two. *She* couldn't.

Blocking the annoying stranger from her mind, Nadja busied herself by packing the leftover bakery goods she would drop off at the local food bank. She glanced up to see her aunt leaning against the doorjamb separating their two stores.

How long had Ivett been standing there? What had she seen? Her dark eyes sparkled as if she possessed a tantalizing secret. Nadja sighed, girding herself for a grilling.

She hoped when she was forty-three she'd look as attractive as her aunt. Ivett's clear, heart-shaped face was framed by dark flowing hair and set off by the most expressive eyes. But Nadja knew she'd never bubble like her aunt—that kind of free spirit didn't lurk anywhere in her body.

"Hmm, who's the tall dark handsome stranger?" Ivett quipped, stepping into the coffee shop. "I don't think I remember seeing him around. And if I had, I think I'd have noticed. He seemed quite engrossed in you."

"Nonsense. He was just a customer." There was no need to tell Ivett about the man's outlandish proposition. The man had no manners — or maybe he was merely another example of American bluntness.

"Few customers, even male customers, stand at the counter and blatantly undress you in their minds."

Nadja gasped. "He wasn't."

She frowned. Or was he? Her cheeks warmed. She wasn't blind. She'd noticed his broad chest pulling at his shirt. But she hadn't considered him any more thoroughly than that. And she didn't think it wise to do so now.

She shook her head. "You must be wrong. He was only interested in the coffee business."

"Right! I don't believe that for a minute, but if you must, go ahead. Your mother has been gone for nearly two years now, Nadja. It's time for you to get on with your life."

"I am. Look at this place." She swept her gaze around the shop. "This was only a dream eighteen months ago. But with the inheritance from my mother and your and Uncle Steve's help — this is a reality."

"Your dream is a reality because you worked twenty-six hours a day on it with very little help for the first eight months."

"I couldn't hire help until I got the place up and running."

Ivett blew air through pursed lips, and Nadja prepared herself for what had become an all-too-familiar lecture.

"You could at least show some interest in a man."

"I don't even know his name."

"I don't only mean him. But he'll be back."

"He's probably already dumped the book in a trash can."

"Poppycock. If you thought he'd throw the book away, you'd never have let him walk out of here with it. You may not be certain he'll return it, but you know he won't throw it away."

Nadja shrugged, grabbed a towel, and began wiping down the counter for a fourth time.

"You know you can't get rid of me that easily. That little trick of aloof annoyance may work on men, but it doesn't work on me." Ivett placed her palms on the counter. "He'll be back because he's curious about you."

"Ivett!"

"I didn't say he's in love with you. I didn't even say he wants to sleep with you — though I expect that thought crossed his mind — I'm just saying he's curious. And a curious man usually comes back for more. Keep a man curious, and you can have lots of fun."

"I don't need that kind of fun. I don't need complications."

"Girl, this is the year two thousand and five. You've been living here for four years—how many dates have you been on?"

Nadja shrugged. "You keep better count than I do. You tell me."

"Four." Ivett held up four fingers. "And two of those don't count because Pastor John only wanted to make sure you got out now and then. And I don't know what you did to stop him from nosing around more, but he wasn't much of a catch anyway. You've been cloistered like a nun—first because of caring for your mother, and then because of setting up this shop." Ivett paused for breath. "The shop is booming now. You can take some time and enjoy yourself."

"I *do* enjoy myself," Nadja protested. "I go to every play, ballet, or musical performance I can get to at the college or the community playhouse. I love the nature trails. And I run."

"And how often does a man escort you?" Ivett shook her head. "I know you've made some friends. And many of the strongest patrons of the arts find you intriguing and support-ive—but you're always withholding."

"I am who I am."

Ivett tapped her fingers on the counter. "I'm not giving up. Sometimes I wonder how we can be from the same family."

Nadja gave her aunt a half smile. "Me, too. You know I very much appreciate your concern and help."

Ivett looked around, probably double-checking that they were alone. She leaned forward and spoke softly. "Maybe I shouldn't have given you that crystal dildo two years ago. I gave it to you to tide you over—not to replace a man."

Scowling, Nadja huffed, "You know I don't like calling it a dildo. It's my magical crystal wand."

"Did you ever try the rabbit I gave you?"

"I don't want to use anything mechanical. The crystal is natural and communicates its own vibrations. And I've told you before, I do enjoy it. It warms me."

"Not as much as a man would. I'm sorry I gave it to you."

"Don't be sorry. Maybe I simply haven't found a man who intrigues me enough to make time for him."

"There's my doorbell. I'd better go see about my customer." Ivett gave Nadja a disgusted frown. "Maybe you need to lower your intrigue expectations."

Nadja chuckled as Ivett exited. It was hard to stay angry with Ivett. The woman had turned half the world upside down to get Nadja and her mother to emigrate from Kiev to Northern Iowa. Nadja loved her more than anyone, other than her mother.

She shuddered. But Ivett could be annoying. She did pry too much. She'd love to play the role of the matchmaker. But to Ivett's dismay, Nadja had refused to be a pawn in that game.

Intrigue? Were her standards of intrigue too high? She shook her head. *Nope.* If she were to get involved with a man, he'd have to be more than a little intriguing. He'd have to be able to capture her imagination on a number of levels.

And the bedroom was hardly at the top of her list. She'd had sex with a few guys in her younger years. She still didn't know what all the fuss was about. None of them even came close to doing what her magic crystal wand did for her.

She glanced toward the exit where the dark-haired stranger had left. Had he really been undressing her? What had he meant about *buying* her? And why had he taken a book with him?

Her brow furrowed. That did mean he'd be back. But why? He must know she had no intention at all of selling the shop.

His eyes had sparkled with mirth when she'd told him she wasn't for sale. Few men she'd met had ever displayed a real sense of humor. They had one interest—getting her in bed. When they discovered she wasn't quick to acquiesce, they made a hasty retreat.

But the stranger had laughed when she'd rebuffed him. He'd left, but he would return. He had her book.

She cocked her head to the side and pursed her lips. Maybe the stranger *had* inched up her intrigue ladder a wee bit. Wouldn't Ivett be pleased? But then, she wasn't about to tell her aunt.

The following morning, Kevin Langley scowled at his typical breakfast of two pieces of toast and a banana chased down with steaming hot coffee. He ate better when he was on the road, but it felt good to be back in his St. Paul house. It was his sanctuary from the hectic pace of his world.

And it provided a home-like atmosphere when his seven-year-old visited. He peeked out the kitchen window at the swing set he and Danny had built the previous summer. They'd had a lot of fun putting all the pieces together. Danny's screams to be pushed higher and higher still filled his ears.

He stared into his coffee cup and shook his head. It had only taken a little over two hours to drive back from her coffee shop. He'd been able to think about little else but the proud statuesque blonde since he'd left. Women seldom affected him that way—anymore, at least.

Since his divorce two years earlier, he'd mostly only tip-toed around women. Once burned was one too many times for him. He'd maintained a fairly healthy distance from any woman he thought might be interested in anything more than sex. And he'd even become rather bored with sex. He shook his head. That was a terrible fact to acknowledge, even in his most private thoughts.

He grimaced. What was it about the Nadja woman that stuck with him? He'd never known a taller woman. He was six feet even, and he hadn't had to look down at her. She'd had a sultry, modulated accent—probably Eastern European. Maybe one of those tiny countries whose name he couldn't remember or pronounce.

Even in a rather drab dress, she had a body that screamed sex. Full breasts. Broad hips. What man could look at her and not undress her? Perhaps a happily married man, but he even doubted that.

She must have more men than she could count. Sexy. In a word, Nadja of Nadja's Literary Cappuccino was about the sexiest female he'd ever seen.

Yet she carried herself with aplomb. She projected an air of innocence that failed to fit her body. And she certainly wasn't one of those women who relied solely on sex to get ahead.

Her coffee shop had been put together by someone with a lot of passion and heart—and by an individual who was not afraid of working hard for what she wanted.

The ambiance of the shop had attracted him even before he'd paid much attention to its owner. Kevin smiled. His boss would like that. After all, Kevin had been sent to Jefferson City to evaluate the coffee shop, not necessarily the woman who owned it.

As district manager for Java Beans, it was his job to determine whether it was economical and feasible to set up a franchise in Jefferson City, Iowa. That would be easier to achieve if they simply bought out as many competitors as they could. Or they could move in and take a chance on lowering their prices to drive competitors out. That was riskier for all involved—such price wars could backfire. In his business, as well as in his personal life, he liked to keep risk at a minimum.

Her shop radiated her personality—or at least his assumptions about her personality. Commitment to the arts. Clearly, she'd established a gathering place for folks interested in the arts. He couldn't place the classical music that had been playing, nor could he identify the artists of the various art pieces hanging on the wall. What he'd seen of her books suggested an eclectic range of interests—arts, history, geography—so she was no prude. Several of the paintings were semi-nude models, female and male. Tasteful, but still not what he'd expected to find in Northern Iowa.

But neither had he expected to find such a stunning woman in Northern Iowa—or anyplace else, for that matter.

He spied the book he'd borrowed sitting on the end of the counter. He leaned over to retrieve it. *KIEV* was its title.

He hadn't really paid much attention to what he'd pulled off the shelf. His interest had been much more focused on her reaction.

He chuckled, remembering how she'd wanted to get rid of him. He opened the book and studied numerous pictures of majestic, gilded onion-domed buildings and snow-covered fields. There were no words. He flipped to the back of the book and frowned. It had words all right, but in letters totally unfamiliar to him.

He went back to the front of the book and found a map. Kiev/Kyiv. Kiev, Ukraine. He scrunched his mouth. Did that mean Nadja was from Ukraine?

Not necessarily. But it did fit. If someone had asked him where Ukraine was located, he probably would've said Russia. He peered at the map. He wouldn't have been too far off.

He leaned back on his kitchen stool. He'd heard about the stereotypical sexy blonde bombshell from Russia but figured that was just so much smoke or hype.

He shook his head and sighed audibly. That image didn't fit her—not really. Sexy? Absolutely. No debate about that. But she'd done nothing to flaunt her natural sexiness. If anything, she'd tried to hide it behind an ill-fitting wardrobe.

And she'd taken great umbrage at the thought that she might be for sale. Not that he'd ever suggest such a thing—to her or any other woman.

Her sophisticated, short-cropped blonde hair was efficient as well as sexy. He'd noticed three or four broken fingernails. A woman wanting to flaunt her sex would've taken better care of her nails.

He pushed the book away and refilled his coffee cup. Nadja of Nadja's Literary Cappuccino was turning into a puzzle. He had a professional obligation to understand her better. If it turned out he'd have to cajole her into selling, he needed to know where her vulnerable spots were. If he had to set up a franchise across the street to compete with her, then he'd have to know how best to accomplish that.

And he had a personal reason for wanting to know what made the tall blonde who carried herself with an erect, appealing pride tick. He had to return her book. Maybe honesty would be the best approach for getting to know the voluptuous blonde.

She'd moved so fluidly—like a dancer, or an athlete. Certainly, like someone comfortable in her own skin. He closed his eyes. Would her skin warm under his touch?

He blinked his eyes open. He'd better scrap those fantasies and stick to business. He didn't know what it would take to get her out of her coffee shop, but he wouldn't fail. He might've had a failure or two in his personal life—but he never failed professionally.

By late the following Tuesday afternoon, Nadja had scrubbed her counter several times. She didn't like being this edgy. She glanced toward the shop doorway. Since the man who'd borrowed her book hadn't shown up earlier, she fully expected him today. Perhaps it was women's intuition. She'd thought he might be some sort of traveling salesman who passed through Jefferson City on Tuesdays.

Why did she find it annoying that he hadn't returned her book yet? Many people held on to books for longer than a week. But she was pretty sure he couldn't read Ukrainian. And she really had expected him to return the book. She considered herself a fairly good judge of character. While she probably wouldn't trust the stranger with her life, she had thought him trustworthy enough to lend a book to.

She glanced at the doorway again and fought back a smile. There he was. Had she conjured him up?

He walked toward her with the book tucked under his arm, grinning his welcome. "Bet you didn't expect to ever see this book again," he teased, placing it on the counter in front of her.

Like the last time, he was dressed in a sport coat with a loosely knotted tie. She hadn't remembered the soft luster of his brown eyes.

"I trusted you to return it." She folded her hands at her waist.

He nodded. "Maybe you're too trusting."

"Hardly," she snickered. "I'm quite skeptical of people, actually."

"But you trusted me?"

"With a book."

"I see." He cast his gaze around the room. "It's six o'clock. I always seem to show up at closing time."

"Twice is hardly always."

"You *are* skeptical. Let's try this a different way. I suppose you won't let me pay for the loan of the book."

"Of course not. Don't be silly. It costs me nothing to let people borrow my books."

"What I'd really like to do is take you to dinner. I have business matters to talk to you about."

"Dinner? No. Why would I want to go to dinner with you? I don't even know your name."

"Kevin Langley." He extended his hand.

She took it reluctantly and quivered from the sudden jolt that zipped from her fingers to her elbow. She eyed him cautiously. If he'd been aware of the spark, he didn't show it. She never reacted that way to a man.

Consternation spread across Kevin's face. "I have to talk with you, or I may lose my job."

"Why would that happen?"

"There's your skepticism again." He paused. "I bumbled things badly last time, but I really do have to talk with you about selling your place." He held up his palm to stop her from interrupting. "I know you don't want to sell. And I'll try to honor that, but I've got a boss who wants me to talk with you. And even if you don't want to sell, you should probably listen to what I have to say. The coffee market in Jefferson City is going to get another player—a big player."

"You! You're going to compete with me?"

"Not me. My company. I'm a district rep for Java Beans. My job is to evaluate this town for a possible franchise."

"Java Beans. Goodness." Nadja fought for breath. Could she survive such stiff competition? "So a final decision hasn't been made?"

"That's correct." He flashed an eyebrow. "You may even be able to provide convincing information why it wouldn't be advisable for Java Beans to do business here."

"I doubt that. But you're right. I should probably learn more about what it is they want to know." She looked sharply at him. "But no matter what, I'm not for sale."

"I understand your position. And I may try to change your mind, but it's nothing personal. It is business, but"—he studied her for a long moment—"I won't lie to you."

"Somehow I didn't think you would."

"So, are you ready for me to take you to dinner?"

She shook her head and put the towel away. "I will pay for my own dinner."

"Okay, if you must."

"I must."

She stepped out from behind the counter to join him, and he gazed at her with masculine approval. She had worn a pretty print dress — but of course that had nothing to do with her expectation that he'd drop by before the day was done. "What do you want out of all of this, Kevin Langley — other than keeping your job and not lying to me?"

"That's it."

"Good." She tilted her chin at him. "You don't want to have sex with me?"

"Why" — he sputtered — "why would you ask a question like that?"

"You've not thought of having sex with me?"

"Now hold on. I didn't say that." He shook his head. "You have me trapped. That's not fair."

"It's nothing personal." She stopped in front of him to look at him eye to eye. "I'm just — what do they say — clearing the air. This is my body, Kevin Langley of Java Beans. When I choose to grace a man with my body, it becomes very personal. I'm not into casual sex. And when I even listen to a man talk about buying my shop, that, too, is very personal."

Kevin shuddered. "Damn, you do believe in being blunt. I'll try not to feel emasculated."

She shrugged her shoulders. "Nothing personal."

"So I'll try to control my growing admiration for you and my enthusiasm for your coffee shop. I wouldn't want to be misconstrued as being too personal. And by the way," he squinted at her, "I'm not into casual sex either. Tried that. It might be fine for some people, but not me. If we ever have sex, Miss High and Mighty Nadja — which I highly doubt — I can guarantee you it will be very personal."

She couldn't hold back a laugh. "I didn't mean to offend you. I only wanted to be clear. Do you still want to go to dinner with me?"

He hesitated only fractionally. "Sure. I still have to lay out the proposition for you—the business proposition. And maybe now I can ask you some personal questions I've been curious about without you thinking I'm trying to get into your panties."

"We'll see." She ushered him to the exit and locked the door behind them. "I'll drive." She felt strangely giddy. She'd fully expected him to run for the exit when she told him there'd be no sex. Most men did.

She knitted her brow. What did he want to know about her? She smiled as he followed her toward her car. Surprisingly, he continued to intrigue. Now, what did *she* want to learn about *him?*

CHAPTER TWO

Giving the menu a quick once-over, Kevin avoided looking at the blonde sitting on the other side of the booth. He counted himself lucky to be alive. Was the woman enraged at him, or did she normally drive like a demon? Fearing for life and limb, he'd made no attempt to engage in conversation, and neither had she.

He'd order the grilled walleye. That ought to be safe enough. He peeked up at Nadja, who gave him a hard stare. She was a specialist at projecting innocence, sexiness, and danger in one amazing package.

He reached for his coffee and sipped. Not bad for restaurant coffee. He glanced around the spacious eating area and smiled. Nadja wasn't taking any chances. She'd brought him to a well-lit, fairly noisy sports bar. Hardly a setting that would engender a romantic mood.

And romance was the furthest thing from his mind — until he looked at her and felt himself drawn into her soulful eyes. Was she a witch? She had to be one of the most absolutely stunning women he'd ever met. And he was drawn to her *eyes*. Cripes, maybe he was getting old. At that moment, those beckoning eyes bored holes through him. Romance was definitely *not* on Nadja's mind.

One of them had to break what was rapidly becoming a painful stalemate. Thankfully, neither of them had to blink first, because their perky waitress chose that moment to take their orders.

Nadja looked a little more comfortable once their orders

were placed and the waitress disappeared into the kitchen.

"Nice place," he volunteered. "Do you come here often?"

"Yes, I do. They serve good food and the staff is friendly. Now tell me about this proposition you think I need to know about. I will tell you again, I am not for sale."

"Nor do you want a large-scale competitor."

"True."

"Isn't that why you agreed to listen? You hope to convince me not to proceed. Or perhaps to learn something that will help you torpedo Java Beans's plan to move into the area."

"Of course," she said smugly. "Why else would I bother to have dinner with you?"

Kevin closed his eyes briefly. He tried to wait until he counted to ten before responding. He counted by twos. "You're not very healthy for a guy's ego."

She hesitated a moment. A wisp of a smile crossed her lips. "No, I suppose I'm not. So are you going to talk to me about this business thing, or are you going to sit there and nurse your wounded male ego?"

He laughed easily. "I'm not that wounded, and since you're not about to volunteer to be my nurse, let's talk business. As I said, I'm here to assess the pros and cons of setting up a Java Beans franchise in this part of Northern Iowa. Being a regional hub makes Jefferson City a logical place for locating the store."

"But why my shop? Wouldn't your company want to build its own? I thought that's how big corporations did things. Erect their cookie-cutter buildings and start running the locals out of business."

"Bitterness does not become you." He ignored her rigid posture. "We don't want to move in that way in smaller communities. That sets up exactly what you just described. We want to be part of the market, but we'd prefer to blend in, so to speak. We look first at locals to see if anyone is interested or willing to sell—that is, people who own shops that meet our specifications."

"And I do."

He hurried on, not wanting to consider her specifications too closely. "You have an ideal location, and your store fits our square footage needs."

"You," she squeaked, "know my square footage."

"You'd be amazed about the range of information that's part of some public record. Yes, I've done a lot of homework on Nadja's Literary Cappuccino. Tax rate, debt, profit, and so on."

Nadja's scowl could've turned lesser men into pillars. "And I thought we left the snoops behind in the old country. Tell me, what do you know about the owner of Nadja's Literary Cappuccino?"

"No need to get testy. Not enough. Not nearly enough." He glanced about quickly. No one sat in any of the nearby booths. "I have done a little research on the owner since we last spoke. I did blunder my way through that initial meeting. And again, I do apologize."

She sat across from him in stony silence, waiting for him to continue.

"Your full name is Nadja Ivett Petrov. You are twenty-nine years old. Unmarried."

"What does that have to do with anything?"

"We know you're not supporting a family. Let's see, you came to Iowa from Ukraine four years ago, in two thousand and one, with an ailing mother. I was sorry to learn she died over a year ago."

Nadja blinked back tears.

"She was fortunate to have such a loyal daughter and sister." He smiled. "Yes, I know why the door between your two shops is left open. That should offer a sense of security, if you ever need it."

"I've felt that need of late," she said coolly. "Go on."

"You've operated the Cappuccino for seventeen months and two weeks. Miraculously, you turned a profit after the first nine months of operation. That's well ahead of expectations and certainly attracts my company's attention and interest. You have a prime location."

"Have you considered the possibility that the shop's success has less to do with the location and more to do with the ambiance I offer?"

He leaned back and sighed. "Yes, I have worried about that some. And if you don't sell, I will have to worry about that even more. You do make an able competitor."

"That's good. I'm not for sale."

"You are a broken record."

She frowned. "Broken record. What does that mean? I'm still learning this country's idioms."

"It means you stubbornly repeat yourself."

She grinned. It was the first genuine grin he'd seen from her the entire evening. "I readily confess to being stubborn. Continue, please."

He stopped long enough for the waitress to put their food platters on the table and to sample his grilled walleye. To his surprise, the walleye melted in his mouth. "Delicious. This is excellent food."

"I'm glad you like it. There are many fine things in this small town."

"I'm beginning to appreciate that fact." He put down his fork. "Are you even a little curious about what we are prepared to offer you?"

"Only because I feel like laughing."

He stared at her for a long moment and grinned. "You're right. I haven't heard you laugh. Well, if this is what it takes, it may be worth it. We are prepared to pay you thirty thousand dollars over the fair market value for the Cappuccino and its contents. The appraisal can be made by a person of your choice."

She scowled.

"You're not laughing?"

"This is not a laughing matter, and you know it." She pushed her grilled chicken aside, hardly having touched it. "Why would you pay me more than I am worth?"

"In the long run, we save money by not having to find another location, or go through zoning issues, or build, or run a losing business for however long it would take to drive you out of business."

"Pure economics."

He nodded.

"I could sell to you and set up in another location six months later. My loyal customers would follow me."

"Maybe. Java Beans would probably build a clause into the sale contract about future competition."

"If I don't sell, how long do you suppose it will take before Java Beans has a franchise here?"

"Depends." He shrugged. "I'll have to spend much more time scoping out possibilities. I have a meeting with a realtor tomorrow morning. And I'll meet with a member of the Chamber of Commerce for lunch. If we fast-track it, maybe nine months. More likely twelve to eighteen months."

"I see." Nadja's nose twitched and her chin jutted out. "And if I agree to fuck you, will you go away and tell your superiors that setting up a franchise here would be a very bad idea?"

Kevin couldn't close his mouth. Had he heard her correctly? Of course he had. His fingers curled into fists. He reached deeply for breath. "Whatever gave you such an idea? Do you really think I can be bought with sex?"

He winced. Her stare was fixed, not giving away at all whether she was bluffing. What would she do if he said yes?

"Would you really do such a thing?"

"I'd do anything to protect what's mine." She brushed her throat with her fingers. She lowered her hand, letting it graze a breast. Kevin swallowed hard at the sight of a shadowy nipple. "I do not make such an offer lightly." She reddened slightly. "I have not fucked a man since moving to America, but I realize this is how business is often done in my country and here. I will do whatever is necessary to save my shop. It's only sex, only fucking. It's not making love. No big deal."

"That's not how business is done here." He spat the words out. "At least, it's not how I do business."

"But you've been admiring my body since you first met me," she stammered. "I thought . . ."

"I'd have to be blind not to notice. I'd have to be made of stone not to appreciate your beauty."

"But you're rejecting me?"

"Absolutely. I'd never take advantage of a woman in that way. I wouldn't be able to live with myself."

She gnawed on her bottom lip. "I think that makes you a better man than most I've met."

"Then you've hung out with some poor excuses for men. And why would you think, if I agreed to have sex with you, that I'd keep my half of the bargain—that I wouldn't disappear?"

It was her turn to shrug and look away. "You said," she began, her words so soft he had to lean forward to hear, "that you wouldn't lie to me. Maybe it's intuition, but I trust you."

"Shit!" he roared and looked sheepishly about. "I don't understand you. You don't have casual sex, yet you offer to fuck me as if it's a bargaining chip. And you'd trust a guy who'd have sex with you as part of an agreement."

"Sex is not that big of a thing." She peered at him thoughtfully. "I speak from experience. I don't know what all the fuss is about. It is my body. I can withhold or give as I choose."

"You amaze me. I hardly know you, and yet we have some of the most outlandish conversations I've ever had with a woman." He roughly raked his fingers through his hair.

"Then your answer is no," she pressed on.

"Yes. I mean yes, it's no!"

"And you will continue working on this scheme to locate a Java Beans project here."

"Yes, that's part of what I'm paid to do. You know it's not personal."

She smiled brightly. "And I will do everything in my power to see that you fail and that my shop thrives. You know that's not personal."

"Touché. I expect you to be a formidable adversary."

"Are you married?"

"What?" Kevin nearly rose off the bench seat.

"Are you married?"

"You offered me sex and thought I was married?"

"It didn't matter then." She shrugged. "It matters now."

"Well, I'm not. I was. I have a seven-year-old boy, Danny."

"Danny." She smiled. "That's a nice name. Does he live with you?"

"No." He paused and took a deep breath. "He lives with his mother in the Cities. I see him every other weekend. And he spends his summers with me. That can be a bit hectic with my travels, but we make it work. What is this leading up to, Nadja? I trust I'm not amusing your idle curiosity. These are very personal questions."

"I know." She pursed her lips and stared at him until he started to shift uncomfortably. "I have an extra ticket to tomorrow night's play at the college. If you want to come along, you'd be welcome."

She'd floored him this time. What was her game? Was she still trying to work her Faustian bargain? "Are you asking me for a date?"

23

Her lips curled into a tiny smile. "I'm not sure about that. But it does occur to me that if I can keep tabs on you while you're here, I might learn something that will help me keep my shop."

Kevin cocked his head. "Develop a relationship with the adversary and see if you can learn any company secrets."

"Sort of." She glanced down at her uneaten meal and back up at him. "And you intrigue me."

So she *was* interested. What a rollercoaster ride! "Intrigue? Well, you're more than a little mysterious to me, too. Sure. I wasn't planning on staying over another night. But why not? I'll extend my reservation when I get back to the motel. But you're sure this isn't a date?"

"Pretty sure."

"You'll let me know if you change your mind?"

He was certain she had no idea she'd wet her lips before whispering, "Yes."

With annoyance, Nadja scowled at her reflection in her bedroom mirror. What had gotten into her? While she might be bold in some matters, she was not bold when it came to men. Why had she invited him to the play?

She needed to stay in contact with him. She might still be able to convince him this wouldn't be a good site for his franchise.

She cupped her breasts in her hands. Goodness, she'd even offered to fuck him if he'd go away. She smiled, remembering the shock on his face. He certainly hadn't expected that offer.

He'd turned her down. Intriguing, indeed. How many men would reject such an opportunity?

She crawled into bed, appreciating the coolness of the satin sheets against her nude body. She enjoyed the fact that he found her mysterious. It had been so long since she'd stopped long enough to engage in banter with a man.

He scared her. Obviously, he threatened her future. Yet a part of her found him fun to be with. She closed her eyes. Not only that—he was incredibly handsome. Her nipples suddenly pebbled, and she rolled one between her thumb and forefinger. It tightened until she ached.

She glanced at the bedside stand. She hadn't used her crystal wand for some time. Maybe she should use it while fantasizing about Kevin Langley.

She shook her head and turned over, tucking a pillow between her thighs. Fantasizing about Langley would make him become much more personal than she wanted or needed. Maybe she'd dream about him instead.

Late Wednesday afternoon, Steve Chambers looked up from the charts on his desk to see his old college roommate standing in the doorway. He swallowed. These days, Rick Adams didn't stop by unless he wanted something. Steve knew he owed him, but for how many years did he have to pay him back? It'd been twenty-two years now.

Rick swaggered into the room and plopped down on a soft chair across from Steve's desk. "Heard you had a client this morning."

"I have clients most days," Steve said evenly, not bothering to ask his old friend not to light his trademark cigar. It wouldn't do any good anyway. Instead, he pulled out a desk drawer and retrieved the one ashtray he kept just for this purpose.

"This fellow represented an out-of-state corporation. According to the rumor I heard, the guy was particularly interested in the Henderson property your wife and her niece share."

"That's right." Steve leaned back in his chair and cast a

curious eye at the man who'd gained far more pounds than he himself had since college. At least that was one thing—though Rick had also amassed many more dollars from land development.

Steve had done some of the property work for Rick. But Rick had other dealings, which seemed rather murky, that Steve had had no part in. So why was Rick interested in the old Henderson building?

"The guy was down from the Twin Cities looking at possible sites for a Java Beans franchise. Nadja's place is only one possibility." He shook his head. "I told him she wouldn't sell. He laughed and said she'd already assured him of that."

"Too bad." Rick's voice held a threatening hitch. "Maybe it's best not to be too hasty." Rick paused to blow a perfect smoke ring. "How long has it been, bro? Nineteen eighty three—twenty-two years?"

Steve scowled and tried not to shake. "I suppose that's about right." He knew the time to the week. Hardly a day had gone by since the death of his college sweetheart that he hadn't thought of her, or the aftermath of her death.

"Figured you hadn't forgotten . . . and the fact that you still owe me."

"I didn't kill Mary Beth, Rick, and you know it."

"I've always taken your word for that, buddy. Never doubted you. Though I'm not sure the Sheriff's department would've if I hadn't provided you with an ironclad alibi." He puffed on the cigar until the end glowed. "Nope. The boyfriend is always the prime suspect, just like you were."

Steve remained silent. They had rehashed Rick's points many times over the years—usually when Rick wanted something from him.

"I've always meant to ask—have you ever told your wife about Mary Beth's untimely death?"

He shook his head slowly. "That was ancient history by the

time I met Ivett."

Rick's eyes twinkled. "I wonder if the Sheriff's department would think so. Cold cases are in the news these days. And I'm surprised you haven't told your Russian wife—but then I guess she's probably quite used to people keeping secrets."

"She's from Ukraine. What do you want this time, Rick? Cut the bullshit. What do you want from me?"

"The Henderson building—pure and simple."

"What?" Steve's gut clenched, and he struggled to keep his voice steady. "Ivett and Nadja own the building. I don't own any of it. Ivett bought it before we were married, and she sold half to her sister when she moved here."

"I don't give a damn who owns it. I want it. Have for a long time, but I'm a patient man. One of the things I've learned in the land business is if you wait long enough, an opportunity arises, and you better be prepared to strike. And Java Beans is my opportunity."

"You're not making sense, Rick. Java Beans may be interested in buying Nadja's share, or even possibly leasing the place from her. Most likely they'll have to go elsewhere. My niece is stubborn."

"I've noticed." Rick's fair complexion reddened. "I don't give a shit about Java Beans. But if they can dislodge Nadja and maybe even your wife, then I'm all for them. I'd give them no more than six months before they'll be begging me to buy them out dirt cheap."

"But why that property? The women have sought historic status for the building."

"Yeah, well, they're not going to get that as long as I have some influence in this town. They're running artsy craftsy crap there. In the right hands, given that location, that property could be worth millions in a few years."

"You're kidding."

Rick shook his head. "I keep my ear to the ground. I don't

give a hoot about the building, but I want that land. I already own land on both sides of it. That's the only parcel of land on that block facing Washington I don't own."

"Millions." Steve's brain spun. "There aren't many ways even that piece of property could become that valuable." He sighed. "Maybe a casino, but even you can't seriously believe this city is going to accept a downtown casino."

"I didn't say that. Let's just leave it at this: I know a lot of things you don't know. And the high and mighty citizenry of this town can be bought. I've been working my fingers into some pies for a long time. And Java Beans gives me a perfect way to get my hands on that building without having to go up against the so-called cultural arts community. Sometimes those people make me gag. And your wife and her niece are right at the center of it all."

"Yeah, well, they probably wouldn't be too fond of you either."

"I'm not here to win a popularity contest. I'm here to collect on a debt. I want you to convince your wife and her Amazon niece to sell to Java Beans. And I'll take care of ousting Java Beans in due time. Remember, I'm a very patient man—to a point."

"I certainly can't guarantee doing that, even if I wanted to. Both of those women are headstrong and very committed to their businesses."

Rick shrugged. "Hoped you could be convincing. At least do this—don't show this Java Beans guy any other promising pieces of property. You can do that for old time's sake, right?"

Steve couldn't avoid Rick's glare. "I suppose I can do that."

"You also try to talk those women into selling. If I have to, I can use other means to help convince them—but because we're friends, I'd rather not resort to those."

"Now see here . . ." Steve rose to his feet.

Rick stood and stared at him levelly. "I want that property, bro. This is an opportunity to get it without anyone getting hurt. Understand?"

Steve nodded, not trusting his voice.

"Or I could always rethink the night of April twenty-fifth twenty-two years ago and wonder aloud about whether I was sober enough to know you were asleep in our frat house. And those Russian women are really quite attractive. I'd hate to see either one of them harmed in any way."

"I've got the picture." Steve kept his voice level. "I'll do whatever I can."

"That's what I wanted to hear, bro. And that's exactly what I did for you all those years ago. Seems almost like yesterday."

Steve ignored Rick's extended hand and slumped back down in his chair as Rick left, closing the office door softly behind him.

He laid his head in his hands. Why was he still paying the price for something he'd never done? He should've told Ivett long before now. How could she forgive him for keeping such a horrific secret from her? He loved her and he didn't want her to lose her shop, but he didn't want her hurt, either. Even if he told her now about Mary Beth's death and how Rick had helped confirm his alibi, she'd only dig in her heels more about selling the property. Telling her might very well increase any danger she might be in—and Nadja, too.

CHAPTER THREE

A t least she'd conceded the armrest to him. Kevin grinned at the actors on stage. Why should that little victory be so important to him? He sat in the aisle seat, able to stretch his legs out. Nadja sat next to him, a bit more cramped, with her hands folded neatly in her lap.

She'd picked him up at the motel and they'd come directly to the theater. Apparently, dinner beforehand would've made her feel like they were on an actual date.

So why was he here? There'd been little time to talk before arriving at the college. He didn't think she had plans to invite him back to her place afterwards. And he wasn't about to cheapen whatever might develop between them by inviting her to his cramped motel room.

He sniffed the air. He couldn't place her subtle scent. She'd dressed as if it were a date—but then maybe she always dressed up for the arts. She'd chosen to wear a simple but attractive pink V-neck dress that showed off her ample bosom. She'd used a large piece of white jewelry to gather the dress just below her breasts. His gaze—and probably everyone else's in the vicinity—was drawn to her cleavage. The dress fell to about two inches above her knee. In her seat, it had traveled much farther up her thighs.

What would she do if he rested his palm on her bare thigh? He chuckled softly. Probably jump out of her skin or slap him into the aisle. Why did a woman who was not on a date and had no personal interest in him dress so provocatively?

Hell, Nadja would look provocative in a sweatsuit. He

could only imagine her bursting out in a bikini. His semi-hard cock stiffened until he had to shift in his seat to relieve some strain.

To his chagrin, the audience stood as one. When had the play come to its end? He applauded. Nadja clapped her hands and whistled. He glanced at her. Maybe that was a European thing. She glowed with enthusiasm, with passion.

Until she turned to look at him. It was as if she'd drawn a curtain to cover her emotions.

"Wasn't that fun?" She flashed him a brief smile.

He nodded. Hopefully, she didn't expect a detailed critique of the play. He could describe how she breathed after laughing, or how she sat tensely when the heroine was threatened, or how much he'd wanted to comfort her as she sobbed when the hero nearly died, or how her boobs rose and fell when the heroine and hero finally conquered the demons that had kept them apart.

Nadja parked in front of Kevin's motel and deliberately left the engine running, making it clear she had no intention of prolonging the evening. "So, you return to St. Paul in the morning?"

"Yes, unless you want to have an early morning coffee."

She shook her head. "No, I run early in the morning. And I have to be at the shop by nine."

"Another time, perhaps. I'll need to show up at my office by ten or so." He gave her one of his boyish smiles. "You're a runner?"

"Yes, long distance. I've tried a few marathons."

He whistled softly. "A serious runner."

She shrugged. "It keeps me fit."

Kevin coughed. "I won't argue with that. I'd figured you for a dancer or an athlete."

She furrowed her brow. "Why is that?"

"You move with fluid ease. And your carriage is erect."

"Carriage?"

He chuckled. "You have good posture when you walk and even when you sit. Some might describe you as prim and proper. I think you're simply comfortable with your body."

"You are quite perceptive." She couldn't conceal a grin. "I danced ballet for most of my life."

"Really?"

"We have a tiny company here in Jefferson City. I do it because I love it and it helps me stay in shape."

"But you were much more serious about it at one time?"

"Oh yes. I was being groomed for the Russian ballet until I was fifteen."

"What happened then?"

"It was nineteen ninety-one—Ukraine became independent." Her words were clipped. "Training in Russia would've cost way too much money. I danced in regional companies in Ukraine until I got too big."

He frowned. "Too big. I thought tall dancers were most desired."

"I didn't mean tall. These," she said, hefting her breasts. "My tits got too big."

Kevin's cheeks flushed.

Why did her touching her breasts embarrass him so? They were only tits. He'd been staring at them much of the evening, and at her bare thighs. She could've tugged her dress down more, but she took a perverse delight in watching Kevin Langley—the man who wanted to buy her—squirm. She should ask him the names of the hero and heroine in the play they'd just attended. She'd bet he couldn't tell her.

"They don't look too big to me," he stammered, glancing at them quickly before staring out the windshield. Slowly, his head turned until his focus was once again on her.

"Thank you," she replied. "But they are too—how do you say it—too pendulous for a dancer. They swing about too much. My tits can become a distraction."

"Oh."

"You are quite funny when you blush so much. When will you be back?" His gaze rose from her bosom to her eyes. Had he heard her question?

He blinked a couple times, and she waited calmly. "Friday, maybe. I should see what the town is like on a weekend."

"Weekends are often quite busy." She tried to think through the coming weekend. "There is a Celtic band playing Friday night at the Cappuccino. The fairgrounds will host a dog show. I love to watch the working dogs."

He shook his head, seemingly unaware of such events.

"The working dogs include the rotties, pinschers and boxers. You've never been to a dog show?"

"Nope."

"I work on Saturday, but the shop is closed on Sunday. I'll take you Sunday, if you'd like to see the dogs."

"Why not? You're a dog lover. Do you own a dog?"

"Not since we came to America. There's not been time. It's one of my biggest regrets. Maybe someday." She compressed her lips. "I'm sure you'll have meetings during the day on Friday. Why don't you drop by the Cappuccino Friday night? The music starts at seven-thirty."

"I'll be there."

She softened her lips before leaning over and kissing him on one cheek and then the other. "Good night," she whispered. "I will see you Friday."

He curled his fingers around the door latch and turned back to her. "Hmm, kissing me on the cheeks—does that make this a date?"

She broke into a large smile. "I'm not positive. Don't misread a European custom." She hesitated and then leaned across the space separating them to brush her lips lightly across his. She settled back in her seat and quietly watched his eyes sparkling.

"That's an American custom," he said, "for ending a date."

"Don't be so narrow-minded," she teased. "I believe that custom is fairly common worldwide for ending a first date. Good night," she added quickly. "I'll see you on Friday."

"You bet you will," Kevin said, opening the door.

She watched him until he entered the motel. She hadn't planned on their evening turning into a date. But it had. How? When? Why?

It had seemed like such a natural thing to kiss him. It had only been a kiss, and not much of one at that.

So why did her lips still tingle?

Even her crystal wand couldn't soothe the sensations still lingering on her lips. She'd tried to ignore Kevin's effect on her. But sleep would not come.

Nadja wet the smooth crystal in her mouth. She closed her eyes and sucked on it as if it were a popsicle. Her throat muscle worked steadily until she withdrew the crystal, slid it down her chest, and let it rest atop a swollen nipple.

She didn't open her eyes. She hardly breathed. She'd swear the crystal had increased its vibrating. Her nipples were beyond puckering.

Cupping a breast with one hand, she shifted the crystal lower, then guided its tip around the rim of her navel. Her breathing became more ragged. Vibrations stretched across her belly upwards and downwards. Would his tongue be as effective?

She opened her eyes and parted her thighs. She watched her crystal friend make its way downward until it teased her labia. She licked her lips, trying not to think of Kevin but failing miserably.

She tilted the crystal and eased it inward. Her loins clenched and relaxed. Her brow knitted, and she smiled as the magical crystal traveled her depths. She slowed, teasing herself. Then she withdrew the crystal and let it play across her vulva.

Too soon she lost the will to wait. She refitted the crystal back into her pussy. Briefly, she allowed its vibrations to fill her. Had it ever been more alive than tonight?

Those vibrations spread to her chest, her thighs, her toes. She couldn't stand much more. She propelled the crystal on its journey.

She brushed fingers over her clit twice and then yelped to no one in particular. She curled into a ball and withdrew the wand and cradled her crystal lover between her breasts.

Would Kevin want to cuddle after lovemaking — or would he be like the others, reaching for a smoke or making a hasty exit? She wasn't nearly ready to find out, but he was making his way up her intrigue ladder quite nicely.

She squeezed a pillow tight. Why wasn't he intimidated by her? Most men were — whether because of her height or because of her frankness.

Nadja grinned. Her aunt had been trying for years to get her to soften her direct approach to things, with little effect. She had grown to despise people who did not speak the truth or hid behind bureaucracy and arcane rules. Some might consider her rigid in her ways, but she prided herself on being honest and straightforward.

She could become quite determined when she wanted something bad enough. She'd never been short on perseverance, whether in ballet, running, caring for her mother, or setting up her coffee shop. But her perseverance had never been put to the test in matters of love.

She'd never met a man who was worth the effort. She stretched languidly. Until, possibly, now.

Kevin wrestled on the sagging motel bed, half-asleep and half-awake. He hated being so indecisive. When Nadja had brushed her lips across his in the car, he had fought the urge to take her in his arms and show her how she deserved to be kissed.

She was slicing him into little pieces, and she probably didn't even realize it. She had dressed to seduce, though she hadn't tried to seduce him. Had she actually realized how that dress accentuated her figure?

Had she purposefully taunted him by hefting her breasts? *Tits too large,* she'd said. He'd like to be the judge of that. He swiped at his perspiring forehead. And they swung when she moved. He flashed to an image of loving her from behind, with her breasts swinging so much he'd have to reach around and steady them with his hands. "Shit," he muttered.

He sat up and swung his legs over the edge of the bed. His cock stood up as if to salute her image. He ruffled his hair. Damn, why had he ever given up smoking?

He stood, walked to the window, and parted the curtain to stare out at the darkness. He breathed deeply. He could still smell her scent. He wet his lips. Her faint taste still caressed them.

Kevin turned back toward the bed, trying to ignore his arousal. Maybe he should go into his boss's office tomorrow morning and tell him Jefferson City wasn't a good site for Java Beans. Then there'd be no reason for him to return to the place.

He shook his head and crawled back under the covers. He didn't really know whether this was a good location or not. It was too early to tell.

And he didn't like running away from a woman, particularly from Nadja of Kiev. So she was a long-distance runner.

He used to run in high school and college. He'd cut back on it after his first year of marriage, then given it up entirely after being promoted to middle management. There never was enough time for running.

Maybe it was time to get a new pair of running shoes.

And she liked dogs. Danny begged for a dog, but his mother didn't want one. And Kevin had no way to manage a dog, given the amount of traveling he did for work.

What would Nadja think of Danny? His breath caught in his windpipe. What would Danny make of Nadja?

Whoa, there. That was way down the road. And it wasn't at all clear the road even stretched that far.

He welcomed sleep at last, trusting the road would bring him back to this place and to her the following Friday. That was all he could count on for the moment. And strangely, that was enough.

"Nadja should find a man, get married and have a passel of kids. Isn't that the American dream?"

Kevin Langley frowned at Steve Chambers, who was driving him out to see yet another property. Since when had Fridays become such long days? The past week had dragged, but this day seemed to have no end.

He'd see her later in the evening, at seven-thirty. Even if he could have come earlier, he wouldn't enter the Cappuccino until the appointed time. He didn't want Nadja to think he was overly eager.

He tried to focus on the realtor. He hadn't remembered Chambers being quite so preoccupied and uncomfortable the previous week. Of course, at that point he hadn't realized the realtor was Nadja's uncle. "I didn't get the impression she was looking for a man." He kept his voice even, as if he were only idly curious. "Are you certain she wants a passel of kids?"

Chambers turned left onto a one-way road. "She should," he said, without averting his gaze from the road. "Maybe then she'd give up that damn coffee shop."

Kevin absently studied a row of drab houses and small shops as the realtor slowed the car. "This doesn't look like the part of town we'd want to locate in. And what makes you think Nadja would sell her shop if she married? That shop sounds like a dream come true for her."

"Humph. She and Ivett both suffer from some gene that says they have to do something creative to be happy."

"Ivett is your wife? Nadja's aunt?"

"Yeah." Chambers turned and smiled broadly. "Ivett is the best thing that ever happened to me. I've never met a more passionate woman. But she's as passionate about her arts and crafts store as she is about me."

"Maybe Nadja is like her aunt," Kevin said, trying not to think too explicitly about Nadja's passion. "Maybe their determination goes back to growing up in Ukraine. That had to be a challenge."

"Yeah," Chambers said, his voice trembling slightly. "Ivett almost didn't make it out. Nadja and her mother waited until they were out from under the thumb of the old Soviet Union before moving."

"Sounds like they had a hard time of it."

"They don't talk a lot about that life." Steve gave him a quick look. "Too bad your company doesn't want to buy the entire Henderson building."

Kevin glared hard at Chambers, who smiled and waved at a man on the sidewalk. "But your wife owns the other half of the building?"

Chambers shrugged, keeping his focus glued on the road. "She shouldn't work so hard. She doesn't have to. I make plenty of money for both of us." He glanced at his passenger. "I've often seen Java Beans next to some sort of bakery. Is that coincidence, or is there a partnership between the two companies?"

"The two have a working relationship. Sometimes it's to both companies' benefit to move in together. It's often an economy of scale issue."

"It's possible, then, you might be interested in the entire building."

"Possible. Probably not likely, actually. Trying to deal with one pissed off woman is enough."

Chambers chuckled. "I can understand that. Well, here we are. This is known as the Janson place."

Kevin got out and leaned against the car. He shook his head in disbelief at the ramshackle building begging to be torn down. "It should be called the dump." He wheeled on Chambers. "This is hardly downtown, Steve. I thought you said last week there was a place for sale right across from Nadja's."

"The owner took it off the market." The realtor blanched. "I'm sorry. Downtown properties are often bought word-of-mouth before they even get listed. And then some folks are holding out because they believe the boom has just begun. Maybe you shouldn't give up on Nadja so quickly."

"I haven't given up on Nadja. Maybe you should work on your wife. If she's willing to sell, then maybe Nadja will sell also."

Kevin wanted to laugh—it looked like Steve Chambers found the task of convincing his wife to sell almost as onerous as he himself found the task of convincing Nadja.

Hours later, Kevin sat at a table in Nadja's Literary Cappuccino nursing a latte, letting the soft Celtic music wash over him, and very much savoring this other side of Nadja. She was an easygoing, laughing, sparkling hostess. She moved comfortably among the almost standing-room-only crowd.

She'd hired extra help Friday and Saturday nights, freeing her up to make sure her patrons were enjoying themselves.

The strain of spending the afternoon with the realtor had diminished immediately when Kevin walked into the shop and she greeted him with a bashful smile and a kiss on each cheek. She hadn't seemed particularly bothered that others were watching.

She'd guided him to a small table in the corner that she'd reserved for herself. That had been her base of operations the entire evening. She supervised the baristas, made sure the musicians weren't overextending themselves, and flitted from table to table chatting with customers.

Nearly everyone called her Nadja. But she didn't seem to favor anyone in particular. No man seemed to catch her eye. He frowned. Nor woman. He hadn't considered that possibility.

"And you must be Kevin—the predator."

Kevin looked quickly at the dark-haired woman beaming at him. She had incredibly white teeth and a smile without limits.

She pulled up a chair without being invited and extended her hand. "Hi. I'm Ivett Chambers, Nadja's aunt. She told me about you. Do you really want to compete with Nadja?"

Speechless, he watched Ivett bat her eyelashes at him.

"Be careful. Nadja is used to winning. She usually gets what she wants."

Kevin blinked at the woman, who didn't look old enough to be Nadja's aunt. "Are you trying to scare me, or tease me?"

Ivett laughed easily. "Maybe both. Nadja's strong-willed. She won't sell the coffee shop any more than I'd ever sell my store." She leaned over and squeezed his fingers. "But there is a catch in her voice when she speaks of you that I haven't heard before. You intrigue her as a man. That hasn't happened since Nadja brought her mother to America."

"I see." Kevin fumbled with his napkin, suddenly feeling uncomfortable.

"I doubt that. But be that as it may, be careful with her." To his surprise, the woman's eyes turned cold. "If you hurt her, I will cut your balls off."

"What the . . ."

"Forgive me," she purred. Her eyes flashed the same kind of fire they'd had when she first sat down. "I have some gypsy blood coursing through my veins. Sometimes it just bubbles forth." She sobered. "I know I'm an interfering aunt. Nadja may look strong and even impenetrable at times, but she has a vulnerable side. She's been hurt before. She can never do a thing halfway. If she decides to love you, she won't hold back anything to protect her heart. You will have to do that for her."

"Jesus," he whispered, glancing over at Nadja, who was poking fun at the keyboard player. He'd never seen her so un-inhibited.

Ivett followed his gaze. "Yes. Nadja can be a lot of fun. Maybe it's her role as hostess, but she comes out of her shell on Friday and Saturday nights." She pushed her chair back from the table, leaned over and kissed him on the cheek. "It's not too late to walk away from her. But if you don't soon, then you'd better be prepared for the long haul. If Nadja decides she wants you, you won't be able to run fast or far enough. Nice meeting you, Kevin. Enjoy."

He nodded as Ivett disappear into the crowd. Had the woman tied his tongue in knots? He blinked. He'd certainly been warned. Not told to stay away — just warned.

He tried his best to smile when Nadja took the seat her aunt had just vacated. "I love this place," she said enthusiastically, "especially when it's filled with people enjoying themselves like tonight."

"And you are the glue that makes it happen."

She gave him a questioning frown.

"You're everywhere. Tending to everyone's needs. Listening to their stories. Laughing at their jokes."

She shrugged a shoulder. "Maybe I like an audience."

"I don't know about that, but I sure do like to watch you. You seem so relaxed tonight."

"I'm sorry I haven't been able to spend more time with you, but I saw you met Ivett."

He tried not to wince. "Yeah, she dropped by. She's quite the lady."

Nadja gave him a curious smile. "She can be quite protective of me. But she's full of love. I don't know what we would've done without Ivett and Steve." She paused. "I've noticed you watching me most of the evening. I like that." She ran a finger down his forearm. "Now I want to know, how often have you undressed me in your mind?"

"What!" he nearly shouted. "Where do you come up with these ideas?"

"I watch American movies to brush up on my English," she said innocently. "That's how I learn about American men. They undress women in their minds."

"I'm not sure that's a skill only known to American males."

"So, how many times?"

"Damn, Nadja. I try not to do that."

"Too bad. Sometimes imagining something is good. I expect you'd be disappointed if you ever saw the real me."

Kevin cleared his throat and glanced around the room. "I doubt that very much. Am I going to see the real you?"

She looked quite pensive, mulling over his words. "I haven't decided. I should check on the baristas." She got to her feet to tower over him. She leaned down and brushed her lips across his. "I'll let you know when I decide."

He watched her sashay toward the counter, hoping his tongue wasn't hanging out. Fortunately, the table hid his erection. The woman was going to be the death of him yet. He'd had a perpetual hard-on almost from the moment he'd met her. What had Ivett said — it wasn't too late for him to get out of Dodge?

Once behind the counter, Nadja turned and flashed him a broad smile.

He braced himself in the chair. He didn't have to stay. His life had been dull but sane before stopping in Jefferson City. He glanced over at the counter. Nadja was busy giving instructions to a barista. She looked completely focused and serious again. And then she peeked over and tossed him another warm smile. His heart melted.

Damn, he wasn't going anywhere. He had to at least show her how a woman deserved to be kissed.

Later that evening, Nadja shuddered, sitting on her living room couch. Kevin sat next to her. He was too close. He was too far away. Her skin warmed and then just as quickly chilled. When had she become such a tease? She never toyed with men. She never bantered with them. Not like this.

Was it Kevin's seemingly boundless patience she was testing? Or was it his perseverance? Maybe it was *her* perseverance.

She raised the wine glass to her lips and peeked at him. They'd exchanged views on a wide range of topics. She'd been surprised by his varied interests. But he hadn't even tried to put his arm around her.

"Do you miss Ukraine?"

"Yes. I miss the high hills, the beautiful buildings, and the dancing."

"But you don't plan to go back?"

She shook her head. "Not to live. This is my home now. I have my shop, and Ivett and her husband. And I can speak my mind without worrying about what others may think." She paused. "At least most of the time."

He nodded and studied her thoughtfully. "Nadja."

"Yes?"

"I don't read minds very well. Are you going to jump out of your skin if I kiss you?"

She wet her lips but couldn't smile. "I'll try not to."

He placed an arm around her shoulder and turned her chin toward him with his other hand. She held his gaze as he dipped his head until his lips slanted across hers. It was a soft kiss. Not at all demanding. His lips coaxed hers into responding. She draped her arms around his neck. She feared she might dissolve in his arms.

He leaned back only enough to whisper, "You taste like cherry."

"My lipstick," she explained.

"I like cherry."

"Maybe you'll want to taste again."

"Oh, yeah."

Again, his tongue flicked at her lips—testing, tasting. He licked the corner of her mouth and etched his tongue along its width. She parted her lips slightly, and he separated them farther with his tongue.

She closed her eyes and let him work his wonders. No one had ever taken the time to kiss her like this. Her entire body responded. Her nipples pebbled. Her thighs opened and closed. Had he found an erotic switch on the roof of her mouth she hadn't known she possessed?

He tapped her tongue until she responded in kind. She moaned, enjoying this novel tongue play. He gradually withdrew his tongue into his mouth, and she chased it with hers. He chuckled and trapped her there. He suckled her tongue as if his life depended on satisfying her.

Tears came to her eyes. He let her go and pressed his

tongue back into her mouth. She kept her eyes tightly closed and suckled his tongue as he had done to hers. She tightened her grip on his head. She couldn't get enough of him.

His hands roamed the length and breadth of her back. They cupped her buttocks. Her eyes popped opened, but she didn't yield her hold on his tongue. His eyes remained closed. Perhaps he'd lost himself in the moment just as she had.

She closed her eyes and returned to their dance of tongues. Her breasts ached. Her rigid nipples sought relief.

As if he could read her every need, his palm settled over a breast. His thumb grazed her nipple and then depressed it as if it were a button.

She broke their kiss and arched her neck back. His lips trailed the chords of her throat. Shortly, they replaced his thumb on her nipple. She struggled for breath as wetness from his mouth drenched her blouse.

She clutched his head tight. His mouth poured heat over her body. Her loins tightened. She hadn't realized he'd worked a hand inside her blouse until his finger grazed her bare skin.

She chewed on her lower lip, trying to keep up with what was happening to her, to them. His finger found its way into her bra and tapped on her nipple. "Kevin," she moaned, "I . . ."

There was no end to the thought or the sentence. Her body had shifted into its own gear. Her hips moved in unison with the finger tapping on her nipple. She clung to his neck and let it happen. "Goodness." She stiffened.

His finger withdrew. She opened her eyes and saw him unbuttoning her blouse. He reached for her bra clasp. She covered his hand and met his questioning stare.

She shook her head. "I can't. I'm sorry. I'm not ready for this."

He nodded and backed away. "Could've fooled me. Guess

you did. Guess I'd better head over to the motel."

She didn't bother buttoning the blouse but rose to her feet when he did. She took his hands in hers. "You are an incredibly patient man. I'd understand if you don't come back."

His smile threatened what little reserve she possessed. "Oh, I'll be back." He pecked at her nose. "I hope you're getting the picture."

She frowned. "What picture?"

"When we make love, it will be something to make a fuss about. It won't just be fucking. And it will be personal."

"It already is." She brushed her lips across his. "You're not going to give up on me?"

He straightened his shoulders. "I don't give up easily. I probably can be as stubborn as you."

"Uh-oh, we may be in trouble. Good night. Will I see you before tomorrow night?"

"I doubt I can make it tomorrow at all. I've got a fairly packed schedule. The mayor invited me to a party he's holding for some local politicos tomorrow night. But I am keeping Sunday open." He started to leave and stopped. "I forgot to tell you I brought my running shoes. Do you run on Sunday, and what time?"

"Great. Of course I run on Sunday. Seven."

"Seven! On Sunday morning?"

She nodded.

"Damn, you are a slave driver. I'll be here."

"Good—I won't leave without you."

He waved and let himself out.

Nadja blew air between her compressed lips. She cupped the breast he'd so recently caressed with passion she hadn't been aware of.

Kevin Langley had really begun to scare her. Not because of his interest in her shop. Not even because of his interest in her body. He scared her because he displayed a deep river of passion that just might match her own.

Even when using her crystal wand, she hadn't dared to probe the depths of that passion. Certainly, no man had ever bothered to try.

Kevin Langley had proven he was capable of doing that. But should she let him?

She blinked back tears. What if he didn't like what he found? What if she didn't like what *she* found?

CHAPTER FOUR

Breathing hard, Kevin stopped on the jogging path, hunched over, and grabbed his knees. Was this his punishment for having erotic thoughts on a Sunday? He glanced up at a smiling Nadja and shook his head.

"We won't run as far as I typically do." She stretched a hamstring. "You'll need to run more often if you plan on keeping up with me."

Wasn't that the damn truth? He'd thought he was in better shape. He did work out at motel gyms when he traveled, and he jogged now and then around a lake in St. Paul. But Nadja was a long-distance runner. He grimaced, still gasping for air.

She appeared rather intimidating in her powder-blue sweatshirt. She must have had on one of those fancy sports bras, because she looked nearly flat-chested. That was a visual loss.

On the other hand, he'd become quite familiar with her ass undulating back and forth as she ran fluidly ahead of him. While aware his feeling wasn't rational, he'd become jealous of her sweatpants hugging that butt. Did she have any idea how her movements mesmerized? She must have an entourage of male runners following her each day.

He glanced along the trail. Fortunately, this morning she only had an entourage of one. He couldn't decide what was more painful—his burning thighs or his straining erection.

She brought a water bottle to her lips. She sipped; a small rivulet spilled from the corner of her mouth. She started to brush it away.

"Let me." He ran his finger across her lips.

She again brought the water bottle to her lips. This time more water spilled from her mouth and her eyes sparkled.

He didn't require a written invitation. He tilted her wet chin and licked his way from her chin to her lower lip. She parted her lips, and more water spilled from them. He lapped at it and then locked his mouth over hers. The water she'd been holding in her puffed-out cheeks flowed into his mouth. He swallowed. He hadn't realized how thirsty he was.

He clutched her rear between both hands and ground her loins against his. There was no way she could avoid feeling his hard cock. She flinched and then let him draw her closer. He held her tight, afraid to move. He didn't want to frighten her, and this wasn't the place to go much further anyway. He squeezed her butt, and her eyes popped wide open. They were clouded with an emotion he couldn't define.

She drew his tongue into her mouth and he closed his eyes, letting her take whatever she wanted. Her arms tightened around him. Her pelvis rubbed against him. She was obviously aware of his arousal. His eyes shot open; hers were shuttered. Was she aware of what her body was doing? He ran his palms over her bottom and patted it. How could a woman's ass feel so tight and yet be such an inviting cushion?

One of them had to stop or they could be in world of trouble, if not hurt. With effort, he backed out of their embrace and held her at arm's length. She gave him a furtive glance and then looked down at their feet.

"I'm sorry," she stammered, "I don't know what came over me."

He chuckled. "I think it's called lust." He reached for the water bottle and turned away from her. He sipped and then swallowed. He willed his cock to shrivel before he turned around to face her, but he knew that was impossible.

He faced her and handed the bottle over. "Do you want to

go further?"

She blushed. "No—we'd better head back." She broke into a smile. "If we run much farther, I may have to carry you back to the car. And it doesn't look"—she pointed at his crotch—"like you should be trying to run right now."

"Sorry about that. You're right. Maybe we should walk for a while." He brushed the back of his hand across her forehead. He was burning up, and she was cool. "Guess I'll have to work harder at staying in shape."

"You're in fine shape." Her lips curved into a faint smile as she lowered her gaze again to his midsection. "And you certainly seem firm enough." She peered at him without a hint of humor. "You may need to work on your endurance if you want to be around me very much."

He grabbed her by the hand and headed down the path, and then stopped suddenly.

"What is it?" she asked.

"Are you always more bold in a public setting than in a private setting?"

"I don't know what you mean."

He shook his head. "I think you do. It's safer out here. Isn't it?"

She shrugged.

"You enjoy playing with me, don't you?"

She frowned. "You don't want me to play with you?"

"I didn't say that. I very much like you playing with me." He lifted her chin but made no move to kiss her still puffy lips. "But you must remember you are not playing this game alone."

"I do know that." Her voice trembled slightly. She brushed a finger pad across his cheek.

"You're comfortable playing at level one. There will come a time when I will want—will need to play at higher levels."

She nodded. "I know that, too. But don't rush me. Please?"

"I'm trying not to. I really am." He swung her hand in his. "The morning is a-wasting. Let's keep going."

Humming to herself, Nadja checked the bacon and stirred the eggs. She cocked an ear toward the stairway. The upstairs shower was still running. She closed her eyes, trying not to imagine Kevin standing naked in her shower. Her skin warmed. He'd seemed quite sizeable when he'd crushed her body to him near the running path. More substantial than her crystal wand.

She hugged herself, not believing she'd actually rubbed her crotch against his. And then she'd made an obvious reference to his arousal. It pleased her to know she'd brought that about, but she was not usually brazen with men. What had come over her?

Was it his tenderness? His fingers, his lips, his tongue promised so much more. They promised an ecstasy Ivett had talked about.

Didn't she deserve to experience that kind of ecstasy at least once in her life? She didn't want to deceive herself by thinking Kevin could maintain any long-term interest in her. But he was no bumbling boy—nor was he a demanding old man.

She'd thrilled under his touch. And she had a hard time not touching him in the same way. She shivered and returned her attention to the eggs.

Moments later, a deep male voice taunted, "If you don't stop whipping those eggs pretty soon, we may have to add rum and have eggnog."

She whirled to protest. Her voice caught somewhere in her throat at the sight of him standing in the kitchen doorway wearing only sweatpants. She couldn't stop staring at his solid bare chest, still damp from the shower. She noticed a thin line of dark hair below his navel and stretching lower yet. She swallowed hard. His bare feet only added to the effect, making him the most desirable man she'd ever seen.

"If you keep staring at me with that hungry look," Kevin warned, "we'll be moving up another level or two very quickly. Those shorts you have on and that T-shirt will hit the floor only seconds before you do."

Her hand flew to her throat, and she shook her head. "That won't be necessary," she stuttered. She stumbled toward the refrigerator and reached for the orange juice.

"I'm sorry," he said, quietly. "I didn't mean to scare you."

"You didn't. I scared myself."

"Sorry, but I left my duffle in the living room. I'll slip into fresh clothes. That might help remove temptation for both of us."

"I'll put the food on the table and get the paper." The memory of him standing there nearly naked, his sweatpants tenting before her eyes, was more than enough temptation to last for a while. At least food and the newspaper would be a distraction. But temptation would remain with her unless she could purge her memory bank.

Once the eggs were finished, Nadja opened the kitchen door and reached down for the Sunday paper. Her arm froze. She couldn't breathe. With effort, she grabbed the paper and reread the headline over the right hand column: *Java Beans Buyout?*

She scanned the article quickly, gagging at each word. How could he do this to her? She'd never said she had the slightest interest in selling.

Smiling and wearing jeans and a blue shirt, Kevin re-entered the kitchen. "This should be less tempting."

She glowered at him, and he stopped mid-step.

"What? What's wrong?"

"I didn't expect encouraging your interest in me would

stop you from pursuing your plans to locate a franchise here — but then, I didn't expect you to lie about me, either." She flung the paper at him. "I think you'd better leave now."

He picked the paper off the floor. His focus moved quickly down the front page. "What the . . . No one interviewed me for this article."

He looked up at her with a pained expression. "You never said you'd consider an offer."

She crossed her arms under her breasts and shook her head. "I want you to leave, Kevin. I can't think straight with you here."

"Sure," he snapped. "The going gets tough and you want to run. I've seen this kind of thing in other towns. Someone wants you to sell and is using the local paper to make a point. It could get worse. But I'm not behind this story."

"I didn't know you wanted to buy the entire building. Was that another little secret?"

"I don't. We don't. At least I don't think the company would want to do that. Too risky for a small market. Your uncle mentioned that possibility when he was showing me some rundown property."

"My uncle?"

"Yeah, Steve Chambers. I don't remember telling him whether we'd be interested or not. It was idle conversation." He scowled. "I thought."

"No matter; I want you out of here."

"I'm going. When you cool down, you can call me if you want. Don't count on me calling you first. I don't like being called a liar." He whirled and left the kitchen. The entry door closed with a bang.

Tears streamed down her cheeks as she bent down to retrieve the paper. She reread the article with blurry eyes. It was true the paper only cited an unnamed source. If it wasn't Kevin — and she wasn't ready to believe it wasn't — then who was it? Her uncle? She frowned. He might prefer to have Ivett at home, but it didn't seem possible he'd stoop to airing their family disagreements in a newspaper. And if it was him, he'd better be wearing full body armor to ready himself for battle with his wife.

Nadja dumped the cold eggs and bacon down the garbage disposal. She wished it was as easy to erase her memory bank. And what if Kevin hadn't been the source? Then she'd just done him a wrong they'd both regret.

She shook her head. At this point, he might not regret it at all. He'd gotten rid of a confused woman without even having to work at it. She hated being confused.

"Sounds like someone is trying to railroad us into a deal," Asa Sheridan said, staring thoughtfully at Kevin.

Kevin nodded at the elderly president of Java Beans. "That's possible. It's happened before. Small towns want the benefits of a nationally recognized chain in their community." He glanced at Carolyn James, Vice President and heir apparent, who continued to scowl at the article.

She looked over at him. "Maybe. How much do you know about this Nadja woman?"

Kevin didn't like the feel of his skin warming under her stare. "Some."

"I see." Carolyn cleared her throat. "I'm sure you've heard the old adage not to mix pleasure with business."

"Sometimes it can't be helped."

Carolyn smiled knowingly. "I can attest to that. I wouldn't be happily married if I hadn't ignored that little piece of wisdom. But back to this situation." She glanced down at the paper. "The quotes from the unknown source seem aimed as much at her as at drumming up support for Java Beans."

"I agree," Kevin said, "but it doesn't make any sense.

Nadja seems to be well-liked, and she's put together a gathering place for people in the arts."

"Not everyone, I suppose, is attracted to the arts—even in Jefferson City."

He ignored her bias about small-town culture. "I imagine you're right about that. I really haven't had much opportunity to explore any of this in depth." He sighed. "Let's just say that when Nadja discovered this article, I became persona non-grata."

"Ah," Sheridan said, "the wolf in sheep's clothing. Only Nadja didn't think you were a sheep."

"Most women don't," Carolyn pointed out quietly. "Seems like we have three choices. One, we can walk away from the possibility of setting up a franchise in that area and write it off as an idea that had little merit. Two, we can continue having Kevin scope out the area—maybe expand our original geographics. If we do that, you may want to hook up with a different realtor. There have to be more options in a city that size than one little downtown shop."

Kevin nodded. "And three?"

"We try to sort out what the hell is going on with this woman whom you believe won't sell no matter what. If we do set up a franchise in Northern Iowa, we don't want the Java Beans reputation sullied because someone is trying to settle a score with your Nadja woman."

Kevin frowned. The Nadja woman had suddenly become *his* woman. Would Nadja agree with that assessment? Probably not. But he was furious at the possibility someone might be using him to hurt her.

"I'm not ready to accept the first option," Sheridan interjected. "We need a presence in Northern Iowa. If not in Jefferson City, then I want to know where." He coughed. "Seems to me options two and three are quite intertwined. And I definitely concur we have a reputation to protect. I assume you agree."

Kevin cleared his throat. "Of course."

"Then I want you to spend some time down there until you can ferret out what the hell is going on."

"You don't want to send someone else?"

Carolyn chuckled. "Do you think Nadja will trust anyone else we might send in your stead?"

"No."

"Then I guess it's up to you to get back into her good graces enough to figure out what is happening with her shop."

"That's a tall order."

Carolyn stood, clearly calling an end to their meeting. "You're man enough to pull this off, Kevin. She's only a woman."

"Right," he muttered, not liking Carolyn's challenging grin. Too bad he liked her and respected her so much. She was certain to be the next president of the company and had already talked to him about moving up to a vice president position. But sometimes she enjoyed watching him squirm more than he liked. And she was obviously enjoying herself right now.

As soon as she opened the door to her shop, Nadja realized she was in trouble. Her aunt was pacing back and forth in front of the counter. She had a newspaper rolled up in one hand. Her hand was clenched in a fist, and she was cussing in Ukrainian.

"I would've stormed your house yesterday," Ivett fumed, "but I didn't trust myself. I feared I might kill that bastard Langley."

When she paused for breath, Nadja took the opportunity to duck behind the counter and busy herself with making coffees.

"You can't escape me that easily," Ivett declared. "He was with you yesterday, right?"

Nadja sighed and blinked. "Until I told him to leave."

"Good for you, girl. The son of a bitch, thinking he was going to buy me out, too."

Nadja set the coffee beans aside. She shook her head and tried desperately not to cry. She *never* cried. "Kevin was not the source."

"Right!" Ivett smacked the paper against the corner. "And lakes freeze over in the summer."

"He said he was never interviewed."

"And you believe him?" Ivett stared, disbelieving. "But you just said you kicked him out."

"I panicked. I needed space to think." She turned away from her aunt's glare to fill a pot with water. After she inserted the coffee container and pushed the button, she faced her aunt and, with surprise, saw that she'd calmed some. Ivett could nurse anger for days. "I thought back through everything he'd said to me about the shop" — she quickly glanced away — "and about other things. Kevin wouldn't purposely lie to me."

"Wow!" Ivett blew bangs from her brow. "I don't know whether to be more pissed, relieved, or pleased. Your rosy cheeks say much more than your words. He's chipping away at you. Isn't that a hoot? Mr. Swashbuckling Salesman sweeps introverted Ms. Iceberg off her feet."

Nadja glowered. "I am still on my feet."

"Sort of like Professor Hill conquering Madam Marian the librarian."

"I am no Madam Librarian," Nadja huffed. "And I always thought Marian conquered the professor anyway."

"A matter of interpretation, I'm sure. So if your beau is to be believed . . ."

"I said I believe him."

"But you haven't told him that?"

She shook her head and once again tried to hold back tears.

Ivett chuckled. "That should be interesting. Chip, chip. The salesman gains some ground. I assume he hasn't gotten into your panties yet."

"Ivett! How . . ." Nadja's fingers curled at her throat.

"You're not glowing enough. You're too on edge." Ivett reached across the counter and brushed the back of her fingers against Nadja's cheek. "I am so pleased you are opening to him. It's been too long. You are such a precious flower. And I'm pleased Kevin Langley is taking his time with you. Maybe he appreciates how special you are." She sobered. "Not all men are like Gustave."

Nadja shook her head, not wanting to think even for a moment about her old coach. Her lips curved into a small smile. "If Kevin were an impatient man, he'd be long gone." She furrowed her brow. "But my overreacting to the newspaper article probably means I'll never see him again." She hugged herself. "Oh well."

"If he's as patient as it seems, I don't think he'll let a misunderstanding stay in the way for long. And if he does, then you'll have to act. I've never known you to hesitate about going after what you want."

Nadja decided it was best to keep her own counsel on what she might or might not do to retrieve her errant knight.

"If he didn't talk to a reporter . . ." Ivett flashed an eyebrow. "I believe you. You're usually a better judge of people than I am. But where did this damn story come from?"

"I don't know. Kevin has met with representatives from the City Council and the Chamber. He hasn't tried to be particularly secretive, but he claims he's never expressed an interest in buying the entire building. The only time that came up was in a conversation with Steve."

"Steve?" Ivett stilled. "My Steve?"

"Uh-huh. I don't know how he decided on Steve as his realtor, but he was surprised to learn of my relationship to him. Why are you turning several shades of purple? Are you all right?"

"I'll survive, which is more than might be said for my husband. You don't suppose he's seeing this Java Beans interest as a way for me to give up working? He's harbored some resentment about this shop since before we married, but I never thought he'd go behind my back to force me out."

"I don't think he'd do that. He loves you too much."

"And I love him," Ivett spat out. "That doesn't mean we don't have some major disagreements."

Nadja nodded. She'd witnessed more of those disagreements than she'd wanted, but Ivett and Steve always seemed to enjoy making up afterward. She could only hope Steve hadn't gone too far this time—if indeed he was behind the story.

"I'll take care of my Neanderthal husband. You'd better think about how you're going to take care of your lover." Ivett stuck her tongue out. "Bye for now." Ivett sauntered out of the café and into her own shop.

Returning to her coffee urns, Nadja was pleased she didn't have to listen in on how her aunt would deal with her uncle. Maybe the guy had a penchant for being skewered.

She pursed her lips. How to deal with Kevin? Lover? She smiled softly. She hadn't used that label to describe him. Maybe. Seemed likely. If she could get him back. What would that require? She had little experience in groveling.

CHAPTER FIVE

Rising from the living room couch to answer the doorbell, Nadja frowned and tightened the sash of her robe. She checked the mantel clock. It was nearly eight-thirty. She'd put away the dishes, showered, and had been engrossed in her current novel. Rarely did she have visitors this late in the evening.

She flipped on the porch light and peeked out a window. Her heart kicked into high gear. Did he always show up unexpectedly? And she hadn't yet decided what to do with him.

She opened the door and stepped back. She did her best to show no emotion. If he broke off with her tonight, she wouldn't give him the benefit of witnessing her pleasure at seeing him.

"May I come in?" Kevin said, haltingly. "I hope it's not too late. I was late getting away from the office. Maybe I should've waited until morning. But after the other day, I didn't want to risk having your customers witness you tossing me out of your shop."

"I wouldn't . . ." She stopped speaking as soon as his eyes lowered. She smiled to herself when he began to redden. Apparently, he'd only just she was wearing her lounging robe.

At last he raised his chin and wet his lips. "Damn, those slippers are absolutely amazing."

Now it was her turn to blush. She didn't have to peek down at her pink bunny slippers, long ears and all. As a girl, she'd always been fascinated with bunny rabbits. Maybe she still was. But she didn't need to explain her choice of slippers to him.

"Come in," she said, her voice just above a whisper. "I've wanted to call you, but I didn't know how." She grimaced. "I made a mistake. I know you didn't talk to the newspaper reporter."

"How do you know that?" Kevin folded his arms across his chest.

She tried her best to ignore her memory of him standing bare-chested in her kitchen. She failed miserably. "Because you said you wouldn't lie to me."

"And you trusted that?"

"Once I had time to think about it, yes." She brushed back tears. "I'm sorry I panicked."

"I know." His voice was soft. "Let me." He wiped away her tears. "You were badly frightened. It was best for me to leave — though I wasn't thrilled about that at the time." He gave her a quirky smile. "I guess we both needed some space for reflection."

She nodded, grabbed his hand, and led him toward her kitchen. "You want some coffee, or wine?"

"Wine would be great. That would be relaxing."

She led the way to the kitchen where she grabbed an open bottle of wine from the fridge. "Hope you like Pinot Grigio. It's what I have left."

"That'll be quite fine. Maybe it will help me unwind. I did speed more than I usually do getting down here. I wasn't at all sure you'd even talk to me."

Nadja chewed on her lower lip, then handed him a glass of wine. "I think I'd like to do more than talk, if you want to." She paused. "Maybe a little of this," she whispered, rising on her toes to slant her lips across his. She parted before he had a chance to react. "Why don't we take our glasses into the living room?"

They settled on the couch, and she held a glass in one hand

and intertwined the fingers of her other hand with his.

He squeezed. "Do you have anything on under that robe?"

She grinned, certain he'd wanted to ask that question ever since he'd gotten over his initial nervousness. She shook her head and squeezed his fingers back. "I wasn't expecting company."

"And if you'd known I would ring your doorbell this evening? Would you have worn something else?"

"It would not have made any difference." She blushed and glanced away.

"Unless you chickened out?"

"That could've happened, I suppose." She jutted out her chin. "But you're here now. And I'm not running away this time. And yes, I am naked under this robe. Does that fascinate you?" She saw no need to inform him that she'd become very wet, almost as wet as when she played with her wand.

He brushed a finger across her willing lips. "More than I can say. Before I kiss you, I need to let you to know I met with my bosses at Java Beans. They are no longer interested in buying your property. They remain committed to setting up a franchise in the Northern Iowa area. But they are not at all pleased about someone misrepresenting them in the paper."

"I don't want to talk about that now." She pushed back a lock of hair from her brow. "I thought you came to see me. I want you to see me. All of me."

She held his gaze steady and guided his hand under her robe until her hand and his cradled a breast. She moaned when his fingers came to life. She left him there, wrapped both of her arms around his neck, and leaned across to kiss his partly open mouth. She swallowed whatever verbal response he made while his fingers continued caressing her breast. They cupped it and teased her nipple.

She thrust her tongue between his lips, relishing the role of aggressor. She sucked on his tongue until his moans filled her ears. Then she broke away and pushed his head downward. "I love the way you play with my tits. Now I want you to see me, all of me."

Together they parted the top of her robe until her breasts stood out before him. His immediate adoration caused her toes to curl.

"They are splendid," he said, reaching out to rub the back of a hand against each nipple. "I never had the honor to love such beautiful breasts."

"They are not too large, too pendulous?"

His eyes gleamed at her. "You're kidding. No, you're not." He cupped each breast and lifted them slightly. He shook his head. She could tell his breath had become ragged.

He said nothing more but lowered his head to kiss first one aching nipple and then the other. He kissed them as if they were sacred objects. Tears formed in her eyes. She'd been so conflicted about her breasts for years. Kevin wasn't conflicted at all.

She arched forward as he took one breast deep into his mouth. She shuddered and combed his hair with her fingers. He didn't stop. She didn't want him to.

He moved his lips to the other breast. She winced for the one he'd just left. It was damp and bereft. His warm hand soon covered it, and he caressed the nipple.

She tossed her head from side to side and whimpered. He was turning her into mush. And she loved it. "Goodness," she murmured, surprised by the sudden buildup in her loins. Clutching him to her bosom as tightly as she could, she welcomed the approaching relief. Her hips leapt off the sofa once, twice. Then just as quickly, she stopped writhing in his arms. Her scent filled the air.

He raised his head and pecked at her lips. "You have incredibly sensitive breasts."

She shook her head. "I don't usually come that way. I don't

know what's happening to me."

His eyes filled with pride. "Maybe it has something to do with me?"

She ran her fingers lightly across his forehead. "I believe it has a lot to do with you. You're introducing me to a body I didn't know I had."

"Hardly." He pecked at her nose. "Maybe together we're exploring it in ways you haven't before." He reached for the sash. "May I?"

She caught her breath, nodded her chin, and tried to show no fear as he nodded and lowered his gaze. Then he untied her sash and, with slightly trembling fingers, spread the robe.

"Damn," he gasped.

She shrank into herself. What was wrong?

"You're a goddess, Nadja. Why am I so blessed?"

Her skin warmed—he must like what he was seeing.

His fingers skimmed across her moist mound. She flinched and then relaxed, parting her thighs more for him.

He nodded but did nothing to break the spell that had overtaken them. He slid a finger down one side of her labia and then slowly up the other side.

"What are you doing?"

"Familiarizing myself with your sex. You have a beautiful pussy." He winked at her. "And I'm showing you how much fun it can be getting to know me." He massaged her folds between thumb and forefinger.

She flinched.

"Is that okay?"

"Uh-huh," she replied, not trusting herself with more words.

"You're so moist."

She tilted her hips, making her request as clear as she knew how. "I've come once already. I don't know . . ."

He chuckled softly. With one hand he parted her labia and

slid a finger the length of her crevice.

She tried to breathe. She couldn't take much more of this. Pleasure had suddenly turned to torture.

"Ready?"

"I think so," she murmured, without opening her eyes.

Her sex welcomed his finger as if he were a long-lost friend. She moaned her yearning. *Lover,* Ivett had called him. Nadja bit down on her lower lip as his finger explored her depths. A lover he was. A careful, patient lover. Her lover.

"So desirable. You are an amazing woman. So ripe. So ready. So responsive." His words washed over her. His finger began moving in and out of her. She gasped and clutched her breasts.

"Come for me, Nadja. Don't hide from me."

His words became a jumble—she could only concentrate on the music of his finger playing her like a fine-tuned musical instrument. A second finger entered her. She stiffened. "Oh my," she wailed. He didn't let up. And she edged closer and closer to the brink. His fingers curled, begging her to come. She could hear as plainly as if they were screaming to her.

"Let go, Nadja," he said softly. "Come for me. Let yourself go. You're safe with me." He brushed the back of his other hand against her aching clitoris.

She immediately spun out of control. Her hips bucked against him. He chuckled, and she soared out of the atmosphere. Then she grabbed his wrist and held it steady. She couldn't give him any more. She curled into a ball, and he clutched her tight.

Long minutes passed before she opened her eyes to find him watching her, concern written on his face.

"Are you okay?"

She nodded. She grimaced when he slowly withdrew his fingers from her folds. She couldn't explain the sudden emptiness that threatened to engulf her.

Slowly, some strength spread across her muscles — muscles she'd had no control over only minutes earlier. She rubbed his bicep. "I'm afraid I've been having all the pleasure."

He shook his head at her. "If you truly believe that, then you don't know me at all."

She propped herself up on an elbow. Where had her energy gone? She smiled, remembering that other world beyond the curtain. Was that where she'd left it? "But what about you? You need relief, at least."

He followed her gaze to his bulging arousal and shook his head. "Another time. You're exhausted. I'd prefer to wait." He frowned. "Someone has hurt you badly."

She shrugged. She didn't have to ask him what he meant. "It happened a long time ago. I don't want to talk about it."

"I won't press you."

"I know you won't. I'll just say that not all ballet coaches are gay. One of my coaches became quite angry because I let my breasts grow too big. His punishment wasn't pleasant. He was too large. I was too young."

She watched him scowl and sort through her words. She saw anger fly across his face, only to be replaced by compassion. At last he nodded. "Some people can't appreciate beauty — inside or out. You are beautiful, Nadja, inside and out. I'm not sure I'll ever get enough of you."

She smiled with trembling lips. "I know. And I love sharing my body with you. You are such a patient man. Will you stay the night? You can share my bed." She gave him a weak smile. "I can't guarantee anything, but there is tomorrow morning."

He shook his head, gathered her robe tight around her and knotted the sash. "I appreciate the offer, but I'm not sure I'm that patient. No, I'd better stay at the motel tonight."

She pouted. "If you must." She wet her lips and dug deep

for courage. "I may not be very experienced in matters of sex, but I do know how to bring off a man with my hands."

"Jesus." Kevin sprang to his feet. "Whether on purpose or not, you do know how to act the temptress. No, I'll wait. I don't want my first time with you to be that way. I don't want to feel like a teenager in the backseat of a car." He smiled. "But I would welcome a goodnight kiss."

She stood and wrapped her arms around his neck. "I don't know about backseats of cars," she whispered, raising her lips to his.

His chuckle reverberated across her swollen lips. He broke away and patted her rump. "Until later. I'll drop by the shop sometime tomorrow."

"I'll be there."

Neither spoke again. She locked the door behind him and padded off toward her bed. She frowned. Her bed was going to feel much larger than usual. She rarely felt lonely. But she seemed to be having a lot of rare moments lately.

"Shit," Steve Chambers mumbled, glancing into his rearview mirror.

Kevin noticed Steve's change in attitude immediately. Gone was the glib air that all was right with the world. It was replaced by anxiety, if not downright fright. They'd parked in front of another dump of a building Steve seemed intent on showing him. The black Cadillac pulling to a stop behind them provided a diversion, although apparently one Steve didn't welcome.

Getting out of the car, Kevin smiled at the man with a cigar locked tightly between his teeth. The slightly paunchy blond fellow brushed right past Steve and reached out a hand to shake Kevin's.

Kevin shook the man's hand. His grip reminded him of a

wet washrag.

"Howdy, Mr. Langley. My name is Rick Adams." He gave Steve a quick glance. "Steve and I are buddies from way back. Hear you're interested in bringing a Java Beans franchise to our good town."

"Might be," Kevin acknowledged. "If the numbers come together and it feels right."

"I know about numbers. I've been working numbers in this area for people for years. We're always interested in companies that can enhance our community." The newcomer gave Steve a stern once-over. "What are you showing him this piece of shit for?"

Steve glared at his inquisitor. "Trying to show him the range of options available."

Rick shook his head and gave Kevin a conspiratorial look. "You ain't gonna do better than that Henderson building. Nice article in the paper last Sunday."

Kevin kept his features blank. Often he learned more by staying quiet than by reacting to every piece of new information. So how did Rick Adams figure in the overall picture, and why did Steve Chambers resent the overly gregarious man?

"You gonna make a bid on the Henderson building?"

He shook his head. "Doesn't look like it. It's not for sale."

Rick sneered. "Those Russian women will sell. You just have to show some backbone and perseverance."

"I thought they were Ukrainian," he said, looking over at Steve.

"Whatever," Rick spat out before Steve could correct him. "Foreigners no matter what spots they may have. No better than the damn Mexicans."

"Rick! You're talking about my wife and niece."

"Oh, I forgot."

Kevin fought back his temper. Quite obviously Adams had

not forgotten, nor was he concerned about Chambers's feelings or anger. Kevin glared at Steve. Why the hell wasn't he defending his women? This entire situation had a stench about it. "We're not particularly interested in the Henderson building—and we never did want to buy the whole thing."

"Don't give up so quickly. I'm sure we can work something out."

Kevin smiled thinly. "I thought those women owned the building."

"Yes, but . . ."

Kevin drew himself to his full height, towering over the smaller man. "Java Beans is not interested in browbeating women to sell. And we don't want to be sullied by those who do." He looked directly at Steve, ignoring the man chewing on his cigar. "Are we going to look at this property? I've got a schedule to keep."

"Sure. We can look at it right now."

Adams held out his hand. "Here's my card if you can't find a better option for your franchise. They're a lot of businessmen in town who'd love to have a reputable national chain in that building. Call me."

"Don't waste a lot of time waiting by the phone." He nodded at Steve. "Let's go."

Kevin followed Chambers up the sidewalk to the office building that must've seen a better day. Once inside, he whirled on Steve. "You mind telling me what the hell that was about?"

Steve laughed nervously. "Nothing much. Rick thinks of himself as a mover and shaker in the town. He's mostly hot air."

"And you let him talk about Ivett and Nadja that way?"

"Do you think busting his nose would improve his attitude any?"

Kevin shook his head. "I don't know about his, but it sure

as hell would improve mine. I guess every community has its share of gutter snipes."

"Unfortunately, you're probably right."

"This is another dump, Steve. Are you sure you can't show me any better properties? Maybe I should hook up with a different realtor."

Chambers blanched. "Maybe you should. I'll look at the listings again, but I can't find much that has any potential."

"You do that. You look at the listings again. I may make some other calls." Kevin glowered at Steve, who recoiled. "We'll leave it at that, for now. I may have some questions for you down the road, but I expect I know a couple women who should have first call."

Flushed, Steve shrugged. They drove back to his office in silence.

Nadja rested her elbows on the top railing of the nature observation deck. She'd brought Kevin to one of her absolutely favorite places—a public acreage set aside to preserve some of the prairie in the wild state in which it had once flourished across much of the Midwest. This prairie also served as a bird and wildlife sanctuary. There wasn't a season she didn't relish here, and the abundant blooming flowers bursting across the landscape from early spring to late fall seemed to change almost weekly.

She'd often stood on that deck at dusk and watched deer graze their way across the meadow or listened in on the early morning or late evening chattering of birds welcoming the day or the night.

She gave Kevin a shy smile. Probably neither either of them had spent as much time observing wildlife since they'd arrived as they had each other. What was it about him? She couldn't get enough of him. His soft brown eyes pooled like a pond on a still day. Sometimes she didn't even want to try to decipher the emotions they reflected. How could a pair of eyes draw and frighten at the same time?

"So, what's churning in that beautiful head of yours now?" Kevin asked, brushing her nape with the back of his hand.

She inhaled sharply. "Why are you interested in me?" she asked hesitantly.

He took a half step backward. "Why do you ask that? Why here?"

She smiled and turned to stare out across the meadow. "This is a special place for me. It feeds my soul."

"And it's safer than your living room or your bedroom."

She nodded, not daring to look at him. "That, too."

"Aside from being a gorgeous woman, you fascinate me."

She turned her head toward him. "How do I fascinate you?"

"Your work ethic. How you think. Your passion."

"Passion?" She scowled. "You must be mocking me. I'm certainly not living up to what you want when it comes to passion—I'm trying, but . . ."

He shrugged. "You don't rush a good wine or a good whiskey." He curled his fingers around hers. "Or a good woman."

"Are you just being persistent?" She knitted her brow. "You're confident if you hang around long enough you'll find your way into my pussy."

He eyed her steadily. "I already have—or have you forgotten?"

She shook her head. "How could I forget? You were wonderful. And you know that's not what I meant. I will yield. Somehow, you will make it happen—or I will."

"When you really open for me, it will be because we both want it and allow it to happen." He slid his lips across her ear and leaned back and grinned.

She held herself in check. "What happens after we do it,

after we fuck?" she murmured. "After I've given you a most precious part of me — what then?"

She swore his eyes flickered with pain. Her immediate response was to kick herself for causing him such distress, but she desperately needed to hear his response. She knew they couldn't have a long-term future together, but neither did she want to be merely a notch on some guy's belt.

Gently, he placed a hand on each of her shoulders and turned her to face him directly. "I'm not sure what you're looking for, Nadja, but I can tell you this. Yes, I want to fuck you — no — I want to *make love* with you. I don't apologize for that — I know we'll be good together. I don't have a crystal ball. Maybe that's all we'll do. If so, I expect it will be well worth the effort. Where do we go from there?" He shook his head. "I don't know."

He cleared his throat. "One thing you should know. When I get involved with a woman sexually, there are no others. I don't have enough emotional fortitude to deal with more than one woman at a time."

She snickered. "I've never tried being involved with more than one man at a time." She grinned at his arched eyebrow. "And I don't have any plans to try that in the near future."

"Well, that's something." He slanted his lips across hers and backed away. "I believe we've entered into some sort of committed relationship." He held up a palm when she opened her mouth to speak. "An open-ended relationship — neither of us predicting how this will end."

She thrust out her chin. "What if I disappoint you?"

"What?" He looked aghast.

She glanced away. "In bed."

He cradled her chin until she looked at him squarely. "When we make love, Nadja, I am not going to be disappointed." He gave her a teasing grin. "We're not talking about a one-time event. I'm confident we can work together to make it a mutually satisfying experience. I haven't gone away from you disappointed yet."

"Maybe you should've," she huffed. "I haven't given you much at all."

"I hate to tell a woman she's wrong, but you are definitely wrong about that. I have been exhilarated beyond belief. Do I look forward to you being nestled against my body with my cock filling you? Absolutely!" Her cheeks warmed, and he suppressed a chuckle. "But that won't take place until we're both ready. Understood?"

She nodded, not trusting her voice.

"Good. Maybe" — he cleared his throat — "maybe we'd better walk around the meadow. I don't think the park visitors came to watch us."

"I hope not." She squeezed his fingers. "Do you think anyone has any idea what we've been talking about?"

"That excites you — just a little?"

"Maybe. But," she added quickly, "I'd be horrified if they really knew."

"One of the many qualities I like about you is that you can be so damn seductive without even trying."

They held hands as they walked along the tall grasses. Had she ever been more mellow? If they were back at her house, she knew she would give herself to this man. No — she'd *share* herself with him, just as he'd share himself with her. Her skin heated against the chill of the late evening air. Would she ever be more ready than she was right now?

She jerked at the sound of Kevin's cell phone piercing her reverie.

"Yeah." Kevin stopped. "How is he? Damn. When? How did it happen? No, I'll be there as soon as I can get back. It'll take me two to three hours. If he wakes . . ."

Nadja blanched at the sight of tears forming in Kevin's eyes.

"No, when he wakes, tell him Daddy's on his way and that I love him very much. Yeah, you take care, too."

Kevin snapped the cell phone shut and looked wildly at her. She reached out for his hands. He shook back tears. "It's Danny. He's been in an accident. I've got to get back to the Cities."

"Of course," Nadja said. "I'll drop you back at your motel. Of if you want, I'll drive you to the hospital."

"No." He shook his head. "I can make it all right. I'm just in a bit of shock at the moment. But I do have time for a hug."

She moved into his arms and cradled him as best she could. She could sense the fear and anxiety spreading throughout his body. She did nothing to interrupt his sobs other than rub his back in concentric circles.

He straightened and pressed a finger against her lips. "Thanks," he muttered. "I needed that. Guess we'll have to take a rain check on the other."

She nodded at him through her own tears. "The most important thing right now is your son. I'll be ready for you whenever you can come back. I can promise you that." She matched him long stride for long stride as they hurried back to the parking lot.

"I'll let you know what's happening," he said. "Once I know something."

CHAPTER SIX

"Worrying yourself to death," Ivett warned, "isn't going to help the boy."

Standing behind her candy and bakery display, Nadja nodded. "I wish Kevin would call. I wish I were with him."

"You're getting hooked, girl. I'm sure he'll call you when he knows something. If the EMTs are right and it's a severe head injury, it will take some time to know what his actual condition is."

"But it's probably not good."

"It's amazing what people, particularly young people, can overcome."

"I've seen his picture. Danny's such a cute looking kid. And Kevin wants to be a good father. The divorce complicates things, but he and his ex-wife seem to have some sort of working relationship."

"Trauma like this will test most any relationship. I'll stop and light a candle for him on my break."

"I stopped early this morning." She felt a strange awkwardness when Ivett gave her a stern look.

"I thought you didn't believe in any of that stuff."

She began wrapping chocolate chip cookies for display to hide her embarrassment. "I don't," she said, without looking at Ivett. "Not really." She looked up and scowled at her aunt. "I don't know what I believe."

"At least that's an honest answer. I'm old enough to remember how our people maintained the faith even under the Soviets, who did everything to root it out." Ivett shrugged. "Maybe that's why I count myself among the believers. That the faith survived such a harsh regime says something about it."

"I suppose." Nadja again busied herself with the cookies. "I'd like to believe. Mother believed." She blinked. "Her faith didn't help her much."

Ivett chuckled softly. "Your mother would be the very first to tell you otherwise. But I am pleased you stopped and lit a candle for the boy."

Feeling sheepish, Nadja admitted, "I also lit one for Kevin."

"Good. I'll light one for him, too." She flashed a brilliant smile. "And I'll light one for you and Kevin."

"Ivett, hopefully there is a God who cares about Danny, but I don't expect that God to care about what is or is not happening between Kevin and me."

"Perhaps"—Ivett's eyes flashed a warning—"you shouldn't underestimate God."

Scowling, Nadja decided it was past time to change the topic. "Have you talked with Steve about his conversation with Kevin?"

"We talked." Ivett's brow knitted. "I shouted. He listened, sort of. He claims he didn't mean anything by his offhand comment. He was curious whether Java Beans had longer range plans. He swears on a stack of Bibles that he did not talk to the newspaper."

"And you believe him?"

"Yes." Ivett folded her arms under her breasts. "I'm sure he didn't speak to a reporter. He was less convincing about why he'd brought up the idea of Java Beans being interested in the entire Henderson building."

"That means there is someone else out there trying to stir this pot."

"Apparently. I wish Steve would be more comfortable with me working at my store. Sometimes he can be quite old-fashioned."

"You owned the store before you even got involved with him."

"It does take up a lot of time, I suppose. But it's much less stressful than when I worked the trauma center at the hospital." She gave Nadja a quirky smile. "I don't enjoy getting angry with Steve, but it surely is a joy making up. We didn't even make it out of the kitchen."

"Ivett!"

"Now I'm embarrassing you." Ivett winked. "I must be getting back to my place." She turned to leave, then paused and grinned brightly. "You have a solid oak table. You should try it some time."

"Ivett!"

Nadja shook her head and watched her aunt stroll into the store next door. Sometimes Ivett seemed more like a sister than an aunt. Nadja scowled. But she didn't have a sister, and Ivett was the only aunt she really knew, so she had very few comparisons to make. Ivett was Ivett.

The kitchen table? She frowned and checked the coffee urns. How? She shook her head. She wasn't even going to let herself daydream about that.

Trying to focus on the foibles of the hero and heroine in her latest novel, Nadja rearranged her pillows for the umpteenth time. She couldn't find a comfortable position for reading, or thinking, or sleeping.

She closed her eyes. Would her own story be any more believable than the one she was reading? Were she and Kevin as star-crossed as the lovers in her novel?

Were they even lovers? They hadn't even consummated their relationship. She squirmed back against the pillows. Of course, that wasn't Kevin's fault. But he'd been gone nearly twenty-four hours and had not called.

Maybe getting back to the Cities had brought about a

change of heart. *Uh-oh*—would his son's trauma reunite him with his ex-wife? She held her breath. She wouldn't get in the middle of that.

She snapped up her phone on its second ring. "Yes?"

"I've missed you, Nadja. Forgive me for not calling sooner, but this has been terribly exhausting. I can hardly think straight now."

"How is he? Danny. How is he?" The strain in her voice surprised her.

"I'm sorry, I should have started there. Danny is going to be fine. He's out of the coma now. It's almost as if he went away for a while and decided to come back. The injury is not nearly as severe as they feared. Apparently, head injuries are hard to diagnose initially."

"That's what Ivett told me. She used to work in a trauma unit."

"I didn't know that, but she's right. Danny will go home the day after tomorrow. They want to keep him one more day for observation. He's having a blast with the nurses. I think he has them all wrapped around his little finger."

"Sounds like his father." Nadja felt suddenly giddy—maybe Ivett was right. She'd been overburdened by the weight of Danny's injury.

"I've missed you."

Nadja smiled, even though he couldn't see her. "And I've missed you, too. Terribly. I was so worried for your son and for you."

"And for us," he said, without accusation.

"Yes, for us, too."

"You don't know how often over the last few hours I wished I'd let you drive me back here. I figured you would've stayed. But I could feel you still hugging me."

"You're going to make me cry. I doubt your wife would've been as pleased with my presence."

"Maybe. Maybe not. She just told me she's going to get re-married."

"Really?"

"Don't tell me you were worried she and I were going to get back together?"

"I wish you weren't so perceptive."

"It can be a problem at times, but you seem to appreciate that quality at other times."

She wet her lips. "Very much."

"Nadja?"

"Yes?

"I'm curious. I get the distinct impression you haven't been with many men since you came to the States."

She laughed softly. "That's correct. Not many anywhere. And I have made you curious?"

"Yes, why me? When we were on the observation deck, you asked why I pursued you; but why do you let me pursue you?"

She waited a long time before responding. "I wish I knew the answer to that question. But you're right. To be fair, I will try to answer your question. You make me laugh."

"What?"

"I don't laugh at you—you help me laugh. And you appreciate my work—what I've accomplished. Many men are afraid of a successful woman."

"Many men are dumb. We've already established that fact."

"You seem to cherish my body and do miraculous things with it."

"Your body is you."

"Yes, true. And let me see. You are handsome. You stand solid and have a tight butt."

"A tight butt?" He chuckled. "Yes, I have noticed you testing that hypothesis."

"That's no hypothesis. And too often I feel like I am going to drown in your soft eyes. You are sensitive." She cleared her throat. "You don't rush me. You are ambitious and yet passionate." She laughed. "How am I doing?"

"Just fine. Excellent, really. Don't stop on my account."

"And you are so strong when you hold me. I feel safe with you."

"Even though I came to your place wanting to buy you out?"

"Yes, you haven't lied to me and I trust you won't. And Kevin?"

"Yes?"

She closed her eyes and vowed to forge ahead. "I want to see all of you. I want to touch you all over. I want to hold your shaft—no, your cock—in my palm and squeeze you and watch you grow hard for me. I want you to fuck me. I want to make love with you."

"Jesus. You couldn't get me much harder than I am right now. Damn, I wish I were standing beside you."

"Me, too, but I'm not standing. I'm lying on my bed—reading." She smiled at her reflection in a nearby mirror. "You might like to know I'm naked."

"Son of a . . . Do you often read in the nude?"

"Yes, particularly late at night before going to sleep."

"You sleep naked?"

"Of course. Why waste money on pajamas when you don't need them?"

"I can't come up with a single reason."

"You mock me."

"No. You are so refreshing. Are your nipples pebbling?"

"Yes, since I first heard your voice."

"That's nice. Can you kiss your own breasts?"

"Certainly."

"Can you kiss one for me?"

Nadja lifted a breast and lowered her lips until she kissed it. She raised her head and grinned at the phone. "I did, but you kiss her so much better. She misses you."

"Well, I miss her, too. Are you aching for me?"

"Yes," she managed to whisper. She covered her mound with a palm, trying to hold back her quivers. "You know I am. You've made me very wet."

"Could you bring yourself to . . ."

"I'm ahead of you this time—your fingers or mine—I can't tell."

"Are you coming for me, Nadja?"

"Yes, a little. Are you stroking your cock?"

"Yes. Are you rubbing your clit?"

"I will. I have two fingers in my pussy." Nadja used her free hand to play with her clit. "Oh, my. I'm coming. Come with me."

"Oh yeah." Kevin groaned. "Son of a bitch. You're hot even when you're a hundred miles away."

"I'm glad you enjoyed that."

"So. Are you ready for me, Nadja? Are you ready for my cock to be in you?"

"Yes, I am so ready for you. I want to feel your cock deep inside me. I wish you were here. I want to fuck you. Right now." Another orgasmic spasm raked her body as she withdrew her fingers. "Make love later."

"I'll be there soon. Very soon. Then we can fuck or make love or whatever you want twenty-four seven. Sleep tight. Sweet dreams."

Nadja giggled. "Sounds like a marathon—which one of us will run out of stamina first? Good night, Keven. Sleep tight. Sweet dreams."

Nadja rolled onto her side and hugged a pillow. Soon it would be him in her arms. It would be his fingers in her, not hers. It would be his cock filling her. At last. She just hoped reality would live up to fantasy.

As soon as Nadja unlocked the door to the Cappuccino and closed it behind her, she stepped on an envelope she hadn't noticed initially. It must have been propped against the door. She picked it up and frowned. It was an Arts Council envelope. Odd—she hadn't realized they were trying to save on postage these days.

She set it aside and started the morning coffees. First things first. She had two pots going when she peeked at the envelope lying on the counter. It was addressed to the Cappuccino. Most of her correspondence with the Arts Council came addressed to her personally. After all, she was a member of the Council.

She shrugged, picked up the envelope, and slit it open with a knife. Her eyes narrowed at a crudely drawn card. Was this an announcement of a Children's Art Show?

She held the card closer. Her eyes widened. Her fingers shook. It was a cartoon, of sorts, depicting two women carrying suitcases. The caption read, in awkward letters: *Russians Go Home.* One woman was tall with a short crop of yellow hair. The other was considerably shorter with long black hair. Both women were naked. The tall one had huge, grotesque boobs. The shorter one hardly had any at all.

The scream originated in her gut. By the time she dashed into Ivett's store, she'd started babbling in Ukrainian. She seldom spoke the language anymore.

"What's wrong?" Ivett shouted, grabbing the card Nadja thrust in her face.

Watching Ivett decipher the card, Nadja worked at calming herself. She hadn't been this enraged in years.

"Some bastard *is* out to get us." Ivett's voice had turned cold.

Nadja knew her aunt was most furious and most

dangerous not when she shouted fire, but when she turned to ice. She nodded. "Someone wants us gone. Someone is trying to frighten us."

"To look at you, someone is succeeding in that."

"It's only shock. I'll be okay." She glanced around Ivett's shop and saw the work of so many local artists. Ivett was a long-time member of the community. She felt a pang of homesickness when her focus settled on pieces from Ukraine that Ivett handled on commission. "The note said *Russians*. Why are we targets of hate?"

"The newspaper article referred to us as Russians also." Ivett's fingers curled into fists. "I think it's the building. Our ethnicity doesn't really matter. It's a handy scare tactic."

Ivett scrutinized the card again. Her lips curled into a sneer. "I understand why some idiot would give you boobs the size of watermelons, but I at least deserve peaches."

"Ivett! You're offended because your breasts were drawn too small?"

"At least" — Ivett chuckled — "we know for sure Steve is not behind this."

"I didn't assume he was, but why?"

Ivett's face broke into a wide grin. "He knows I shave between my legs. The creep who drew this gave me a black thatch large enough to get lost in."

Nadja giggled. She didn't want to laugh, but she couldn't help it. She reached for the card and checked it again. Sure enough, the shorter woman had a large dark triangle. Nadja frowned. "The tall woman doesn't even have a pubic area."

"The guy can't think beyond your boobs."

"Maybe he was in a rush. How do we know it's a guy?"

"We don't, but I'd bet a lot of money on it. A woman might draw us naked, but even a villainous woman would draw us in a more flattering manner."

"That's not very convincing. Anyway, what do we do

now? What does this idiot expect us to do?"

"We're hardly running away because of a gross cartoon."

"Hardly," Nadja agreed.

"I have a friend on the police force. I'll talk to her confidentially. I expect it's best not to overreact."

"You're famous for overreacting."

"Not when the stakes become very serious." Ivett tapped the card with a forefinger. "And we certainly have that possibility here."

Nadja glanced at Ivett's grandfather clock. "I have to go. It's almost time to open." She grabbed the card, folded it, and tucked it in a pocket.

"Don't let that card get to you, Nadja. Many people in this community love you very much." Ivett hesitated and winked. "When is your lover coming back to town?"

Nadja's heart skipped a beat at the word *lover*. She smiled brilliantly. "He's going to try to get away from the office early today. If not today, then tomorrow."

"You'll show him the card?"

"Of course." She scowled at Ivett. "You don't think he had anything to do with this?"

"Not really. It didn't come through the mail. But do you think it's wise to share it with him?"

Nadja jutted forth her chin. "I don't want to keep secrets from him. I won't have a relationship based on secrecy."

Ivett nodded her understanding. "Yeah, I guess we've both seen enough of that to last a lifetime. Someone's rapping on your door. It's past opening."

Scurrying toward her shop, Nadja did her best to put the card from her mind. She unlocked the shop entrance, smiled, and welcomed her first customer.

She did her best to keep her composure while making two lattes to go, but she found it difficult to shake her dread. Why had the artist drawn her without a pussy, particularly when

Ivett's was so predominant? She knew that art, no matter how crude, carried meanings sometimes unknown even by its creator.

She'd been drawn sexless. *Why?* she wanted to scream. *Why me? I'm not sexless!* Instead, she lowered her eyes, made change for Mrs. Henry, and bade her a good day.

Standing in Nadja's kitchen, Kevin glared at the senseless card. She'd hugged him and inquired about Danny and then handed him the card, saying she didn't want any secrets between them.

Had she been that calm when she first opened the envelope? What did she expect of him? He scowled. Certainly she didn't suspect he was behind the drawing. He looked up at her and saw only a slightly inquisitive, radiant beauty.

"I know you didn't have anything to with this," she said.

She also seemed to read his mind, and that startled him more than a little bit.

"I just needed to share the card with you before . . ." She glanced away.

"This is the product of a small mind." He let out a deep sigh. "I'm glad you showed it to me right away. If you get distant on me, I won't necessarily assume I did something wrong. But someone is certainly trying to scare you."

She tilted her head to the side. "That's true. And it worked for a few minutes, but not anymore. Ivett and I will survive. My family always has. This is our home. We won't give up because of some gross pranks."

He nodded and set the card back on the counter. "Share with me before what?" he asked with a catch in his voice.

"Are you hungry?" she asked, sidestepping his question.

"Only for you."

Her shy smile only reinforced his hope that she was indeed

ready. He'd thought of little else since their last phone call. The miles between St. Paul and Jefferson City seemed to have doubled since he'd last made that drive.

She gave him a slight nod. "Come with me, please."

She cradled his hand in hers, and he let her guide him up the stairs toward her bedroom. Kevin tried to breathe evenly, but to no avail. Nadja walked directly to the bed and pulled back its comforter. Standing beside it, she turned and looked at him through half-closed eyes. She hesitated and then curled her fingers around the top button of her blouse.

She had four buttons undone before she spoke. The clasp holding her bra became visible. His eyes hurt from not blinking.

"I'm not sure there is a good way for a woman to undress in front of a man."

"I'm not sure there's a bad way." He flexed his fingers. "Please, don't stop."

She nodded. When she had the last button undone, she shrugged out of the blouse, letting it fall behind her. She craned her head to the side in her innocent way and unclasped the bra. It, too, fell to the floor. Her breasts tantalized him, the nipples growing taut.

"Jesus," he muttered, not budging an inch. "So stunning."

"I'm going to think I'll have to pleasure myself," she said coyly, "if you don't start undressing."

"Oh." He moved his shaking fingers to his shirt and fumbled with reluctant buttons. No woman had made him feel like a teenager for years.

She smiled. "I'm glad you're trembling, too." She reached for a hidden button in her skirt, and the skirt soon joined the other bits of clothing cluttering the floor.

Kevin swallowed and stared hard at the pink bikini panties. They did nothing to conceal pussy lips puffy with expectation. He waited for her to hook her fingers in her panties and pull them down.

Her eyes glistened as she shook her head. "Not yet. You next."

He reached for the buckle of his belt and tugged on his pants zipper. He kicked the trousers away and did nothing to hide his erection straining against cotton boxers. Her face lit up, and he wanted to kiss her endlessly.

Instead, at last he watched her hook her thumbs over her panties and wiggle out of them. She brushed her blond curls lightly. "We've been waiting for you to return." She glanced at his arousal, then stepped toward him. "Looks like someone wants out — or maybe he wants in." Her eyes seemed to laugh.

He loved it when her eyes laughed. He reached for his briefs.

"No," she said. "Let me."

She fixed her gaze on his, clutched his boxers at the hips, and pulled down. She only slid them halfway over his thighs before she glanced down and gasped. "Look what we have here."

She reached out and cradled his stiff cock in both hands. He rose on his toes, hoping she knew what she was doing. She wouldn't have to do much to make him come before they even got started.

She rolled her thumb over and around his crown. "So soft. And yet so strong. How did he get so big?"

"I think you've had a little something to do with his condition. Now that you've met . . ."

"Do we want to move on?" She shoved his briefs down his legs.

He stepped out of them before saying, "Yes."

He reached for her, and she moved easily into his arms. She fit just right. He couldn't imagine a better fit — well, not quite. He nibbled on her ear and cupped a breast in his palm. Her moans made him grow another inch. She rubbed her moist pussy against his erection. He was surprised she took the initiative.

She leaned away from him, inviting his mouth to travel from her neck to her boobs. He nuzzled the underside of a breast. She stood on her toes. He suckled a nipple, and she mewed softly.

He kissed his way lower to her navel. She clutched his head tight as he bored his tongue into her belly. His hands kneaded her buttocks, and he began to work his tongue lower. Her scent filled his nostrils. He flicked his tongue at her folds, which were already separating for him.

She pulled him up by his arms. "No." Her voice was urgent. "Another time. I need to feel him in me. Now!"

He pecked at her nose. "Show me the way, my lady."

She led him to her bed. He let her settle first. She lay on her back with her legs parted slightly, then extended her arms to him.

He crawled onto the bed and knelt between her widening legs, clutching his cock. "Is this what you had on your mind?"

"Yes," she whispered. "For too long. Fuck me. I'm more than ready." She reached for him and encircled his shaft. "Enter me, please."

He prayed briefly for patience. She deserved slow and easy. She rubbed his cockhead the length of her vulva and then tilted slightly, and he pressed inward.

Her mouth curled into a smile. "Mmm," she moaned. "You don't have to be so careful. I won't break. Fill me."

"But you're so tight." He glanced down at their joining. He was still only halfway there. Perspiration beaded his brow. He licked at his lips.

She twisted her head from side to side. "I want all of you." She hitched her strong legs over his rear and, with more force than he'd been willing to use, impaled herself on him.

God, he wanted to cry. She had all of him. Her heat seared.

She reached for his neck and pulled him into a kiss. Then she nibbled at him and started to giggle.

"What's so funny?" he asked, leaning away from her.

Her laughter bubbled. "Now that I have you where I want you, I'm not sure I want to let you go."

His laughter joined hers. "I might not want to either, but we might look a little strange walking down the street this way."

"True." She sobered. "I started the pill two weeks ago."

He blinked. "Cripes, I was going to ask. I had protection, but our strip show left me brain dead."

"Just wanted you to know," she whispered, pecking at his lips. "You don't have to pull out. You can fill me with your seed."

He nodded.

"You feel so good, but I want you to fill me." She smacked her lips. "Please."

She tapped his ass with her heels, as if to overcome his inertia. He tucked his head in the crook of her neck and shoulder and began slowly gliding in and out.

"Perfect," she whispered, opening and closing her thighs.

"So tight," he sputtered. "I can't last long." He gasped for air. "Come with me, babe." He managed to roll a nipple between finger and thumb.

Nadja didn't have to say a word. He knew she was soaring. They soared together. She raised and lowered her pelvis, meeting him thrust for thrust.

She wrapped her hands around his back; her fingernails dug into his flesh. Like him, she seemed barely holding on by a thread. Then his own thread snapped.

His climax began deep in some mysterious place, causing his hips to churn of their own volition. "Christ," he moaned, pumping into her. "I can't stop."

She grabbed his butt and bucked upward. "Don't stop. Fill

me. Fill me. I feel your seed. Goodness," she cried, "I'm coming. Unbelievable."

Slowly, his hips ran out of energy, settling long after he'd emptied himself into her. He squeezed his eyes hard. She'd caused him to lose control. He couldn't remember ever having been so out of control with a woman.

He didn't want to leave her, not yet. He rose onto his hands to relieve some of his weight and stared at her.

She smiled faintly. "Thank you," she whispered.

"Thank me?" He tried to shake his head clear of lust. "Thank *you*. Is this too much? Do you want me to pull out?"

She shifted her chin from side to side. "No, I love the feel of you in me."

"Good. Let's move to our sides, where I don't have to worry about crushing you, yet we can still cuddle." He tapped her nose with his tongue. "You may get your wish. I may never pull out."

Once settled to their liking, Nadja avoided his eyes and idly played with his pectorals. "You're still quite hard. I've never been with a man who wanted to stay in me after sex." She bit her lip. "I've never been with a man I wanted to have stay in me after lovemaking."

He kissed her hair, her brow, her eyelids, her nose, and he lingered on her lips. "You're going to make me cry. So was this fucking, or lovemaking?"

"Both. I'm afraid I have tears too. Being this emotional is frightening," she murmured. "Just hold me."

She buried her head under his chin. Soon he could feel her sobs quivering across his body. He held her loosely and let her be.

He was in trouble—deep trouble. He kissed the top of her head. She turned him into jelly, without even trying.

He wasn't sure how she distinguished lovemaking from fucking, but in his book they'd just made love. Their climax had nearly unhinged him. And here he lay, wanting immediately to bring her to another soul-wrenching orgasm.

Where would it all end? He shook his head. They didn't need to deal with that question anytime soon. He and Nadja had much to explore before considering endings.

Nadja shivered in Kevin's arms, not because of a chill, but rather from the heat that still permeated every cell in her body. She kept her gaze focused on his dark, matted chest hair. If she dared look at him, he might realize she had transformed into one huge glowing smile.

She wasn't ready for him to witness how their lovemaking had affected her. Yes, that was definitely more than fucking. Ivett was right—lovemaking could be breathtaking. She closed her eyes. Kevin was right, too. The sparks they'd generated were definitely worth the fuss.

She clenched her inner muscles tighter around him as an unspoken *thank you*. His moan was all the *you're welcome* she needed.

But where could they possibly go from here? Her eyes popped open, and her focus drifted to their joining. Several infrequently used muscles felt sore, but nothing matched the ache in her heart. Perhaps it was just as well not to have a roadmap for the future. She was in no rush to reach the end of the road. She slid her lips across his shoulder and wiggled against the hands cradling her butt.

Reflexively, his fingers tightened on her flesh. Then, to her dismay, she heard his soft snores. Too bad—she'd been ready for more. She smiled and closed her eyes. He made a surprising, comfortable pillow. His drive from the Cities must have taken a lot out of him.

Tenderly, she nestled into him, pleased that she'd taken a lot out of him, too.

CHAPTER SEVEN

"Would you like more coffee?" Nadja asked shyly. She wasn't accustomed to feeding a man the morning after. And Kevin didn't seem in a hurry to leave.

She'd already called to have Sara open the Cappuccino. The barista had worried that she might be ill. Nadja had assured her she was quite fine, but she didn't know when she'd get to the shop. She grinned, wondering how often her employees had called in seeking backup because a lover lingered. What a nice problem to start off the day.

"Sure, I'll have some more" Kevin's eyes twinkled as he shoved his plate aside. He hadn't left a crumb of eggs or bacon. "Am I keeping you from work?"

She shook her head. "I took care of that. One of my staff is opening this morning."

"Bet you're seldom late."

"Never." She pulled on the sash of her robe.

"But you are this morning."

"I'm making an exception."

"I'm glad." He heaved a sigh. "I don't want to be away from you. Not yet."

She tried to hide her grin by peeking down at her coffee. "Me either."

"Are you naked under that robe?" His eyes took on a deep, dark luster.

She held his gaze without giving a hint of an answer. "I'm not telling."

He grinned. "Nadja turns coy after recovering from

lovemaking. I like that. Are you going to slap me if I find out for myself?"

She moved her chin slightly left to right, not trusting her voice.

He hesitated.

She stifled her impatience. What had she done to intimidate him? She placed her palms down wide apart on the table, giving him plenty of room.

He pushed back his chair and stood. She stayed still in her chair. Surely he wasn't leaving? He walked around the table to stand behind her. His kisses mussed her hair while his hands slid over her shoulders and inside her robe until each held a breast. She squeezed her eyes tight and moaned her pleasure.

"I like you this way. Your skin is so warm and toasty. I hope you never put clothes on under a robe."

"I won't," she murmured. His fingers toyed with each nipple. "I love the feel of your hands on my tits." She twisted her head around, searching for air. His lips sought her ear. She steadied as his tongue skittered across her earlobe.

She wanted to kiss him in return, but he wouldn't let her. He removed his hands from her robe and stood her on her feet beside her chair, not letting her turn around. His hands dropped to her sash. She smiled to herself. She could kiss him later.

He cradled his crotch against her bottom, making her keenly aware of his arousal. Her loins constricted and softened. He parted her robe, and his fingers trailed downward until his palm cupped her pussy. Her hips pressed backward, straining against him. She blushed, surprised by her own wantonness.

"Don't be embarrassed," he cautioned. "I love it when you're spontaneous. And you're wet already." He nipped at her neck. "I suspect spontaneity has not been a highly valued quality on your personal character list."

"Hardly," she acknowledged, dropping her gaze to the oak table and suddenly remembering her conversation with her aunt. "Until you came along. I don't understand it," she cried out, trying to hide from herself more than from him. "I never do anything outrageous."

He chuckled in her ear. "I'm glad I'm helping to change that little fact. Spontaneity can be a gift. You haven't been disappointed yet, have you?"

"You know I haven't," she murmured, perhaps too quickly.

"I can hear the little wheels in your head spinning. What would you like right now? Right here."

"Here?" She nearly choked.

"I may be a patient man, but I don't think I can wait to go upstairs to have you naked."

"But I am."

"Not entirely. You're stalling, Nadja. What do you want?"

"I'm not used to men asking me what I want."

He didn't respond.

She expected he'd wait until she fainted from desire before speaking again. "You remember last night?" she finally said.

"You think I'll ever forget?"

"You were going to use your tongue before I said I needed you in me."

She could feel his lips spreading into a grin across the back of her neck. "I do recall that," he whispered. "I gave you a rain check, I believe. So?"

"Don't make me beg. I want your tongue. Please lick me."

He turned her around to face him. Her gaze darted away from his, and his lips settled over hers in a brief kiss. "I like a woman who tells me what she wants. That's much better than guessing. You want my tongue in your pussy?"

She parted her lips and nodded. "I also like being

surprised."

"Me, too. And I like surprising you."

He drew her robe down over her shoulders and laid it on the kitchen table behind her. "Lean back on the table," he whispered. "I'm not finished with breakfast. I have developed an overwhelming thirst for you."

She blushed. Had Ivett been a prophetess? "Will it hold me?"

He laughed. "It's made of oak," he said, helping her sit on the table. "I'll catch you if you fall."

She wasn't about to parse those words out. She settled back against the tabletop and quivered as his lips traced a line of wetness from her neck, between her breasts, around her navel until it reached the apex of her loins.

"Breathe." He chuckled. "I'd hate to have to explain why I had to take you to the emergency room wrapped in your robe."

"Don't tease me," she wailed, placing a hand on either side of his head. She flexed her pelvis. "I need to feel your tongue."

His tongue settling in her crevice provided his only response. It was the only response she wanted. She curled her fingers in his hair and moaned.

Kevin lifted her legs and scrunched her back farther on the table until it bore all of her weight. He dipped his tongue into her cleft and she shrieked. She clutched his head between her hands and kept her legs wrapped tightly around his back. He had no way to escape.

His burrowing tongue gave no indication of any desire to flee, but she wasn't taking any chances. His fingers grazed her clit, keeping pace with his probing tongue. She started to pant. "I'm breaking apart," she whimpered. "Outrageous." Her torso strained for release. "Faster." Nadja heard herself babbling in her native tongue.

She clung to him, sinking her fingernails into his shoulders and bucking against his tongue. She felt herself release.

"That's it, babe, come for me."

He alternated lapping at her pussy and then sucking in on its folds.

"Good grief." She arched against him, "I've never . . ."

She shuddered, amazed as yet another contraction and release overtook her body. It was as if he had breached a reservoir deep inside her that she never knew existed.

His fingers dug into her ass as he lifted her butt off the table and sank his tongue even deeper. She heard him slurping her juices as a child might drink a soda from a straw.

Another wave crashed from her loins to her brain. "That's it," she moaned, trying to pull away from him.

He settled her back on the table. His tongue and lips left her. He kissed her clit again, and she shuddered.

"You are an amazingly expressive woman. I'm not sure I can get enough of you. I wanted to crawl right in. Damn."

Feeling suddenly empty, she lay back and flung an arm across her eyes. What might it take to pull herself together? He pulled forward until her butt rested on the edge of the table. She felt the tip of his hard erection prodding at her entrance, and her eyes popped wide open. His smile warmed her; he was studying her reaction. Yes, that might just do it.

Without further finesse, he plunged into her.

"Oh!" She tried to focus only on pleasure as his width stretched her vagina.

"I'm sorry," he muttered against her throat. "I couldn't wait."

"Don't be sorry," she responded, weaving her fingers through his hair. "I love how you fill me. Don't hold back. Empty into me. Don't wait for me anymore. Just give me your seed."

Her encouragement sent him into churning spasms. Trying to hold him back would've been like trying to stop a swirling tornado.

She opened herself wide, pleased to be his receptacle, raking her fingernails down his chest as he continued to slam in and out of her. She hoped he felt a portion of the pleasure he'd given her.

"Christ," he shouted, "I'm coming."

"Yes, pump that cock into my cunt. I feel you coming. Fill me up."

When Kevin opened his eyes, they were glazed with bliss. She flexed her legs, still locked around his rear, helping him finish. "I want all you have."

At last his hips stopped pumping. With ragged breaths, he blinked at her and refocused. "You are incredible. Hope that wasn't too much for you."

She wiped perspiration from his brow. "Me? You did most of the work. I'm fine. Splendid, actually." She winked. "Though I do expect breakfast is over."

"I'm sated," he managed to say, pulling out of her. "Maybe lunch or dinner."

She chuckled—he sure was optimistic. Before sitting up, she grabbed a napkin and patted her pussy. "I'm not sure how I'll ever be able to serve guests dinner on this table again without remembering this image."

"I hope you don't."

Glancing away from the doorway to Ivett's shop, where she knew her aunt stood, Nadja scrubbed the counter with renewed vigor. She'd managed to avoid her aunt for half a day. Another twenty minutes or so, and she would've been on her way home. She'd sent Sara home an hour ago, and she'd been closed to customers nearly half an hour. Maybe she should've skipped some of the deep cleaning. She sighed. No matter. She'd have to face Ivett sooner or later—it might as well be sooner.

Ivett nearly skipped over to lean provocatively against the counter. "Thought you might come across the way to tell me how he was."

Nadja looked up at her aunt trying to project a bland *whatever do you mean* pose.

"Don't try that *who me* innocence on me. Come on, Nadja — as hard as you're trying, you can't stop glowing. I'm glad it was good for you."

Nadja gave up and leaned back against the opposite counter that held various blends of coffee beans. She nodded and then smiled broadly. "It was heavenly. Far beyond anything I'd imagined."

"Good. I'm happy for you. So is he as big as he looks?"

"Ivett!"

"More enjoyable than your magic crystal?"

Nadja nodded. "Oh, yeah."

"Is he staying with you, or did he go back to the motel?"

"With me."

"My, my, we are progressing."

Nadja frowned and grabbed the washcloth. "But I don't know where we're progressing to."

"Maybe it'll be good not to know for a while."

Nadja shook out the cloth. "I wish I was as comfortable with uncertainty as you are."

"And did you watch the tapes I loaned you? Did you find them helpful?"

"You can be overbearing, you know."

"I never noticed."

"I'm sure you haven't. Yes, I watched the tapes. I learned some things. Some of those positions I would never have thought of. And I consider myself quite nimble, but I'm not sure I can twist around like some of those women do. And I'm still not totally comfortable with words like fuck, cock, cunt, and asshole, though they do seem to turn him on" — she felt her cheeks redden — "and maybe me a little."

"Uh-huh. Dirty talk between a man and a woman who care for each other can be a huge turn-on, especially in the heat of the moment. Maybe you should watch the videos with Kevin. He might enjoy them, too."

"Never! And don't you dare tell him you loaned me educational sex tapes. I won't forgive you if you do."

Giggling, Ivett, covered her mouth. "I wish you could see yourself right now. Your eyes are huge and your mouth is hanging open — but you're still glowing. Don't worry. We're allowed a tiny secret now and then."

"Yes," Nadja agreed, "a tiny secret."

"Did you show him the card?"

"Of course. He was furious. He wanted to storm right out and confront Steve."

"But you had other things on your mind."

Nadja nodded.

"I'm sure Steve didn't have anything to do with the card. He was shocked when I told him about it." Ivett knitted her brow. "Actually, he seemed more frightened about it than I was. I was pissed, but not particularly frightened."

"I'm sure Kevin will talk with him. I can't stop him."

Ivett shrugged. "No problem. Steve can take care of himself. Have you wondered about the card being in an Arts Council envelope?"

"Yes." Nadja emptied the last remaining coffeepot and began scrubbing it. Ivett might want to talk all night, but she had other places to go. She'd agreed to meet Kevin back at the house at seven-thirty. They hadn't decided whether to eat out or in. Her skin warmed at the memory of breakfast.

She shook her head. "The Arts Council envelope probably means nothing. They're available at the museum, the playhouse, and the dance studio, at the very least. They may even be sitting on display at the library. I can't recall."

"In any case, they're too available to be a clue."

"I would think so." Nadja glanced at the clock. "I've got to hurry. I told Kevin I'd be back before now."

"Sorry to keep you." Ivett beamed. "Time goes faster when you have a love in your life."

"Maybe." Nadja's gaze followed Ivett as she retreated toward the adjoining doorway. "Thanks for the tip about the kitchen table."

Without turning around, Ivett shouted, "Yes!" and pumped her fist into the air.

Nadja bubbled with laughter as her aunt disappeared into her shop. At least Ivett should complain less often about her niece not taking her advice.

Nadja stopped mid-step. There she was laughing again. What was getting into her? She hugged herself as images of Kevin in his hard, glorious nakedness flitted before her. He was making a habit of getting into her. Thank goodness! She bent at the waist laughing, gasping for breath.

"Cut the crap, Rick." Steve glared at his old college buddy. How many times over the years had he wished he'd gone anywhere else to college? Anywhere.

For his part, Rick sat nonplussed behind his glass-top desk. The décor of his land development office matched Rick's personality: overpowering and overreaching. "I know you're behind that stupid card my wife and Nadja received."

"Do you, now?" Sneering, Rick steepled his fingers. "You must be a genius in disguise. And what if I was? No harm done. Too bad they're not packing yet."

The sudden hardness in Rick's eyes sent a shudder down Steve's back. He'd seen that look on a few other occasions. It inevitably boded trouble. "How far are you going to go to get those women unnerved?"

"Unnerved?" Rick relit his cigar, inhaling several puffs to fire it up. "I don't care about their nerves. I just want that damn building. They can move back to Russia or into the next block as far I care. I just want them out of that building—sooner rather than later. Don't you have any influence over your women?"

Steve shook his head and squeezed the bridge of his nose. "You've got to be kidding. Sure, they listen to me politely—and then they do whatever they damn well please."

"You should train them better."

"They're not animals to be tamed." Not that he could imagine Ivett tamed, and he certainly didn't *want* her to be. Rick was the one who needed a leash. "There must be other buildings downtown that will meet your needs."

Rick glowered. "You don't know anything about my needs. But if those women don't sell to Java Beans, I don't want you holding me responsible for what happens next."

"What the hell do you mean by that?" Steve crossed his arms and waited, a chill advancing up his spine.

For a moment, Rick's face softened. "We've been friends a long time. I know you think I'm a bastard most of the time. And I admit I do enjoy holding your rather large secret over your head, but we've had plenty of good times too." Rick glanced down at his desk. When he looked up again, his eyes had hardened like steel. "I wouldn't want to see your women hurt, but maybe you should know I'm not in this deal alone. Some of our old Chicago friends have a keen interest in that building."

"Oh shit!" Steve gulped. His pulse raced. He'd met some of Rick's Chicago friends. That explained a lot. Rick wasn't in a much different position than he was. They were both pawns.

Rick stood. "I probably should've remained quiet about that. But maybe now you understand the seriousness of the situation."

Steve nodded. *Think!* Was Rick bluffing? Was he in this alone? Did he want the Henderson building only out of greed? Or were some Chicago heavy hitters applying their own kind of pressure?

"Trying to scare them may be one thing," Steve groused. "But if either Ivett or Nadja gets hurt, there will be hell to pay."

Rick squared his shoulders. "I'm shaking with fear." He arched an eyebrow. "But then maybe I have underestimated you all these years. Maybe you *have* killed before."

Steve felt blood draining from his face.

Rick smiled grimly. "Do what you can, Steve. If you can get those women out of that building, there won't be anything to worry about."

Running a forefinger down the length of Nadja's nose, Kevin grinned when she grabbed his finger with her mouth and gently bit down on it. She looked so pleased with herself, lying beside him on her bed, so pleased with them. And why shouldn't she be? They'd just finished making love for the second time since dinner.

He smiled even more. She happily described the first round as a sound fucking, because they both had been so eager and animalistic. The second time was gentler and softer — definitely lovemaking.

He expected she was like him — not wanting to fall asleep for fear of missing out on something. He didn't know about her, but he knew he'd finished making love for at least a little while — yet he'd never get enough of watching Nadja.

She moved so effortlessly. He'd begun to learn her moods. Nadja, as he'd expected, was a woman of deep passion. He loved to hear her soft giggle; he loved to watch her eyes flash with surprise. He loved to hear her calling his name out in the throes of ecstasy, and he loved to hold her shuddering body as she rode her orgasms. When she sat astride him, she moved and swayed like the dancer she was.

He reached across the short distance where they lay to cover a breast. She placed her hand over his and grinned softly. She squeezed his fingers around her breast. Would he ever grow tired of her tits—yes, pendulous tits—swaying primitively, elegantly as she glided up and down his cock? Absolutely not!

"You seem to be in deep thought," Nadja whispered. "What are you thinking about?"

He closed his fingers around her breast. "You. Me. Us."

She blinked. "And?"

"That I'll never tire of you."

She sobered and stared at him for a long moment before saying anything. "Never is a very long time."

He kissed her cheek and grazed a rising nipple. "Are you always so practical?"

She flinched. "I shouldn't think you'd have to ask that anymore. I haven't been very practical the last day or two. I even went in to work late."

"Yes, you must still be wondering how that happened." He chuckled. "I don't suppose it ever occurred to you before this morning you could serve pussy cream on your oak table."

Her cheeks pinked, and she reached between them to cradle his flaccid cock. "I haven't forgotten why I was late. And I dribbled more than pussy cream on the table—this guy saw to that. Actually, my aunt had suggested my oak table might offer some interesting possibilities."

"Ah, that's why you weren't too shocked. Perhaps I should thank Ivett the next time I see her." He shook his head as Nadja's fingers slid suggestively along his length. "Sorry, but my cock won't be ready for a while."

She giggled. "Me either, but I do like holding him when he

is soft. And I love watching him twitch and harden. Is that so bad?"

"Not at all. You have to be the most unusual woman I've ever met."

She draped a long leg over his and tugged him closer. "You better tell me what you mean by that. That could be good or bad."

"Good, believe me." He closed his eyes.

He'd better tell her about Danny soon, or he'd be in big trouble. Why hadn't he said anything earlier? When had there been time? They'd been so into each other, literally and figuratively. At least they were sated for the moment. "Did I tell you what caused Danny's accident?"

She immediately dropped him from her hand and scooted up the bed to sit back against pillows. "I think you just changed the subject, but I do want to hear more. I thought he was hit by a car while riding his bicycle."

Kevin propped himself up beside her. "That's right. Danny dashed out of the house without putting on his helmet."

"Oh my. Why?"

"His mother"—Kevin tried to keep the strain out of his voice—"had just told him she was remarrying, and that he was going to have a baby brother or sister."

"Oh my gosh!" Nadja covered her mouth with a hand. "And he became angry? He doesn't like the man she's marrying?"

"I expect it was shock more than anything. Danny has seemed to get along with the man fairly well. I've met the guy." Kevin shrugged. "He seems okay."

"Okay? So how do you feel about all of this?"

"That she could've handled it better." He glanced away from the bed. "It's not like she doesn't know about birth control."

Nadja curved her fingers around his chin and turned him

to face her. "How do you really feel?"

"Mad as hell, that she'd put our son in that kind of danger. Sorry for her, because she's whipping herself. Strange, because another guy is screwing my ex-wife—not that there haven't been plenty of others. Relief that she's getting married before me. Free." He gave her a whimsical smile. "Having her remarry frees me even more than receiving the divorce papers."

"There's no more fantasy about getting back together."

"That's right."

"Maybe that's part of what set Danny off, too."

"Probably. Anyway." He leaned over and placed a reassuring kiss on Nadja's lips. Would she agree to his plan? "Elizabeth is getting married in two weeks."

"Two weeks! That is sudden."

"But she is pregnant."

"Yes, I suppose that does necessitate moving quickly."

"But that's not all. Elizabeth wants me to take Danny for the next few weeks after he's fully recovered. She wants more free time to prepare for the wedding, also so she and her new husband can go to the Caribbean for their honeymoon."

"Oh." He could see Nadja mulling this news. She chewed on her lower lip. "Then you will be away for quite a while?"

He shook his head and arched his eyebrows.

"You want to bring Danny here?" She placed a hand over her heart. "I'd love to meet your son, but you and I hardly know each other."

"I beg to differ on that point." He brushed the back of a hand across her breast.

"But . . .won't it be cramped at the motel for weeks? For a boy, that can't be much space."

"I hoped," Kevin sighed, "we might be able to stay here. You have a large yard," he rattled on. "And plenty of room. Danny is a good boy. He's not a difficult child."

Her eyes rounded. Her body stiffened. He wished he could read minds as well as she thought he could. "But . . ."

"You'll love Danny."

"But . . .he might get the wrong impression . . .about us."

"Oh." Kevin's breath caught. "That you might be auditioning for the role of stepmother?"

"Yes." Nadja blushed profusely. "I know that's ridiculous, but I wouldn't want him to misunderstand."

"It's not like he hasn't seen me with other women."

"But did you take him to live with them?"

"No," he admitted. "I'm not sure I'd trust my son with any of them."

"But me?"

Her voice had risen to a near shriek. She wasn't afraid of Danny, or of even having Danny here for a while. She was afraid of herself. Why did he find that so endearing?

She shook her head vigorously. His heart sank. He hadn't counted on losing her this soon.

"I don't want to set your son up with expectations that will never happen." Fright clouded her eyes. "I won't set myself up that way."

"But I don't want to lose you . . ."

"Ssh." She inhaled sharply. "You're right. A hotel would be hard on a seven-year-old boy. Maybe you could stay with Ivett and Steve for a while." She smiled demurely. "That might even give us some private moments. We'd have a built-in babysitter."

Kevin guffawed. "Don't tell Danny he needs a babysitter. And we'd have plenty of so-called private moments if we stayed with you. Danny isn't awake twenty-four hours a day."

"I'm not ready for that."

"But . . ."

Her warm hand squeezed his bicep. "I'm not making a

moral judgment about having your son in the house when we're making love. From what you tell me, he is probably quite aware of what goes on between a man and a woman. But I don't want to be cast into the role of the wicked stepmother."

"I think you'd make a fantastic stepmother . . ." Kevin stopped mid-sentence. Where had those words come from? He'd never considered that as a real possibility. "And you're hardly wicked," he said, trying to bail himself out of trouble. "Though I do enjoy when you get a little wicked with me."

She nodded and gave him a half-smile. "I believe what you're doing is called backpedaling. That's okay with me. I know you had no intention of presenting me to Danny as his future stepmom. Why don't we take this a little step at a time? I'll talk to Ivett. I'll be surprised if she doesn't welcome you and your son with open arms. She loves children." Nadja sobered. "Her biggest disappointment in life has been her inability to bear children."

"Maybe having Danny there will be too hard on her."

"She'll probably spoil him dreadfully."

"And you won't?"

She winced. "Let's try that arrangement. If it doesn't work, we'll come up with something else. Maybe after I've spent time with Danny, I'll feel more comfortable having both of you here as guests. I just don't want him getting wrong ideas about the future."

"Or me?"

"Or either of us." Nadja lowered her eyelashes. "All of this talk has made me very sleepy. Do you think you could hold me for a while?"

"For longer than a while." She turned onto her side and nestled her butt against his crotch. He cradled her in his arms, a breast cupped in each hand, and brushed his lips along the nape of her neck. "I love . . ." His voice broke up. He squeezed her tight. "I love the way you curve into my body."

She wiggled her butt. "Me too," she said, softly. "Now hush up. We have to get some sleep. I can't be late for work tomorrow."

He kissed her shoulder and settled his forehead on her body. What had gotten into him? He'd caught himself before saying the words he'd regret later. He did love how she fit against him—but that was different.

Biting her lip hard, Nadja welcomed that pain. It might help release the pain in her heart. Hadn't he nearly said he loved her? She opened her eyes and closed them tight. Would hearing those words be more painful than not hearing them?

She lay still, not wanting to encourage more conversation or more cuddling. When had she lost her moorings? She was a no-nonsense woman, used to doing things her way and not at all used to holding her tongue. Suddenly she knew too well what that odd expression *tongue tied in knots* meant.

Would she ever be able to think straight again? Kevin wanted her to meet Danny. She wanted to meet Danny. She was curious.

She shuddered. She already had a bond with the boy. After all, she'd lit a candle for him.

Maybe she should go back and light a candle for herself. She was in deep trouble. Very deep. She'd nearly responded with the same words before Kevin managed to correct himself. At least she hadn't embarrassed herself by being too quick to respond.

At last, she felt the relief of sleep creeping over her. She wondered if Ivett knew whether taking a man into your life could ever occur without complications.

CHAPTER EIGHT

"I'm glad you could meet me here," Nadja's uncle told Kevin. The man's features were pinched with strain—maybe that explained why they had to meet in such an out-of-the-way place.

Kevin nodded at Steve and glanced around the isolated gravel pit just north of the Minnesota border. "This isn't exactly on the way to anywhere."

He squinted at the handmade target some hundred feet away. Judging by the number of bullet holes in it, Steve must've been waiting there for some time. Kevin glanced into the open trunk of the realtor's car and whistled softly. "I haven't seen that much firepower in one place since I left the army."

"Sometimes it pays to be prepared," Chambers said, gruffly. "You want to try your hand?"

Kevin shook his head. "Maybe later. I assume this isn't your next idea for a location for Java Beans."

"I wanted to talk privately."

Glancing around the desolate pit, Kevin nodded. "Looks like you've achieved that goal. What's up?"

Steve flushed. "I think the women are in trouble." He swallowed. "Real trouble."

Kevin cocked his head to the side. "Nadja and Ivett?"

"That's right."

"So why are you telling me?"

Steve frowned, clearly not expecting the question. "Ivett told me you and Nadja are involved—romantically."

"We're involved, that's for sure."

"And you have had a hand in sparking this trouble by coming in here, wanting to buy Nadja out?"

"All right," Kevin drawled. "Maybe you'd better tell me about it."

"I don't know all the whys and wherefores, but somebody wants that Henderson building real bad."

"Rick Adams?"

Steve looked down at his feet before answering. "Yeah, but apparently there are people behind him. Chicago mobsters."

"Son of a bitch!" Kevin scowled at Steve and began to pace. Sometimes he thought best on the move. Shit. What kind of avalanche had he triggered? Java Beans couldn't have started all of this. Someone had been lying in wait. An interested buyer could've been waiting to set up an office, a pharmacy, or a pizza joint. It didn't really matter. Java Beans was, unfortunately, the first to show up. So why did people in Chicago want to get their hands on that particular building in downtown Jefferson City?

He stopped pacing and glared down at the bullet-riddled target. It would have to be a legitimate enterprise. To launder money? To be a conduit for drug shipments? Probably wouldn't be enough local clientele for prostitution. Not that there wasn't prostitution in small towns, but there likely wouldn't be enough dollars to attract the mob. Dollars. Gambling? Perhaps. He'd have to do some more digging to come up with the reason. He glowered at Steve. But to look at Ivett's husband, his friend's buddies already had him more than a little scared.

Kevin stepped over and peered back into the car trunk. "Three revolvers, one bolt action rifle, and a double-barrel shotgun. Do you really think using those weapons is going to hold up against people who make a living by force? Have you ever shot at a target that was intent on shooting you first?"

He watched in disgust as Steve shook his head. "Give me that damn Colt."

Kevin ignored the tremor in the man's hand as he handed him the gun and several cartridges. Kevin calmly loaded the weapon and rapidly fired six shots at the target. Together they punched out a large hole in its center. He handed the smoking weapon back to Steve, who continued gawking at the target with his jaw ajar.

"You're damn good," Steve muttered with a trace of awe.

"Yeah, well, some things you don't forget. Have you said anything about this to Ivett?"

Steve shook his head. "No, I wanted to talk with you first. It was just a feeling, but I thought you might be interested, particularly since you seem rather taken with my niece."

"Let me do a little digging before telling Ivett and Nadja."

"They won't like not being told."

Kevin spat on the ground. "You don't think I'm aware of that? I just want a few days to make some calls." He turned to leave but thought better of it. "By the way, what is Rick holding over your head? You could've gone to the police. You didn't have to show me all those god-awful properties."

Steve turned white. "I'm not telling."

Kevin nodded. "All right. Like I said before, you don't owe me an explanation, but I expect a couple women might think differently about that. See you around. By the way," he nodded toward the car, "if I were you, I'd put those damn guns back in the closet where they belong. It must be months before hunting season."

"I think it'd be fun having a boy around the house for a while," Ivett said, unsuccessful in hiding a wide grin. "What about you, Steve?"

Nadja watched her uncle turn several shades of red. He'd

been noticeably quiet as she'd set forth the possibility of Danny and his father staying with them for a few days or so. "Do whatever you want. You will anyway."

"Steve!"

He slouched in his chair. "I don't mind the boy. I don't like the idea of Kevin Langley hanging around that much."

"Why not?" Nadja blurted out before her aunt could.

"How do you know he's not trying to use you, and now us, to get you to sell your place?"

"He's not. I know that. Is that all that's bothering you?"

"Sure," he spat out. "If you think you can trust him, then it's okay with me."

Nadja glanced quickly at Ivett, who raised and lowered a shoulder. She was sure Steve had lied, but she could sit at her aunt's kitchen table all night without getting a more direct response.

"Okay." Nadja stood. "It's worth a try. They can always go to a hotel."

"Or to your place," Ivett said, sweetly.

"Or to my place. We'll have to see." She met Steve's gaze. "I thank you for trying. I'm sure Danny won't be any trouble."

Steve nodded noncommittally.

Nadja left the kitchen and let herself out. She was still worrying about her uncle's response when she arrived back at her house. She knew Kevin believed Steve had deliberately misled him about real estate. She had no explanation for that. But then she had no explanation for the fear in her uncle's eyes, either.

Maybe the two men could learn to trust each other more over the coming days, with Danny present.

Nadja grinned as she turned the key in her door. She had Kevin to herself for at least three more days and nights. Then he had to go back to the Cities. He'd wanted her to come and visit him in St. Paul. Maybe someday. Right now, everything

seemed to be rushing at her. She might welcome some distance from Kevin to catch her breath and her thoughts.

But not yet.

Kevin had a dinner meeting with a Chamber member from
Lakeside, the next town over, so she didn't expect him back
for another hour or so. That gave her plenty of time to shower
and prepare for their night of loving. She'd never realized
how few hours of actual sleep she required.

Reaching for the key Nadja had lent him, Kevin didn't bother
ringing the doorbell. He assumed she was waiting for him in
her bedroom. She didn't need to traipse downstairs to let him
in.

He stepped into the entryway and immediately noticed
soft light coming from the living room. She must be reading
late. He stepped into the spacious room and gasped for
breath.

Nadja lay naked on the carpet before him on her hands and
knees. Her head rested on a couple throw pillows, and she
turned her face to give him an innocent little smile. Her butt
was slightly raised, and both her puffy pussy and pink rosebud appeared to wink seductively at him.

"Hope you have enough energy left for me," she said, her
voice throaty.

He laughed and tossed his jacket toward the couch. "When
did you turn into a vixen? With you on display like that, I'd
have to be dead not to have enough energy."

He hurriedly unknotted his tie and lost two buttons trying
to get out of his shirt.

"You seem in a rush," she teased, wiggling her ass. "Don't
lose any more buttons because of me."

He kicked his shoes off and then began to work on his belt
and trousers. His hard arousal didn't make it any easier to be

quick about getting the damn pants off.

Her giggles hammered against his ears. "You undress with such grace."

"At last," he muttered. "I'm not convinced you're good for my heart."

Her smile flickered. "Are you going to stand there all night and tell me about your health?"

"No," he groused. "You want me from behind?"

"My, you are perceptive," she cooed, slapping her butt.

He dropped to his knees behind her. "Where has my shy, tentative Nadja gone?" He squeezed her butt cheeks.

Nadja arched her neck and pressed backward. "Nice. She's here somewhere. Do you want me to go find her?"

"You're not going anywhere." He tucked an arm under her and guided his cock to her opening pussy, sliding into her tight sleeve as if he'd never left.

"That's what I've been waiting for," she moaned, pressing back against his crotch. "I've missed this. I've missed you. Don't move. Let me savor this feeling for a moment."

He leaned over her back and kissed her neck. She turned until he could kiss the corner of her mouth.

"Hi," she whispered. "Welcome home."

He cradled her breasts and kissed his way down her spine. "If this is the welcome home I get each time I come back, I'll have to leave and come back a half-dozen times a day."

"Only six times?"

He chuckled. "You really are hot tonight."

"I didn't think you'd ever get here."

"I'm here now." He watched his cock easing in and out of her. "And your pussy really is hot. Damn."

"Not surprisingly. And I can tell you're back. Delightfully so."

For the first time since entering the room, he noticed the wine and cheese sitting on an end table. "I see you've even planned for some nourishment afterward."

"Refueling food."

"Does sleep fit anywhere in your plans?"

She shook her head. "There'll be plenty of time for sleep after you return to the Cities."

"But I don't leave for two more days. Sunday afternoon."

"I'm taking tomorrow off." She arched back, impaling him deeper. "How many times do you think we can fuck in thirty-six hours?"

He groaned—whatever happened to *making love?* "Not enough." He flexed his hips back and forth. "But it's past starting time."

She bowed her neck. "Uh-huh. So sweet."

Sweet! He didn't want sweet. Did she only think he was sweet? She said she wanted *fucked.*

He shook his head to clear it. He could fuck. He leaned over and scraped his fingernails down her back.

She pushed back against him. "Goodness."

He kneaded her butt and changed their angle by placing one foot on the carpet. She slammed back against him. He guided her ass with his hands, becoming mesmerized by the view of their mating.

Looking flushed, Nadja twisted her head from side to side. "I need you deeper. Can you stand?"

Where had she come up with that idea? He'd forgotten dancers were athletes. He said nothing but steadied himself on her butt and gingerly rose until he stood behind her, sinking farther into her. She gasped but remained solidly on her hands and knees. Deeper was no longer a possibility.

"Yes, so deep. I love it," she purred. "You are so strong. Your cock is stretching my cunt." Her back muscles tightened. "Please, don't just stand there—fuck me. Pound me."

His lips curled into a smile. He could do this. Strong was a hell of a lot better than sweet—at least for the moment. How had she conjured up the idea for this position? Ivett? His goddess even taunted him with words. And *he* was supposed to be the experienced partner.

No matter, he couldn't hold this position forever. He began rocking on the balls of his feet. Her little whimpers spurred him onward. He quickly picked up momentum.

Nadja braced herself, keeping them both from falling. "So huge. I can feel you in my throat. Wet your thumb and see if it will fit in my ass."

"What?"

"Do it. I am so open for you."

"Okay." He brought his thumb to his mouth, wet it thoroughly, and pressed it against her anus.

"Oh," she moaned.

"You okay?"

She nodded. "I'm opening more. Push it in."

Kevin tried not to blink as her watched his thumb disappear into Nadja's tight, hot ass. "It's in."

She giggled softly. "I know. You are so good. I am so turned on for you. Now fuck me some more."

He didn't bother with slow. He pulled nearly out and slammed back into her. She remained rock solid still, letting him be the aggressor.

"Yes. That's it. Take me. Make me yours."

He wiggled his thumb in her ass as he pounded her pussy. He knew immediately when she clinched her inner muscles. She had a grip like a silk vise.

Her body shuddered beneath him. "Fuck me. Come with me. Fill my cunt." Her words tumbled out. She wailed, encouraging him, demanding more and more.

He went into overdrive churning into her. His hips pumped erratically until he erupted. He stilled, not wanting Nadja to contort in that position any longer than necessary.

"Ah," she roared, clearly wanting nothing to do with his

gallantry. "Give me your seed. All of it." She pistoned back and forth on her knees until she'd milked him dry.

"Jesus, woman!" he howled.

Laughing hysterically, she collapsed to the carpet, and he tumbled after her. He withdrew his softening cock and curled up beside her, trying his best to slow his heart and catch some air.

She turned her head and smiled happily. "That was fun, don't you think?"

Fun? Thankfully, he still had enough strength to nod his head.

"Not all lovemaking must be mushy." She winked. "You make a good athlete."

"Too bad they don't have sex as an Olympic sport. We could sign up."

She narrowed her eyes. "You mock me again. Didn't you enjoy?"

He draped an arm around her. "I enjoyed very much. But I do think our lovemaking at times takes more out of me than you."

"True," she said seriously. She rose to her hands and knees, and he arched an eyebrow. "Not again, silly. I'll fix us some cheese and crackers and pour the wine. You will be ready to go again in no time."

Nadja spread cheese onto crackers and handed him one. Her joyful smile electrified him beyond belief. He chewed on the cracker and watched her fill the wine glasses. His Ukrainian lover had proved to be a woman of many moods. He hoped he was man enough to match this one. He might die trying, but he could imagine more terrible deaths.

Sitting on her patio, Nadja sipped her first coffee of the morning. Cardinals, robins, and phoebes greeted her with their individual tunes. She listened carefully, distinguishing one species from another. Squinting, she spied the red tuft of a cardinal in the montage of green oak leaves. "I see you," she whispered. "Another proud male."

She lifted the coffee mug to her lips, quite pleased with her antics of the previous night. Her preparations had turned into such a surprising success that she wasn't about to return Ivett's tapes yet.

She hadn't had time to finish the fourth tape about sexual fantasies. She chuckled and stretched her neck. She hadn't realized so many fantasies existed. She'd seldom spent much time dreaming about lovemaking — until she'd met Kevin. Now she hardly thought about anything else.

Could she overdose on sex? She shrugged and watched a chipmunk skitter across the patio in search of food. Maybe she was trying to get her fill of sex before Kevin decided to move on. At least she'd have some quality memories when he did.

The look on his face when he'd stepped into the living room and seen her naked on her hands and knees, fully displaying her treasures for him, was emblazoned on her memory. "Thank you, Ivett," she murmured.

She had Kevin guessing, and that pleased her more than it probably should have. It had never occurred to her to want a man guessing what she might do next. She'd always prided herself on being straightforward and predictable. No surprises.

Hadn't he said he liked surprises? She took another swallow of coffee. He'd sure seemed to enjoy last night's surprise. She hadn't realized how a sprinkling of words like *fuck, cock,* and *cunt* could fuel a man's desire — she smirked — well, even her own. More kudos to her aunt and her tapes. And she hadn't planned on introducing anal play into their lovemaking. That had been quite spontaneous. But then she hadn't gone nearly as far as the tapes had shown. His cock in her ass?

She shrugged. Maybe. His thumb had been absolutely amazing.

They hadn't made it up the stairs to her bedroom until well after midnight. They must've giggled and talked for at least another hour. She hadn't known a lengthy, halfway intelligent conversation could be conducted with a man still buried inside her pussy.

Not only had she discovered that was possible, but that in many subtle ways, she could help him stay hard. Maybe all those years of yoga and ballet had paid off. She enjoyed playing with him. It often only took a squeeze of muscles, the movement of a leg, the scrape of a fingernail, and she could feel his stiffening response. Priceless!

She inhaled deeply. Her newly found powers heightened her senses. She closed her eyes and let the scent of roses fill her nostrils. How could she explain her giddiness? She felt loved.

She glanced over her shoulder and smiled at Kevin as he stepped out of the house with a coffee mug in his hand.

He greeted her with a satisfied smile and pulled up a chair beside hers. "I don't think I've seen you in shorts and a T-shirt. Very nice."

"Thought I'd better get dressed, or we might wear ourselves out."

"That might be a risk worth taking." He gave her a curious look. "I like the green shorts, a lot. They show off your trim legs just right." He frowned.

"What? What's wrong?"

"I love the dangling loop earrings. And I like the yellow tee, too, but—do we really need a bra? Are you trying to hide from me?"

"Of course not." She furrowed her brow and glanced back at the house. "What if someone drops by?"

"Are you expecting anyone?"

She shook her head.

"Me neither. And if anyone did come by, so what? I'm proud of your boobs. Such beauty shouldn't be entirely hidden, even from the casual observer."

He brushed a hand across her cheek, and her breathing faltered. "May I?" he asked, dropping his hand to her waist and lifting her shirt an inch or two.

She turned to face him. The admiration in his eyes caused a tingle to start in her toes and spread upward to her tits. "Yes."

He locked his gaze on hers, hoisted her T-shirt, and easily unclasped the bra. With a flick of his wrists, he had it off her and stuffed in the back pocket of his jeans.

"There," he said, pulling her shirt back down. "Now they are free to be watched and adored. Look," he said, with a trace of awe, "your nipples are rising to say *good morning.*"

"They're probably just cold."

"I don't believe that for a minute."

"Neither do I. I hope you enjoy the view. Do you think we'll ever get used to being around each other without having to look or touch so much?"

"You mean like a couple married for years?"

She couldn't prevent her cheeks from reddening. She swallowed. "Ivett and Steve have been married for over five years, and they still can't keep their hands off of each other."

"Maybe some couples are more blessed than others."

"You and your wife weren't one of those?"

"Hardly. Things changed after the honeymoon, and then the fire just about died once Elizabeth became pregnant with Danny."

"Too bad."

"Yeah." He sighed and looked away. "Don't get me wrong. It took both of us to kill that fire."

"Yes," she said, seriously. "I'm learning that it takes two

people to build the fire. I imagine it takes two to put it out."

"So," he said, giving her a devilish smile, "speaking of building fire, how did you come up with the idea to surprise me last evening?"

She pursed her lips and kept her silence.

"You know the scene of the naked woman on a bearskin rug in a north country cabin with a fire in the fireplace?"

Goodness. Had he watched Ivett's tape, too? She shook her head and looked down at her cup. "I'm not telling."

"It's okay," he murmured, lifting her chin. "I wasn't complaining. You were a visual, tactile, and auditory delight — all night long. Whatever prompted all of that needs to be honored. You've said yourself you're not overly spontaneous." He sobered. "I only want you to know I'm aware of how much risk you took last night to please me — to please us — and I appreciate that very much."

She tried to look away from him, afraid she'd start blubbering at any minute, but he wouldn't let her. Instead, he leaned over and pressed his lips against hers. She closed her eyes. This was better than running from him. One of his large palms settled over her breast. She breathed through her nose. Much better.

He broke the kiss and glanced around the yard. "I hadn't realized how large this backyard is. You've done a super job with shrubs and flowers. Did you add the gazebo, or did it come with the place?"

"I added it. It's a good place for thinking and writing poetry — even during mosquito season."

He smiled at her. "Poetry. Is there anything you don't do?"

She blinked, not quite sure how to take his meaning.

"Danny will love this yard. He'll love you."

"I do hope he enjoys his time in Iowa. This must be a much smaller community than he's used to."

"The only thing you're missing is a swing set."

121

"I'll buy one."

"No, no. I didn't mean that. I'll make sure we bring enough of his favorite toys. Of course, he'll want to bring his bike."

She stroked the base of her throat. "Do you think that's safe? After his accident?"

"His doc says the worst thing we can do now is be overly protective. I'm sure Danny will be more cautious. At least for a while."

Nadja crossed her legs at the ankles, hoping she looked calmer than she felt. She didn't know how she'd manage if something bad happened to Kevin's son while he was visiting her or Ivett. "I hope so."

"Is that your doorbell?" Kevin grunted.

"What?" She looked at him wide-eyed. "Of course it is." She jumped to her feet. "No one expects me home on a Saturday morning."

She'd gotten halfway to the entryway before realizing she no longer wore a bra. Oh well. She hoped the visitor wasn't one of the elderly ladies from the Arts Council.

She peeked out the window and gasped. Worse—it was Ivett! Maybe she wouldn't notice. Nadja grew cold. What was Ivett doing here? She should be back at her store.

Ivett stormed through the door like a whirlwind. "Are you alone?"

"No." She shook her head. "Kevin is on the patio."

"Good. You both need to hear the latest." Ivett led the way to the kitchen and helped herself to a cup of coffee and a cookie. She glanced back at Nadja. "You should go braless more often. I guarantee there'd be no shortage of guys hanging around here."

"Humph," Nadja huffed. "I don't want a bunch of guys hanging around here."

"Maybe one?" Ivett gave her a wicked grin and sniffed the air.

She shrugged. "Maybe one." She smirked. "Maybe I should go get another bra."

"Another one. Now you have piqued my curiosity. Where is the first one?"

"In Kevin's back pocket."

Ivett burst out laughing. "That's a good one. May I suggest not getting another bra unless you simply want to fill his pockets? Let's get outside. I can't spend all morning here, and looking at you . . ."

Nadja blushed as Ivett's eyes focused on her aching nipples.

" . . . I doubt you want me to."

Kevin rose to his feet when he saw Nadja returning to the patio with her aunt in tow. Were Nadja's burning cheeks due to embarrassment or anger? Maybe both. He did his best to ignore her reaction by directing his attention to Ivett. "Good morning," he said as casually as he could.

"Glad to see you're good for my niece," Ivett quipped, pulling up a chair. Once settled, she added, "You appear quite satisfied, too. She must be good for you, too."

"Ivett!" Nadja protested before he had a chance to respond.

He kept his silence — this probably wasn't the time to thank Ivett for her apparently good advice on Nadja's sexual prowess.

"Be that as it may," Ivett held up her palms in surrender, "I didn't come over here to disturb your little love nest."

"What's wrong?" Nadja asked. "You still haven't told me. Now both of us are waiting. What happened? Is it Steve?"

"No, not him. I wanted to get to you before the police or a friend called."

Kevin tensed and saw Nadja's hand fly to her throat.

"Both stores had their windows spray-painted sometime

during the night." Ivett's eyes turned cold. "It wasn't a pretty sight."

"Was there a message?" Kevin asked in a voice that seemed oddly calm to his own ears.

Ivett nodded. "*Russian Bitches Go Home.* That was on both stores. *Buy American* was also on my shop window." She glanced at Nadja.

"What else?" Nadja squeaked.

"A female figure with very large breasts was sketched on the Cappuccino window."

"Oh!" Nadja gasped. "That is so personal!"

Kevin hid his hands under the table and balled his fingers into tight fists. Too damn personal for his liking. Was this the work of Rick and his friends, or some teenage prank?

Nadja rose to her feet. "I must go to the shop."

Ivett grabbed her hand and pulled her back into the chair. "I've taken care of everything. Two guys showed up to clean the windows before I came over here. I've talked to the police and a reporter."

"A reporter?" She blanched. "Oh, no. More publicity."

"I'm afraid so." Ivett stroked the back of her niece's hand. "Maybe it's just as well that our friends know what is happening. They will support us. I know they will."

Nadja nodded, fighting back tears.

"Or," Kevin muttered, "it could bring out the crazies."

Nadja arched an eyebrow. "What do you mean?"

He hadn't realized he'd verbalized his fears. He shrugged. They might as well know what was possible. "Most regions have a rabid far-right fringe that would love to fuel the kind of false pride and hatred those messages suggest."

Nadja wheeled to look at Ivett. "And you are an American citizen!"

Ivett shrugged. "A naturalized American citizen. For some people, that doesn't count."

Kevin squinted. "I take it you are not a citizen?"

Nadja shook her head. "My mother opposed becoming naturalized citizens. I've been so involved with the Cappuccino since she died, it has only crossed my mind once or twice. There hasn't been time."

Kevin flexed his fingers and drew back a lock of hair that had fallen over Nadja's eye. "Ivett is right. Naturalization or not isn't what all of this is about."

"What is it about?" Nadja wailed. "I don't like feeling this out of control. If I had someone to fight, that might help. But this coward is faceless."

"You have any ideas?" Ivett asked coolly. "We weren't having any troubles until you showed up with Java Beans's interest in the Cappuccino."

Nadja blushed, though Kevin guessed Ivett hadn't said anything Nadja hadn't thought about. He kept his temper in check.

Before he could respond, Ivett added, "I didn't mean I think you're behind our troubles. But I do know from Nadja that you have been doing some of your own sleuthing at your company's request."

"That's correct." How much could he trust Ivett? Did she know her husband was up to his ears in this mess, one way or another? "I wish I knew why. It appears Java Beans was an innocent catalyst. Someone or some group apparently wants your building quite badly. They must've been waiting for the right trigger to come along. I expect I provided that trigger. If Nadja had sold to us, Java Beans would never have been profitable. I can guarantee that. Whoever is after you now would have made it impossible for my company to survive here. Within a year, we would've written the place off as a bad decision and sold to the highest bidder."

"And we can only guess who that might be." Ivett glared at him. "But that doesn't explain my shop. You were only after the Cappuccino."

"That's right. But the word got out that we wanted to team up with a bagel company — which wasn't true — and therefore wanted the entire building. I imagine our size made that a fortuitous situation for the person or group who wants the Henderson building. If it hadn't been for that possibility, they would've likely taken things slower. And their fast-track overreaching may be their downfall yet."

"What do you mean by that?" Nadja asked.

"I'm not sure. But whoever's behind all of this, I think they're moving more quickly than planned. Which means they are more prone to make a mistake."

"That's seems true enough," Ivett agreed. "And it also makes them more dangerous."

Kevin inhaled deeply and exhaled before answering. He glanced back and forth between the women. "I'm afraid you may be right. But I doubt they'll risk pushing too fast. Now that this is in the public domain, if I were them, I'd wait to see what happens. Will there be a backlash? Will the community divide? Maybe some of those crazies I talked about will step up and stir the pot. I expect the people behind this would like nothing better than to have others do their dirty work."

"That," Nadja complained, "doesn't sound very comforting."

"I suppose it's not, but you don't want to panic or overreact, either."

"I'm not panicking," she said sharply.

He grinned as she stiffened. It felt good to see her spunk returning. "You want to go to the shop, don't you?"

"Yes. I can't stay here." She lowered her eyelashes. "I'm sorry," she added softly, ignoring her aunt. "I wouldn't be any good here anyway. I have to make sure everything's okay."

"I know," Kevin said. "Don't worry about it. I'll come with

you. It might be best for me to head back home today."

Her raised eyebrows contained more than one question.

"There won't be any more trouble at the shop. The vandals will wait and see if their work has any results. And if I leave later today, I can be back a day sooner."

"Oh." She gave him a half-smile. "I hadn't considered that."

He reached under the table and caressed her bare thigh. "And I have spectacular memories to take back with me. I'll return. You can count on that."

She covered his hand with hers. "I'll be waiting," she murmured.

"Hey, don't forget I'm still here," Ivett yelped. "I've seen enough. I'm leaving." She pushed her chair back and stood. "You really don't need to rush to get to the shop, if you two would like to take more time with your goodbyes."

Kevin held back a smile and gave Nadja credit for not chastising her aunt. Like Nadja, he rose to his feet. "Tell me," he asked, "is your husband, like many of the Iowans I've met, an avid hunter?"

"Heavens no—if Steve ever brings a dead bird or animal into my house, it'd better come from the meat market." Ivett scowled. "Why do you ask?"

"I meant to ask him the other day. I haven't gone pheasant hunting for years. Thought maybe in his line of work, he'd know some farmers who'd let us hunt."

"I doubt it, but you'll have to ask him." She cast an accusing eye at Nadja. "Did you know that your lover shoots Bambi?"

"Ivett!" Nadja wrapped an arm around his waist. "He didn't say he shoots Bambi." She eyed him cautiously. "Do you?"

"Not that I know of." A quick exit seemed desirable. "I need to shower before we head down to the shop. See you in a bit."

Before he reached the patio door, he overheard Ivett ask, "Don't you want to join him?"

"There'll be another time."

Kevin chuckled. And *he* was counting on that.

CHAPTER NINE

"You don't mope well." Ivett sat at one of the small tables in Nadja's shop and sipped an iced coffee.

"It's late—don't you have some place to be?" Refusing to look at her aunt, Nadja finished restocking the coffee bean display.

"Kevin better get back here soon, or no one will be able to be around you. It's been five days. Have you heard anything from him?"

"He's in Minneapolis through Saturday." She didn't really want to talk about him. He'd only phoned once, and that conversation had been cut short because his ex-wife called. She hated call-waiting. Was he having second thoughts about their relationship?

She straightened and swiped at her warm brow. Was *she* having second thoughts about *him*?

"Your glow," Ivett mused, "is definitely missing."

"I don't glow. That's your overworked imagination." Nadja walked around the counter to face her aunt. Closing time had long passed, but how could she throw her aunt out?

Ivett shook her head and smiled thinly. "I don't think you have such a poor memory. You glow—when Kevin is around. Sometimes you bubble."

"I do not!"

"You do. It provides such a nice contrast to your cool, self-possessed exterior. It's been heartening to know you are mortal like the rest of us. And now you even mope."

"I'm sorry if I'm naturally a cold woman." Nadja grabbed

Ivett's half-drunk coffee and wiped the table. Maybe she'd take the hint and leave. Leave her alone. "And I don't glow. And I definitely don't bubble." She stomped around the counter and dumped the contents of the cup into the sink.

She heard the scrape of the chair against the floor as Ivett rose. "Believe what you want. I'll leave you to your misery. But you, girl, glowed and bubbled Saturday morning when I stopped by the house. Your eyes hadn't turned soft because of me. Nor were your cheeks on fire or your nipples the size of small buttons because of me."

Ivett leaned across the counter, making it hard for Nadja to ignore her. "All of that glowing and bubbling because of him, because of what he and you shared probably throughout the night and morning, and because your bra dangled indiscreetly from his back pocket. Try to fool yourself, if you must, but you can't fool me. You're falling in love with him, and that scares the hell out of you."

Nadja's fingers curled into fists, and she worked hard at focusing on Ivett through blurred vision. "I'm not," she protested, half-heartedly. "I'm such a mess."

Ivett scooted around the counter and held out her arms.

Nadja folded herself into the shorter woman's embrace, then sobbed while Ivett rubbed her back and shoulders. "He's only called once. I'm not even sure he's coming back. Maybe he found another woman in Minneapolis."

She hated her sounds of desperation. She despised herself for becoming so vulnerable.

"You don't know that. You're letting your imagination run wild." Ivett stepped back but kept a firm grip on her hands. "From what I saw Saturday, I'd say he's just as infatuated with you as you are with him. I won't believe for a minute that he has another woman." Ivett gave her a sharp look. "Have you called him?"

Nadja shook her head. She'd wanted to, but that had

seemed far too risky. What if he wasn't alone? What if he didn't want to hear from her?

"Do you suppose he may feel hesitant about you—since you haven't called him?"

Her shoulder slumped. "He shouldn't."

"And if I asked him the same question, he'd likely say *she shouldn't*. Guys don't want to do all the chasing. And you cherish your independence so much."

"Yes."

"Maybe you should behave more independently. Don't wait for him to call you. If you want to know if he's in bed with six other women, call him—ask him." Ivett giggled. "And if he is, dump him."

Nadja shook her head and smiled through the tears. "You can be good for the soul, sometimes. You're right. I must stop moping around. I need to take control of myself."

"I suppose that's part of what Kevin finds appealing about you. You're not a carbon copy of those other six women."

"There'd better not be six other women," Nadja huffed, making a face.

"That's more like my Nadja. By the way, I left you three more tapes on the counter. I trust you are watching them."

Nadja nodded, not trusting herself to speak.

"I love it when you blush like that. So did the anal play tape shock you?"

"At first," Nadja admitted.

"But then it intrigued you?"

"Something like that . . ."

"I hoped so. You are your aunt's niece. You really are coming into your sexual own, aren't you?"

"Maybe, but what am I going to do after Kevin moves on?"

"Why do you assume he will? I expect you have a lot to do with that. And if he does, you will be much more experienced for the next fellow that strikes your fancy."

"Right. I don't want to think about that."

"You just keep watching those tapes and planning surprises for your man." Ivett laughed. "Now that you're fired up a bit, I'd better get on home. Steve will wonder what I'm up to if I don't call soon. See you tomorrow."

Absently, Nadja waved at her aunt's back. She glanced quickly around the Cappuccino. The shop was ready for another day.

She shivered. Was *she* ready for another day? She'd prided herself on having enough courage to make her own way in the world. So why was she buckling before a man? She could come up with no reasonable explanation. Now that she'd found one of the male species whose company she actually enjoyed, there seemed a distinct possibility others were out there too—if she wanted to look.

She wasn't one of those soppy females who believed in one *meant-to-be* lover. She grabbed her keys and hesitated.

At least she didn't *think* she was one of those females. Her brow furrowed. Kevin could be replaced. She was convinced of that. But she didn't want to replace him.

She snickered—at least not yet.

Ignoring Carolyn James's penetrating stare as best he could, Kevin studied the shadows of clouds moving across the ground far below his office window. Maybe if he remained still, Carolyn would leave and let him be.

"Do you always brood when you're indecisive?"

He winced. Hoping she'd leave had been futile. "What? Oh, you're still here."

"And nonchalant fits you better when you don't force it."

He turned from the window. "I didn't know you were such an expert about my character."

Carolyn smiled gently. "Professional interest only, I can

assure you."

"I never thought otherwise."

"Yes, I suppose I do know your moods fairly well. I'd better, given how much I depend on you. When will you go back to Jefferson City?"

He shrugged. He wasn't sure he knew the answer to that question.

"You'll have to go back, you know."

"My presence may have fueled the trouble down there."

"It may have, but that damage is already done." Carolyn frowned. "And I'm afraid we all bear some responsibility for that. Have you heard yet from our dear private investigator?"

"Not yet. Amy said it might take several days to get back to us. She had loose ends to take care of before she could make the trip south. Though she said she'd have an assistant begin some computer tracking."

"Excellent. Amy does her job well." Carolyn's features softened. "At one time, I thought you and Amy would make a fine couple."

He shrugged. He figured Amy had already explained their thinking on that matter, but just in case, he said, "You know we dated a few times, but I expect we were both uncomfortable with me dating the boss's sister."

"Too bad."

"I wasn't ready to give up my job. And that's the only way it would've worked."

Carolyn nodded. "I'm sure the two of you made the right decision. If the earth shook when you were together, you would've figured a way around your job."

"You're probably right," he conceded. "Anyway, it's good to have Amy working on this situation in Jefferson City. I won't feel like such a lone ranger."

"Why do I think when you're working in Jefferson City, you're not lonely at all?"

"I didn't say I was lonely." He didn't welcome for a moment the gleam in Carolyn's eyes.

"Your Nadja woman must be quite the lady."

"She is. But she's not *my* woman."

Carolyn arched her eyebrows. "You sure?"

His shoulders slumped. "No."

"Not sure of her, or not sure of yourself?"

"Both, probably. I'm not quite sure what to do with her."

Carolyn chuckled. "Now that *is* funny. She must be very special if you're thinking beyond the bedroom."

"I didn't say that," he countered quickly.

"You didn't have to. Come on, Kevin."

He didn't try to shake her hand from his arm.

"I've known you since before you met Elizabeth. I doubt I've known all your women, but this Jefferson City woman seems different. Women don't tie you in knots like this."

"Maybe I'm just concerned because I may have placed her in jeopardy."

Shaking her head, Carolyn smiled. "You can be a bullshit artist at times. That may work out in the field, but it doesn't work with me." She squeezed his arm. "Don't deceive yourself."

Later that evening, Kevin tipped a bottle of his favorite German beer to his lips and swallowed. He glanced at the phone on his den desk. He should call her. Maybe he should show up on her doorstep and see what she had to say for herself.

It wasn't as if she didn't have his phone number. He'd called her once. True, Elizabeth had interrupted that conversation. He'd be happy when his ex-wife finally remarried. She was a basket case, and he didn't think it was his job to hold her hand as she went through pre-wedding jitters.

He'd pick up Danny over the coming weekend, make sure

the boy attended his mother's wedding the following week-end—he didn't expect his own presence was needed or desired—and then Danny would stay with him for at least a couple weeks. He looked forward to having Danny with him, though he still hadn't decided about accepting Ivett's offer for the two of them to stay with her and Steve. Steve probably didn't have much of a say in that decision. But then Steve probably didn't want to spend time with him any more than he did with Steve.

He eyed the phone cautiously. Should he, or shouldn't he? He jumped as the phone rang. Damn, was he a psychic? But it probably wasn't her anyway.

"Hello."

"Hi, I hope I'm not bothering you."

He smiled. "You're not. I've missed the sound of your voice."

"Apparently not enough to call me."

"I deserved that," he responded to her accusation. "Pull in your claws. I was going to, but I'm glad you called."

"Having second thoughts?"

He frowned. Her directness appealed to him most of the time. "Maybe it is important to pause and reflect a little."

"And?" She failed to hide the catch in her voice. She wasn't quite as impervious as she tried to project herself.

"Given your question, I expect you've done some reflecting, too." She didn't break the silence. "Okay, I'll blink first. Yes, I miss you. Yes, I want to be with you. Yes, I'm coming to Jefferson City as soon as I can get away."

"I will be here for you." She hesitated. "I've missed you, too. And I'm not ready to look for your replacement."

"What! You thought about replacing me?" he blurted out. "Like a light bulb?"

"No, no." Her words tumbled out in a rush. "This second language can still cause me problems. I must not have said that right. I want you. I yearn for your arms. I want you filling me completely. Is that clear enough?"

"Yes." He chuckled. "I like the picture you've painted. Very much."

"When will you arrive here?"

"I have to pick up Danny the day after tomorrow. I'll have to drop him at his mother's wedding the following Saturday. We can either come down this Sunday or next Sunday."

"This Sunday, if you can."

He smiled. He did like her directness. "We'll do that. Is Ivett ready for houseguests?"

"Yes. She's looking forward to it."

"More than Steve, no doubt."

"Probably."

"And how has the citizenry of Jefferson City responded to your plight?"

"Mainly supportive. Ivett and I have each received a couple crank calls, but we hung up on them."

"Good."

"And the newspaper ran a very supportive editorial encouraging its readers to rise above hate. They even listed many of the things Ivett and I have done to improve the community. I'll show it to you when you get here."

"I'll look forward to reading the piece." He glanced around his den, unable to define the sudden swelling in his throat. "Someday, I'd like you to come up and visit me here."

She met his words with a prolonged silence. At last she said, "I'd like that. I'd like to see where and how you live."

"We'll work on it." He glanced at the wall clock. "Unfortunately, I have to make a few more calls tonight."

"I understand. I'll see you Sunday."

"Nadja?"

"Yes."

"Are you wearing your robe?"

"Yes."

"Are you naked under it?"

"Of course."

"Imagine I'm your robe, and I'll do the same. Bye."

Her sultry *I am — bye* caused him to soar with yet another inexplicable feeling. Someday, he'd have to examine his emotional reservoir — but not yet, not now.

Nadja couldn't stop pacing back and forth across her living room floor. She peeked at the clock again. Had she ever been this tightly coiled?

Kevin was bringing his son to her. He'd called when he'd exited I-35 onto the Jefferson City turnoff. She smoothed out her light blue blouse and checked the creases in her tan trousers. She hadn't wanted to look like a schoolteacher, but she didn't want to look too sexy, either. Frowning, she wondered for the umpteenth time what Danny expected of her, if anything.

What had his father told him? She should've asked more questions of Kevin when they last talked, but her mind had been overrun by sexual banter. Clearly, Kevin counted on having some time alone with her. She squeezed her shoulders back and held them in place for thirty seconds. She was counting on some alone time, too. But the biggest hurdle on this visit might turn out to be a small boy.

She sighed with a mixture of relief and nervousness when she heard Kevin's car pull into the driveway. Not wanting to appear too eager, but unable to wait, she opened the door and stepped out onto the porch.

She smiled when Kevin opened his door and gave her a big wave and grin. The passenger door opened, and a small replica of Kevin stared at her with large, rounded eyes. The boy raised his hand and waved weakly, mimicking his father.

Nadja found herself nearly skipping to the car. Kevin quickly pulled her into a hug and kissed her soundly. He must've done some talking to his son. She broke away from his embrace and knelt to greet Danny.

She held out her hand, and the boy puffed out his chest and shook her hand as if accustomed to doing that every day. "Hi, I'm Danny," he said, with dimples threatening to break into a smile.

"Hi, Danny. I'm Nadja. Welcome to my home."

Danny giggled and quickly covered his mouth. "I can't pronounce your name right. My dad tried to teach me. But I can't."

She tucked her hand under his chin that had fallen to his chest. "That's okay. Is Nadia easier for you to say?"

"Na-ia"

"Just about. Na-Di-a."

"Na-Di-a. Nadia." He beamed at his father and then back at her. "I did it. Nadia. But that isn't your name."

"Nadja is often said as Nadia in English."

"Oh. I know English. I'm pleased to be here, Nadia."

"Oh wow!" She glanced up at Kevin. "This young man is irresistible."

"Sort of like his father," Kevin teased.

"We shall see about that. Would you like some pop, Danny?" she asked, taking his hand in hers and leading the way to the house. Kevin followed along behind.

"Sure. What kind do you have?"

She looked down at his questioning face. "I'll tell you a secret. Your dad told me what your favorite drink is, and I have lots of it in the refrigerator. And I thought you two guys might enjoy an ice cream bar after your long drive."

"Oh wow!" His brilliant smile thrilled her. "Dad," he called over his shoulder, "she may be a keeper."

She frowned at Kevin. "What is a keeper?"

"I'll tell you later." His eyes sparkled. "Right now, us guys can't get to your kitchen fast enough." Kevin dropped his hand to the small of her back and guided her toward the house.

She'd have to remember to ask him about *keeper* later. She had no desire to be anyone's keeper.

Hours later, Nadja stood in the foyer of her aunt's house, saying her goodnights to Kevin and Ivett. "I didn't think Danny would ever wind down. He's so, so exuberant. How do you keep up with him?"

"He's not quite as exhausting" — Kevin stifled a yawn — "after you've been around him for a while."

"He'll adjust quickly," Ivett chimed in. "I'm sure we'll have a lot of fun with him." Ivett looked from Nadja to Kevin. "Well, I'll let you two say goodnight. I'll see you in the morning, Nadja. We may have to trade Danny back and forth between the two shops when he can't be with Kevin. The little guy is a firecracker. I was so pleased to see him worm his way onto Steve's lap."

Nadja nodded. "Me, too. Goodnight," she said a little sharply.

"I'm going."

Once her aunt's footsteps grew faint, Nadja moved easily into Kevin's arms. They held each other tight.

"Thanks for accepting Danny the way you have," he said into her hair. "I know that's a lot to ask."

She shook her head against his shoulder. "He's a lovely boy. I'm sure we will find lots of fun things to do."

"And how about me and you?" He lifted her chin. "Are we going to find lots of fun things to do?"

"I hope so," she whispered, slanting her lips across his. What began as a gentle kiss turned quickly into a bruising kiss. Neither could get enough of the other. Their tongues dueled for space as he grabbed her butt with both hands, pulling her snug against his erection. She squirmed against him, teasing, promising.

Holding his face between her hands, she didn't want to risk parting their lips. She balanced on one foot, wrapped a leg around his butt, and squeezed him tight.

His groan filled the cavern of her mouth. And she shuddered in his arms. Reclaiming her tongue, she pecked at his lips and backed out of his arms. "I'd better leave before we embarrass ourselves."

"Yeah," he said, between ragged breaths. "Maybe I'll come by tomorrow night after Danny goes to bed. By then, it'll be easier to get him back onto his regular bedtime schedule."

"He was so cute, negotiating for a later bedtime about a half-hour at a time."

"That won't stay cute for long. Believe me. But Danny's really a good kid."

"I know he is. We'll talk tomorrow. Good night."

On shaking legs, Nadja made her way back to her car. Did Kevin have any idea how much willpower it had taken to leave him standing in the foyer? She remembered the hardness of his arousal pressing against her mound. Yes, he probably did know. That, at least, comforted her.

"Your coffee is better than Java Beans," Danny declared, flashing a smile at Nadja. He was sipping a concoction of mostly warm milk and a little bit of decaf espresso.

Nadja stood behind the counter and smiled back at him where he sat at the nearest table in her shop. It was mid-afternoon, and the flow of customers had lulled. An older couple sat in one corner, engaged in deep conversation. A young college-age couple sat in another corner. Nadja ignored the way the young man rubbed a hand against the inside of the woman's bare thigh. The couple remained oblivious that a world existed around them. She could empathize with them. She caught herself imagining Kevin's hand working its way along her thigh, inching higher and higher.

"You look like you're dreaming."

She blinked and flushed slightly. The boy's words had definitely reminded her that a world existed around her. "No," she said smoothly, "just appreciating your praise for my coffee. You are a charmer."

"Yeah?" Danny drew himself up with pride. "I'm often told I'm just like my dad."

"It must be about time for you to go back and visit Ivett's shop." She wasn't about to engage in a prolonged conversation with Danny about his father.

Danny stood and clutched his decaf latte in one hand. "You're trying to get rid of me." His smile seemed benign enough. "That's okay. Ivett is a lot of fun."

And she wasn't? Nadja tried not to grind her teeth. "There's probably more to do in her store. Perhaps you'd like to visit a hobby store. Do you put models together?"

"Sure." His eyes brightened. "I specialize in anything to do with NASA. My dad helps me with them. Do you do models?"

"Not exactly. Do you see the colorful eggs and the dolls at the end of the counter?"

He nodded, looking at the counter. "Ivett has lots of them in her store, too."

"I make those."

"Really." He squinted at her artwork. "That must take lots of patience. I'm not sure I have enough."

"Maybe you'd like to help sometime."

"Maybe." He didn't look too convinced. "The eggs should be interesting." He frowned at her. "But I don't play with dolls."

She ignored his comment and walked down to the end of

the counter, where she picked a doll up. She began taking it apart carefully while keeping one eye on the boy. As she'd expected, his eyes grew in surprise when she pulled a second doll out of the first, and then a third and a fourth, and finally a fifth.

"Wow!" he squealed. "How do you do that?"

Grinning, Nadja replied, "The individual pieces are made in my home country of Ukraine, and then I paint them, usually on winter nights."

"You're good." He scowled. "Are they all girl dolls?"

"No, you can paint them however you want. I've even seen some painted as football players."

"Really?" Danny stood on his toes to get a better look. "Maybe I could help you." He cocked an eye at her. "But it's not winter."

She found herself laughing easily with him. "I can probably make an exception for you."

He nodded. "My dad says you're a dancer."

"That's right." She wondered about this sudden change of conversation.

"Do you tap?"

"A long time ago. I haven't in years."

"My mother has me in tap dance lessons."

"How nice."

"Except some of it is tough. I want to get good enough to do more step dancing. We're Irish, you know."

"Of course you are." She gave him a puzzled look. "Your mother, too?"

"Yeah, I'm almost all Irish." He flashed a smile that would someday melt the heart of any Irish lass. "Maybe you could help me."

"I'd be delighted to," she said, turning to a customer.

"Don't let me forget," she called over her shoulder. "Why don't you run along and see what Ivett is up to?"

"I won't let you forget," Danny hollered, waving at her as he rushed toward the other store.

With half a mind, she listened to her customer's order and prepared the cappuccino. The other half remained focused on Kevin's son.

She had to take care. The more involved she became with him, the harder it would be when Kevin moved on to another woman. She was an adult and knew about the pain at the end of a relationship. Danny was a seven-year-old and could throw his entire self into a relationship without considering the consequences.

She grimaced. But then he'd experienced his parents going through a divorce—losing her friendship probably wouldn't compare to that.

Nonetheless, she must be careful. She still had her own heart to protect—from both father and son.

CHAPTER TEN

"You should probably be leaving," Nadja murmured later that night. She wasn't really ready for Kevin to go back to Ivett's, but she knew they had to get some sleep, and he needed to wake up where his son was.

"You think loving you once is going to tide us over for twenty-four hours?" He pressed a finger pad against a raised nipple.

She moaned. "No, but at least one of us should be reasonable."

"Reasonable" — he chuckled — "about loving you. I'm not sure reason has anything to do with that."

They lay on her bed. Neither had seen a need to pull a sheet over them after making love. Modesty hardly seemed like an issue any longer. She glanced down at his cock. "He doesn't look particularly eager for more."

Kevin brushed his lips across her brow. "He's just resting. I expect he could be talked into more."

Her heart skipped a beat. Had he suggested what she thought he had? She sucked on her lower lip. Why not? Ivett's tapes made it look easy enough.

"Maybe I should give him a tongue-lashing." The sudden flash of lust in Kevin's eyes provided all the encouragement she required.

She slid down the bed until she was eye to eye with his stiffening cock. If she didn't slip it in her mouth soon, he would be hard anyway. Without more hesitation, she leaned over and settled her lips around it.

She was immediately astonished by its soft texture. How could something that could get so hard be so soft? Wanting to feel his entire length, she took it slowly into her mouth. Quickly, it grew larger and larger until, to her disappointment, she had to back off some. Maybe with more experience she'd be able to manage all of him in his stiff state. This would have to be good enough for now.

Kevin leaned forward enough to twist his fingers in her hair. "You can give my cock a tongue-lashing anytime you want. Your mouth is as hot as your pussy."

She winked at him but did not give up her perch. She wrapped a hand around the base of his length and began to bob up and down his shaft. To her surprise, Kevin wailed in delight. She hadn't realized how powerful giving him pleasure would make her feel. He was clay, and she was the potter. She scrambled onto her knees to try a different angle, hoping to take him deeper.

She closed her eyes and breathed through her nose. He was too thick. Maybe another time. She concentrated her efforts on his upper half. Kevin's groans suggested he wasn't disappointed. Her eyes flew wide as she sensed his crown expanding and his hips beginning to move in unison with her.

"Jesus, no." He tugged at her torso until his cock dropped from her mouth. "I don't want to come in your mouth."

"But you were so close. I know you were. I could feel you getting larger, getting ready to explode." She couldn't explain her sudden sense of loss. She knew she could've finished him. "I wanted you. I wanted to taste you."

He looked at her with the deepest love she'd ever witnessed in another human being. "I know you did. Another time. I didn't want to leave you out."

"I hardly felt left out. I've never tried that before. I had no idea I'd get so much pleasure from having a cock in my mouth."

"I would never have guessed. You had me nearly coming within minutes. I'm sorry. Next time I won't interrupt."

"Next time I won't let you interrupt." She slid his cock back and forth in her palms as if it were a rolling pin. "But since you did so rudely interrupt me, and since I'm already down here, I think I'll just find another home for this fellow."

She easily straddled him and slid his shaft along the length of her wet crevice. She stopped and gave him a hard stare. "Unless you have a different idea."

He shook his head. "You're doing quite fine without my consultation. Damn, you're soaking down there. Sucking my cock excited you that much?"

"I told you I was enjoying having him in my mouth." She smiled and guided him to the opening of her sex. "Now I'm going to enjoy having him in my cunt."

She lifted her arms high above her head and glacially allowed herself to encase his full length. "So big. Maybe sucking on him first made him grow. Exquisite. So full. My pussy thanks you for thinking of her." She wiggled her bottom and began to rise.

"Don't move yet, please." He squirmed beneath her, rearranging their fit. "Let me stamp this view into my memory. You are so beautiful, Nadja. I feel so lucky to cherish you this way."

She felt her cheeks flush. She was unaccustomed to receiving such praise from a man—especially a man she held in such a vulnerable position.

"I want to watch you love me, if that's okay."

She nodded and wet her lips.

"Tease your nipples for me."

She rolled each nipple between a thumb and forefinger until she couldn't stand it any longer. She groaned and stuck her tongue out at him. She squeezed her shoulders forward and held a breast in each hand.

"You said you could kiss your own nipples."

"Of course," she murmured, bringing a breast and nipple to her lips to demonstrate.

She felt him jerk inside her.

"Cripes, what a turn-on. Can you bite it?"

Gingerly, she took a nipple between her teeth. She didn't respond to his hips flexing beneath her. She grinned at him, released her breast, and leaned down over his chest until she'd replaced his nipple for her own. Then she bit lightly, and he howled—a howl of joy, not pain.

His hips rose and fell, driving his cock in and out of her. She looked at him and shook her head, then sat back up until she had him pinned to the bed. "Not so quickly."

"Are you into torture? I'm on the edge."

"I don't think so. But you stopped me earlier when I had you on the edge in my mouth. I thought you were going to watch."

He scowled. "I forgot. Go ahead. Don't hold onto your breasts. I want to see them swing freely."

"Okay. Unless it becomes too painful."

"For me to watch?"

"No, silly. For me. They might look like they swing effort-lessly like pendulums, but they do become heavy." She ran her palms up, down and across her belly, appreciating the tin-gles that built somewhere behind her belly button. "Enough banter." Effortlessly, she rose up on her knees until he nearly fell out of her. "Do you see our mating?"

"I'm hardly blind," he said between ragged breaths.

"Tell me."

"You taunt me. You only have the tip of my cock in you." Kevin's tongue slid across his parted lips; he squinted as if trying to keep her in focus. "He is wet with your juices. He's straining to get back into your warmth. Your clit is coming out as if to see if all is going well. Is it?"

"Very," she replied, easily sliding down his pole until she settled her buttocks against his hips. She smiled evenly, brushing a finger along her exposed clit. "She's more than pleased. I hope you're ready, because I'm now going to ride you into oblivion."

"I'm ready." He gave her a lecherous smile. "Damn, your clit is growing." Then he placed his palms under his head to present a nonchalant pose.

She nodded and thinned her lips. She'd wager he couldn't keep that pose much longer. Not if she had anything to do with it.

She glided up his length and slid back down. She kept up a slow, steady rhythm and watched his mouth tighten, then increased her pace. He kept his gaze glued on their joining, and his lips trembled slightly.

She giggled—he was clearly trying to appear unaffected. She again lifted her arms above her head and slammed down against his hips, while his hands sprang from under his head toward their joining.

"Just watch, remember," she warned.

He hesitated but let his arms rest at his sides and curled his fingers into fists.

She found she loved being watched—maybe that was left over from her dance performance days. Like he had earlier in her mouth, his cock seemed to enlarge deep inside her pussy. Only this time she wouldn't stop for anyone. "Gotcha," she said, not slowing her efforts at all.

"Oh, yeah!" he shouted, arching his back.

She bit down on her lower lip, increased her speed, and tightened her grip around his throbbing cock. He didn't stand a chance—but then neither did she. Her pussy became a magnet for electrical currents pulsating throughout her body. This time her orgasm was not about to sneak up on her. Her entire being announced the coming of a series of waves.

"Don't stop," Kevin moaned.

She laughed, welcoming his spurting into her. She had no intention of stopping—that would be impossible. She continued pumping him until her stickiness joined his. Until the waves stopped pounding against her interior.

At last, completely exhausted and completely sated, she collapsed onto his chest. His arms cradled her. Her lungs shrank and expanded rapidly. She hadn't realized how aerobic lovemaking could be. Her former partners hadn't expected much from her, and she hadn't volunteered much to change their minds.

"You are one exceptional lover," he murmured in her ear.

She couldn't speak. She nodded her assent. Yes, she'd developed some sexual expertise. She doubted he was as surprised as she was—though she'd always been a quick learner. Thanks again to Ivett for the steady supply of tapes.

Kevin smiled contentedly at Nadja, who was teaching his son a basic step dance move. He couldn't have hoped for the two of them to get along better. Coming from Ukraine, she knew many older European dances, including step dancing, in addition to her specialty in ballet.

He admired the stretch of her calf muscles as she rose on her toes. She wore yellow shorts and a yellow T-shirt over a pale green leotard. But she could wear a sack and still look sexy.

Watching Nadja and Danny's reflections in the wall lined with mirrors, he wondered why she hadn't shown this room to him before—her dance practice room. He licked his lips, considering its possibilities. It certainly had plenty of potential for more erotic dances—another set of dances she was rapidly becoming quite adept at.

Kevin figured himself for a fairly passionate fellow, but

Nadja's passion reservoir looked like it would match his. She grinned at him in the mirror. "Danny has a good feel for movement," she announced.

"Must get it from his father."

Her eyes snapped. "That's a possibility."

He watched her kneel at Danny's feet so he wouldn't have to stare up at her. She tousled his hair. "I think that's enough for one day, young man. You're going to wear me out."

"Can we try again later?" Danny asked eagerly.

"Absolutely. But not today."

Danny's face crumbled. "That means not until I come back next week. I have to leave tomorrow for my mother's wedding."

"Ah. That's true," Nadja acknowledged. "The days have flown by. But you'll be back on Sunday. I promise to save some time for a dance lesson or two. Can you wait that long?"

"I suppose." Danny looked at his feet and then back up into Nadja's eyes. "When we come back next week, can we stay with you?"

"What?" Wide-eyed, Nadja glanced quickly from Kevin's son to Kevin himself.

He remained silent. If she planned on waiting for him to bail her out, she'd have a long wait.

She turned back to Danny, whose frown deepened. "I'm not sure that's a good idea. Don't you like staying with Ivett and Steve?"

"Sure, but staying with you would be better." He made a face. "Then Dad wouldn't have to waste so much time driving back and forth after I'm in bed."

Nadja's jaw dropped, and Kevin straightened. His son seemed to be the only person in the room to maintain self-control.

"But . . ."

Danny shook his head. "I'm not a dumb kid," he huffed. "I

know what's going on between you and my dad. Mom has had plenty of guys stay the night. My new step-dad has just about moved in already." He scowled at Nadja. "I do watch television."

"Oh my," she whimpered.

Kevin held back a chuckle when he saw Nadja's hand caress her throat. He'd give most anything to know her thoughts. Maybe he'd better rescue her. He took a step forward.

She held up her palm to stop him. "I'd love nothing more than to have you stay with me, but your father and I will have to talk about the wisdom of that."

"Thank you," Danny squealed, throwing his arms around her neck, clearly already convinced he'd won.

Kevin had no idea whether Nadja knew that, but Danny certainly did. And it pleased him to see her hug his son tight. She'd make a good mother someday.

Chills raced from his brain to his toes. He fought the urge to run. Mother? He flexed his fingers to revive his circulatory system. This wasn't exactly the first time he'd thought they might be getting into something serious, but *very* serious hadn't crossed his mind. He wouldn't try to kid himself.

But he hadn't actually thought of her as a mother figure for his son. And would that satisfy her maternal needs, which appeared quite strong? Would she want her own child? He couldn't imagine going through all of that again.

"Come on, Dad!" Danny chortled. "Join our hug."

On weak legs he made his way to them, fell to his knees, and gathered them in his arms. He was in deep, deep trouble. Danny liked nothing more than what he called family hugs. He hadn't asked for one for over a year. Kevin shut his eyes tight. Danny had never asked any woman besides his mother to join in his precious family hugs.

Nadja couldn't possibly know of this special history, yet

her body quivering against his made it clear she had some idea of the import — or the threat — of this hug.

Later, while Danny played on the swing set she'd bought and put together, Nadja set her wine glass down on the patio table next to Kevin's. She took a deep breath for resolve. "So" — she looked at Kevin — "what are we going to do with Danny?"

He glanced at her and then quickly away. She couldn't decipher what she'd seen, but he clearly knew what she meant. "It's not good for him to get too close to me."

"He's not. He soaks up attention. You saw him with Ivett and Steve."

"True, but I'm afraid he may misunderstand what's happening between the two of us."

Kevin's voice dropped to a mumble. "Maybe he understands better than we do."

"What?" She gave him a shocked look.

"Nothing. Danny's grown up faster than some seven-year-olds. He's got a harder shell than you think."

"Maybe. I don't want to disappoint him, but I don't want to hurt him, either."

"You can't get close to another person without risking getting hurt."

She eyed him carefully. "I'm learning the truth of that day by day, but I'm not sure your son needs to learn it."

Kevin looked sharply at her. "Would you rather have him keep people at arm's length so he won't get hurt?"

It was her turn to look away. She felt blood draining from her face. Wasn't that exactly what she'd done for years? Keeping her guard up. Maintaining a show of strength. Not letting anyone see her cry. She let out a deep sigh. Kevin had seen her cry. And though she hated to admit it, he could hurt her deeply. But would she rather return to who she'd been before he waltzed into her shop and said he wanted to buy her?

She shook her head, attempting to keep the tears at bay. "Okay," she said, shakily. "The two of you can stay here when you come back on Sunday."

No longer able to contain the tears, she added sharply, "But you and I'd better prepare to help Danny pick up the pieces when it's necessary."

Kevin gave her a lopsided grin. "You can count on that." He wiped tears from her cheek. "Thanks for risking."

She shook her head and interlaced her fingers with his. "I still have my doubts about it." She grinned. "But it will be nice having Danny around. This old house could use a child's laughter."

"And how about me? Will it be good having me around?"

"It will. You know it will." She straightened in her chair. "If we're going to play house, does that mean I need to put together a *to do* list for you?"

He scowled. "What?"

"Isn't that why women keep a man around the house? To make repairs and to do lawn work?"

"That's got some possibilities. I'm okay with a hammer — and I've been told I'm quite good at filling holes," he added with a lecherous gleam in his eyes.

"You," she sputtered, punching his shoulder. "Can't you think of anything else?"

He shook his head. "Can't think of anything I'd rather think about. And you?"

She felt his fingers trailing along her inner thigh beneath the table. He leaned forward, and her lips parted to greet his. How could she think of anything else with his lips on hers and his fingers sending tiny electrical charges every which direction? She deepened their kiss and laced her fingers behind his neck.

A boyish scream of *yay* penetrated her haze. She slid her

lips off of Kevin's to look at the source of interruption. Danny stood about ten feet away, punching the air with his fists and dancing a little jig.

"We can stay, right?"

She blinked at the elated boy. "What?"

"You're nearly sitting on my dad's lap. I saw you kissing. That means we can stay with you next week. Right?"

Exhaling, Nadja remembered to reclaim her hands from around Kevin's neck. She nodded at the grinning boy. "Yes, you and your dad will stay with me next week."

"Fantastic! We'll have so much fun, won't we, Dad?"

She swore there was nothing but innocence in Danny's tone.

"We'll take her fishing, right, Dad? Remember, you said there's a big lake near here."

"Sure, son." Kevin again squeezed Nadja's thigh. "Do you fish?"

She shook her head. "Never."

"Good, we can teach you," Danny said. "Have you ever ridden in a boat?"

"Of course."

A grin split Kevin's face. "Will you come with us? What do you think?"

She looked from one expectant male to the other and laughed. She knew Danny was serious, but she thought Kevin was joking. "What do I think? That you're both nuts. And that I'm craziest of all."

She could see Danny hanging on her words. "We'll see," she said, trusting they would forget.

"Fishing! You?" Ivett's eyes rounded into the size of small saucers. "Why in the world would you even consider doing that? It's so, so . . . primitive."

"Danny has his heart on teaching me how to fish, like I'm

teaching him some dance steps and how to paint eggs."

"Uh-huh." Ivett smiled softly and leaned across the counter to pinch her niece's cheek. "So where do you see this going, Nadja?"

Nadja's shoulders slumped. "I don't know," she said, trying not to whine.

"You're falling . . .falling fast."

"I'm sinking." Her voice trembled. "I'm not sure I'll ever breathe normally again."

"You're a survivor. You'll do okay."

"I'm not sure okay is going to be good enough anymore."

Ivett stood back and folded her arms. "What do you want to happen between you and Kevin?"

"I don't know." She twisted her neck from side to side. "I wish I knew. Can't we stay just like we are?"

"Him visiting you, and maybe you visiting him?"

"Sure. Something like that."

"I don't think that'll work. You never were good at running in place. And there's Danny."

Sighing, Nadja nodded her head. "He does complicate things even more."

"If it wasn't him, something else would pop up to move the two of you along. Neither one of you is getting any younger. If this is the right man, Nadja, why punish yourself by not venturing farther down the road with him?"

"I don't know if he *is* the right man. Not really. I don't know how serious he is or wants to be. Where would we live if we did get together? Will he want more children?"

"Ah. That could be a ticklish issue. And" — Ivett's jaw went rigid —"you are the last hope for extending our particular line."

"We don't know that I could have children, either."

"My situation is not genetic. That shouldn't have any impact on you."

155

"Still, I don't know if I want Kevin to be the father of my children."

"You don't think he's a good father."

"I think he's a fantastic father. Maybe he spoils Danny a little, but not as much as I've seen many fathers and mothers do."

"Then what's holding you back?"

Nadja shrugged. "I'm not sure." She grimaced. "But then I'm not sure of much these days." She frowned. "I used to be so certain."

"And that used to drive me nuts." Ivett grabbed her hand and squeezed it. "Trust your gut. Trust your heart. You are of good peasant stock, girl. Trust your intuition. You've got ancestors who delved into the mysteries—a fact you've not wanted to own. But now may be a time when you need to draw upon that pool of intuition that's as much a part of you as your blood."

"Too bad I'm not as religious as you. Maybe that'd make my life easier."

"I doubt that. But don't be afraid of who you are, Nadja. You are a beautiful woman, inside and out. Too bad you can't appreciate that as much as others do."

Shuddering, Nadja looked toward the shop entrance and welcomed the distraction of a customer. She pasted on her usual smile and set about to take and prepare orders.

She placed the money in the till and only then noticed that Ivett had left. Just as well. She'd been cajoled enough for one day. Seemed like everyone thought they knew her better than she did herself—Ivett, Kevin, possibly even Danny.

She glared at the doorway to Ivett's shop. She refused to be rushed or bullied—not by Kevin's wit, not by Ivett's matchmaking needs, and certainly not by a small boy's innocent smile.

And Kevin's intentions remained murky. She knew he

enjoyed being with her. She didn't question that his feelings for her had deepened. But none of that meant he'd thought about anything permanent, with or without a ring.

She peeked down at her fingers. Maybe she should buy herself some jewelry. She'd seldom spent much money on herself. Perhaps a ring or two would blunt some of these uneasy feelings. She shook her head vigorously. She'd buy herself some jewelry, not because that would somehow ease her mind about Kevin, but because she deserved a little more self-love. She scowled at the books lining the far wall of her shop.

And why did she only deserve one sex toy? The crystal wand was never even her idea. It was a gift from her aunt. So many books, and one crystal wand. She knew how to add to her book collection. She had no idea where to even look for another sex toy.

She watched a young man sitting by himself sipping coffee, staring at his computer. He set the cup to the side and began typing.

Nadja nodded. Perhaps she should search the internet. She'd made sure she had wireless capacity for her customers, but she seldom used the computer except to keep track of events happening in Ukraine and to maintain a few far-flung friendships by e-mail.

She busied herself by checking the progress of two brewing pots, then let out a huge sigh. Why bother with how she might search the internet? She didn't need more sex toys. She needed to know what to do with her favorite sex toy — not the magic wand, but Kevin.

She hugged herself. The traffic through the shop seemed slow for a Saturday morning. She pulled up a stool and sat — something she rarely did at work.

Had Kevin helped Danny dress in his new grown-up suit yet? The boy had beamed with pride when he'd told her how he'd be part of his mother's wedding. It did seem that Kevin and his ex-wife had struck some sort of workable balance where their son was concerned. He seemed reasonably adjusted with both of them.

Nadja propped her elbows on the counter and rested her chin on her hands. Not that she knew much about seven-year-old boys. She shuddered. What frightened Danny? She hadn't seen anything yet. He had to have some fears. Everyone did. Did he risk becoming as self-contained as she was?

Pursing her lips, Nadja surveyed the few customers sitting in the main area. Engaged in small talk and serious discussions, they all seemed quite oblivious to the confusion swirling in her body. She was left with the war of words and feelings vying for supremacy within her soul.

She rose slowly to her feet when she saw Ivett beckoning her from the doorway to her shop, her features contorted in suppressed anger.

Nadja checked her customers as she made her way to Ivett.

"Have you seen today's paper?" Ivett asked in hushed tones, looking furtively about the Cappuccino.

"No." Nadja tensed, reaching for the paper Ivett clutched in her hand. "What is it?"

"Check out this letter to the editor."

Nadja scanned the letter Ivett pointed out. She scanned it quickly. She wanted to laugh, but thought better of it, given the pain on her aunt's face.

She shrugged and handed the paper back to Ivett. "I doubt if God cares much about my coffee shop, for good or bad."

"I don't question that, but this writer is trying to fan flames that would suggest otherwise. And with all the gullible people out there, he might have some influence. How is business this morning?"

"A little off. But I have good days and bad days. And I'm not an atheist. I may not be deeply religious, but I'm hardly a non-believer."

"You and I can quibble and even joke about that, but this is different. This is yet another effort to try to smear you and your business. Ivett paused. "And me by association."

"Well, no one would ever question your religious beliefs. You're one of the most active members of our church."

"Be that as it may, most people don't really know us. And some may very well believe what they read in the papers."

"But how does this trash even get printed?"

"I'm not sure. I imagine the paper can screen the language, but it has to take care not to be accused of censorship."

"What do we do now?"

Ivett shook her head. "You could write a letter to the editor in response."

Nadja stiffened. "That won't happen. I'll talk with Kevin about it, but you won't see a letter in the paper with my name attached."

"It probably wouldn't do any good anyway. The damage is already done." Ivett glanced back into her store. "Hopefully, there aren't a lot of people in Jefferson City with such small minds." She brightened. "Besides, those people aren't likely our best customers anyway. Talk to Kevin, but let's sit tight. Maybe this will blow over quickly."

"Right," Nadja agreed, and turned to greet a customer entering the shop.

"Thanks for meeting for lunch." Kevin guided Amy Jacobson to a nearby table in the small St. Paul café.

"I have to eat, too," Amy replied, sitting down and picking up the menu.

She glanced up at him. He'd forgotten how steely blue her eyes could be.

She sighed. "I'm glad to have lunch with you, but I really don't have much to share."

He nodded. Amy had never been one to go slowly. "No promising leads?"

"We're following up on several possibilities. I don't know about promising."

"I assume Rick Adams is up to his kneecaps in this effort to root out Nadja and her aunt."

"Let's get Nadja out of the way first. I went to the Cappuccino a couple times. I made no attempt to interview her, since you indicated you wanted me to remain discreet."

"She makes good coffee."

Amy laughed easily. "I expect she makes much more than good coffee. The two of you have become a known item in the community."

He scowled. "Really. What are people making of that?"

"Some can't figure out who is trying to use whom — her using you to stop you from buying her out, or you using her to convince her to sell."

"None of them are right."

"I know that. That's not something you would do, and I highly doubt you'd get involved with someone who would try to use you in that way."

Amy paused while the waitress stopped by and took their orders. "She's a beautiful woman," Amy said, picking up where she'd left off. "I do find it ironic, if not downright amusing, that I'm helping you and my sister. Former lovers usually don't team up to solve mysteries."

"I told you before, I trust you. I didn't know who else to turn to. I hope this isn't upsetting you."

"Hardly. We weren't going anywhere, Kevin. We both knew that, and over a year has passed. Working together on this caper may actually be good for us, even for my sister, who I think still harbors hopes for the two of us."

"Your sister can be stubborn."

"And we can't?" She held up her palm, forestalling any

reply. "Anyway, Rick is well above his kneecaps in Nadja's troubles. We certainly know he wants the building. We've pretty much established that he drew the card she found under her door. But we've not been able to establish more than a causal link between him and Chicago. We know of prior relationships with several Chicago mob types, but nothing that makes this push on the Cappuccino obvious."

"Blind alley?"

"Still working on it. Motive remains unclear. No doubt someone wants to make a lot of money, but so far nothing beyond that."

"What about Steve Chambers?"

Amy glanced quickly away from him and then held his gaze steady. "I was waiting for you to ask. You're not going to like this." She pulled a folder out of her briefcase and handed it to him.

He opened it, and the headline of a newspaper article screamed at him: "Boyfriend Questioned in Death of Co-ed." The story went on to report the murder of Mary Beth Ryder. Steve had been her boyfriend. According to rumor, they were about to be engaged.

Tight-lipped, Kevin scanned the remainder of the article. "Holy shit! That explains a lot."

"Thought it might. Sorry."

He shook his head. "Don't be. At least we know what Rick is holding over Steve's head. He provided the ironclad alibi for his roommate. How convenient — then and now."

"You think Steve actually killed the girl?"

He shrugged. "I doubt that very much, but he must've been scared as hell that no one would believe him. And I'll bet you anything Rick has hardly let a day go by without reminding his buddy how much he owes him."

"Then that leaves another mystery unsolved."

"What do you mean?"

"Who killed the girl, and why?"

"You don't think that's directly related to the building." He hesitated. "Or do you?"

"I have no idea, but the question has to be considered. There are a lot of loose ends for what simply looks like an effort to strong-arm a couple women out of their shops."

"Have you talked with the police?"

Amy shook her head. "Not yet. I'm trying to figure out who I can trust. Rick Adams is a lifelong member of the community, and certainly must have friends on the local police force."

"Friends who would help him?"

"Don't know, but we can't rule that out yet."

The waitress set a hamburger deluxe before each of them. Kevin grinned to himself. Hamburger probably wasn't a favorite of Nadja's—he'd never seen her eat one. Maybe he and Danny would have to introduce her to their favorite American cuisine.

After the waitress moved on to another set of customers, Kevin said, "I think Nadja said something about Ivett having a friend on the police force—a female detective, I think."

"Check that out. I may be able to draw on that contact. I'd like to ask some questions off the record."

"Okay." He bit into his hamburger. "When do you plan on going back down there?"

"Not sure. Depends on whether I drive back and forth the same day or stay over." She munched on a french fry. "This is costing you and Java Beans some dollars."

"Not a problem. All of this business has dragged Java Beans's reputation though a lot of crap. Can you imagine someone from Jefferson City sending newspaper clips to the next small town we try to move into?"

"Not good publicity."

"Exactly."

"I'll keep you posted, and you do the same for me if you discover anything new." She gave him a half-smile. "Nadja strikes me as the marrying kind."

Kevin jerked from a slouch to attention. "Is that a private investigator observation?"

Amy shook her head. "Nope, call it woman's intuition. From what I've learned about her and from what I've seen of her in person, she strikes me as a woman who sets out and claims what she wants."

"You two probably have that in common."

"Only, she wants you."

"You don't know that. You haven't even talked to her."

"Didn't have to. Nadja was floating. This business with the Cappuccino would hardly make her float. I expect only a man could cause her to float that way." She winked. "And you are the only man in her life, right?"

His mouth fell open. "Of course I am." He scowled. "You're not telling me she's seeing someone else?"

Amy bubbled with laughter, then lifted the water glass to her lips and swallowed before replying. "I wasn't hired to spy on Nadja's private life. If you want that info, you'll either have to ask her — or, if you don't trust her, then you'll have to pay me a considerably larger fee."

He never had liked being teased, and Amy clearly delighted in his discomfort. "Speaking of paying" — he pulled out his billfold — "I've got this." He checked the bill and laid down a tip. "I trust Nadja," he said evenly. "She doesn't need anyone spying on her private life."

"Good." Amy slid out of the booth. "I don't like that kind of work anyway." She giggled. "I never know when I'll bump into an old lover."

He stood and watched her saunter out of the café without another word of goodbye. He shook his head. Strange, he hadn't realized how similar Nadja and Amy were in some ways. Nadja had a much softer side. And while Amy worked at solving mysteries, Nadja was mystery personified. He sighed. Did he have enough time to solve her bewitching mysteries?

When had he begun to see her as one of the figurines Danny enjoyed helping her paint? Like them, she consisted of many layers. Would he ever get to see her innermost layer?

A seductive tune, whose name he could not recall, began playing in his head. While he might never have enough time for adequately exploring his enigmatic lover, the process definitely had its rewards.

Chapter Eleven

Nadja set a salad in front of Ivett, who had stopped by after church. She was curious whether her aunt had lit a candle for her, but not curious enough to ask.

"Looks delicious," Ivett said. "When are Danny and his father getting here?"

"Late this afternoon." Nadja poked a fork at her salad. "I'm still not sure it's a good idea for them to stay with me."

Ivett smirked. "It was safer for you with them staying at my place."

"Maybe, but I'm looking forward to having them here, too."

"I believe I detect more than a little ambivalence."

Nadja shrugged and focused on her salad.

Ivett giggled. "Too bad your grandma isn't alive. She'd have some advice for you."

"Ah, Babushka." Nadja looked up and grinned. "She could be forceful."

"Forceful? That's almost funny. She'd tell you hourly how it's your duty to God and country to marry and have babies."

"I wouldn't listen."

"You seldom did, to her great despair." Ivett frowned. "I'm afraid your grandmother never did understand why I can't have children. Somehow she believed I decided not to."

Nadja wanted to reach out and soothe her aunt's pain, but she knew that was the last thing Ivett would welcome. "Grandma could be very judgmental."

"For good and bad." Ivett's chin jutted forth. "I do miss her.

Women were always the backbone of our culture. The men could go off and get killed in the wars or escape to the local bars, but the women had to carry on no matter what."

"Do you ever think about moving back?"

"To Ukraine?"

Nadja nodded at her aunt, whose eyes had grown large.

"Never! This is my home." Ivett sighed wistfully. "I'd like to visit more often. I can write it off as a business trip, but finding time is hard. How about you?" Ivett scowled crossly. "Surely, you're not thinking of moving back?"

"Not really," Nadja said softly. She glanced about her kitchen. "This is such a lovely place. Mother and I bought this place because the yard with its many flowers reminded her of her home." She shook her head and spoke more firmly. "No, I won't move back. I wouldn't want to leave this place."

"Not even for the right man?" Ivett's eyes sparkled with mischief.

Nadja groaned. "Sometimes you act like Babushka."

Laughing warmly, Ivett replied, "You're probably my only chance for matchmaking."

"I hope you don't take that ancient art seriously."

"I'd say you're doing fine in that area by yourself." Ivett's face lit into a broad smile. "But I do think I deserve at least a little credit for helping."

Nadja felt her cheeks burn as images of the crystal wand — Ivett's educational tapes — lying nude on her oak table with Kevin standing between her legs all skittered across her mind. "You have helped very much," she said, her voice turning husky. "And I thank you. But no more. I don't want you interfering. I can't foresee the future, and neither can you."

"I'm only afraid you are unwilling to consider the future."

She shrugged her shoulders. "Whether I am or not is none of your business."

Ivett recoiled.

Aware her tongue could often be too sharp, Nadja quickly added, "I'm sorry. You're my family. The only family I have. I don't want to exclude you in any way, but you must let me make my own way with Kevin."

Ivett exhaled before speaking. "I know. I don't have as much patience as you do. I want to know *now* what's going to happen." She smiled weakly. "And I know that's not possible."

"I don't even know. I'm not withholding. And I will keep you informed, but I don't want you trying to pull any strings. I am not a marionette."

"I know, I know." Ivett stood and took her empty plate to the sink to rinse it. "I'd better get going. Thanks for the lunch."

Nadja stood and hugged her aunt. "Thanks for listening."

Ivett turned to leave and then retraced her steps. "Have you ever made love under the stars?"

"What?" Nadja squeaked.

"Your gazebo would offer a splendid opportunity." Ivett flashed an eyebrow. "I left two more fantasy tapes on your couch. Bye."

Once she heard the entryway door close behind her aunt, Nadja burst into laughter. So much for Ivett not interfering — if planting seeds could be considered interfering.

She glanced out the kitchen window toward the gazebo, and her breasts suddenly ached. She'd loved watching the night sky and picking out constellations since she was a little girl. It had never occurred to her to share that passion with a man.

Trying not to be too obvious, Nadja peeked at her men, who were leaning over the table trying out different pieces to find the right fit in the jigsaw puzzle. It was a puzzle from Ukraine, showing one of Kiev's oldest buildings: a large cathedral with blue star-spangled onion domes surmounted with golden spires. Her lungs expanded with pride. Her people had erected buildings to survive the calamities of the centuries—flood, drought, or war.

She'd been pleased to learn Danny enjoyed working on puzzles. She couldn't remember a time when she hadn't, particularly in winter months. While this was a very warm Iowa summer night, the puzzle provided her and her guests with a low-key evening, precisely what she'd hoped for.

Danny had seemed a bit more subdued than she remembered—perhaps the effect of going to his mother's wedding. Kevin had also been pleasantly mellow. She grinned faintly. This might be the first time he'd visited her without trying to get her naked in the first hour of arriving—not that she hadn't been ahead of him on more than one occasion.

And they were *her* men. She breathed easier confessing that fact. At least, for the moment they were. She tried not to think beyond the moment. She'd spent most of her life planning ahead, trying to get from one step to the next, and now she wanted to slow down time. If she could, she'd stop the hands of the clock.

"I've got one," Danny shouted, pressing the curved piece into one of the golden spires.

"You sure do," Nadja praised. "Good for you."

"This is a tough puzzle. The edges were easy enough, but the rest of it is hard."

Kevin beamed at her. "That's often the case, son, with most anything of value in life. Once you get beyond the edges or the surface, the real work really begins."

Making a face at him, Nadja looked quickly at Danny. He searched for another piece and didn't seem the least aware of the byplay between the adults at the table. She ignored Kevin's sage comment. This didn't seem like the place or the time for a prolonged discussion of surfaces and interiors. She watched Kevin check his wristwatch.

"It's almost bedtime, Danny."

"Dad!"

Nadja smiled. The whine wouldn't gain much for Danny tonight—Kevin was probably thinking more about *his* bed than Danny's.

"Big day tomorrow," Kevin responded, smoothly ignoring his son's feigned distress. "You go to the Cappuccino with Nadja in the morning. I assume you'll find things to do there."

"Sure." Danny beamed at his father. "Have you told Nadia about our surprise yet?"

Kevin glanced quickly at her. He looked like the little boy who'd been caught sneaking into the cookie jar. "No, not yet." He frowned at Danny. "Maybe you should tell her."

Though maintaining her outward cool, Nadja felt more than a little curious about the intrigue between father and son. Given Kevin's caution, she wasn't convinced she'd like whatever they'd cooked up.

"We're going to take you fishing," Danny said, as if offering her the opportunity of a lifetime.

She tried her best to look happy. Fishing! All of this intrigue . . . about fishing. She knew Danny and his father enjoyed fishing, and they'd even joked about taking her along, but she hadn't taken them seriously. Now she looked at their faces. They weren't joking at all. "When?" she squeaked.

"I called the marina. I can rent a boat tomorrow or the next day, but after that they have some sort of huge fishing event coming in to prepare for the weekend. All boats were reserved months ago. Maybe I should've brought my own."

"You own a boat?"

"A bass boat. I didn't want to bring it down just to fish one afternoon."

She frowned. "Of course not."

There was so much she didn't know about Kevin. And Danny was still looking at her with expectancy. She quickly thought through the work schedules for the coming week. "Tomorrow would work better for me. Barbara is coming in at three. I can probably get her to come in earlier, if that helps."

"Let's plan on me picking the two of you up at the shop at two o'clock."

"How long will this take?" Why couldn't she sound more pleased with this adventure?

"I'll pick up supper from the deli. No need for you to bother packing anything."

She read that as no need to give her an excuse to change her mind.

"The best fishing is often just before dark," Danny piped up. "You don't want to rush the big ones."

Nadja gawked at Danny, and Kevin laughed at her. But again, the boy seemed completely innocent.

"Okay," she said, mustering a grin. "I will try this once, but don't expect too much. I don't find the thought of killing pleasant."

"Don't you like to eat fish?" Danny asked, his face a picture of disbelief.

"Yes," she admitted, "I do."

"Someone had to kill it."

She sighed and gave Kevin what she hoped was a meaningful look.

"Time for pj's and brushing teeth," he said, apparently getting her message.

She wasn't quite sure how to handle Kevin later, but at the moment that seemed easier than dealing with this father-son duo intent on getting her to enjoy fishing.

"Bedtime. You do want to go fishing tomorrow?" Kevin teased his son.

Nodding quickly, Danny returned the pieces he'd been sorting to the box and followed his father toward the stairs.

Nadja followed behind in case they needed anything.

Surprisingly, it only took a few minutes before Danny climbed into bed wearing superhero pajamas with his teeth brushed and his cheeks freshly scrubbed.

"You know what we forgot?" Danny gave his dad a pout.

"What?" Kevin groused.

Nadja said nothing—maybe Kevin was finally losing patience.

"Books. We didn't bring any of my favorite books."

"Damn. We'll buy some tomorrow."

"Wait!" Nadja interrupted. She turned and ran down the hall to her bedroom. Returning shortly, she held out three children's books to Danny. "Will these do? Ivett told me she thought you might like them."

Danny's eyes bugged as he looked at one book and the next, bringing a smile to Nadja's face. It looked like the books met with his approval.

"Yes, I've wanted this one." He gave her a strained look. "But with all the work on the wedding we didn't get to the bookstore. Would you read me the first chapter? Can she, Dad?"

Looking bemused, Kevin nodded. "If she wants to." He glanced at her, his eyes bright. "I'll go get ready for bed."

She frowned at his exit and then turned back to the boy. Why did she feel so nervous? He was only a little boy. "I thought you read your own books."

"Of course I can read, but I like to be read to."

"I'll make a deal with you. I'll read a chapter to you tonight if you'll read the next chapter to me tomorrow night."

"It's a deal." He extended his hand to her.

She quickly found herself caught up in the dangers of a world comprised of dragons, werewolves, and monsters she hadn't known existed.

Danny grinned, showing his clean teeth when she finished

reading. "I like the sound of your voice. Some kids laugh at people with accents. I like yours—a lot."

"I'm glad," she murmured, tucking the covers under his chin.

She stood to leave.

"Aren't you going to give me a goodnight hug?" he asked plaintively.

"I'd be happy to," she said, leaning back down. He leapt into her arms, and she thought her heart might burst. She stepped back. "Sleep tight. See you in the morning."

Nadja stumbled out of the bedroom and slouched against the hallway wall, gasping for breath. She had to find her balance. Kevin threatened her in ways she'd begun to understand and even welcome. She couldn't begin to fathom why a boy who probably didn't stand four feet tall threatened her so.

Kevin sat propped against the headboard and watched Nadja enter the room. She was so preoccupied she startled when she saw him. Had she really expected him to use one of the other bedrooms?

At least he'd put on a pair of boxers—not that the thin fabric did much to conceal his arousal. He'd been lying there, considering what he might do with her, for what seemed like an hour—though he knew it couldn't have been more than fifteen minutes or so.

She made no progress toward the bathroom or the bed. Instead she plopped down on the nearby Queen Anne chair. He had been eyeing it and assessing its possibilities. But Nadja didn't look ready to try out the chair in any of the ways he'd been considering. Given her stark stare, he figured his best strategy was to remain silent, since escape didn't seem plausible.

"Why am I being forced into going fishing?"

"Forced." He struggled to keep his voice from showing his irritation. "No one is forcing you."

"You didn't ask me—you waited until Danny wanted to know. You knew I wouldn't be able to tell *him* no."

Kevin folded his arms across his chest. "You may be right," he acknowledged. "Though I didn't really plan it that way."

"Why is this so important? That I go fishing."

"Danny wants to teach you something. You're helping him with dance steps and painting. Fishing is something you apparently know little about."

"That's true," she agreed grudgingly. "Did you fish as a family?"

He frowned at her.

"Did Danny's mother go fishing with you?"

"Elizabeth? She tried it once before we married. She never stepped into a boat again."

"I see."

He wondered what she saw that he didn't. Maybe that was her woman's intuition kicking in again.

"And you eat these fish?"

"Of course. You told Danny you like to eat fish. Haven't you ever eaten fish that were freshly caught?"

"No."

"Do you have any idea how sexy you look when you blush?"

"Don't change the subject." She glanced away and then back at him. "I don't want anything to do with making the fish."

"Making the fish? I don't understand. Oh, I'll cook them. That's no problem."

"That's not what I mean," she snapped. "I can cook. I don't know the English word. I won't touch them. I won't fix them—you know, cut off their heads and . . ." She turned up

173

her nose.

"Oh!" Kevin laughed. "You mean you don't want to clean them. That's the word you're looking for."

"Clean?" She looked incredulous. "That hardly seems like the right word for . . .for that."

"You may be right." He sat up straighter. "Now that we have that out of the way, are you going to get ready for bed?"

"Yes." She stood. "I don't like being outnumbered."

"I'm starting to understand. I'll try to be more careful about that, too. We don't want to spook you."

Her puzzled look suggested she didn't have a clue what he meant by *spook,* but she shook her head. "Good."

He watched her grab her robe and enter the bathroom. Once she'd closed the door, he could breathe again—though suppressing his laughter proved difficult. He did have a hard time imagining Nadja cleaning fish.

She looked much more appealing when she came back to the bedroom, her cheeks rosy from scrubbing. Her eyes held a twinkle they had not had only a few minutes ago.

"I won't watch those fish getting cleaned," she sputtered.

"You won't have to. I'll make sure of that." He gave her a level stare. "Now, do you think you are ready to join me in bed?"

She tightened the sash of her robe and shook her head slightly.

He exhaled. "What is it now?"

She scowled. "Danny," she whispered.

"Damn, you knew he was coming back with me. He knows we're sleeping together."

"I know, I know."

He held his breath as she warred with conflicting emotions.

"I want to go see the stars."

"What! Now? What the hell?

"I want to see the stars." She licked her lips provocatively.

"You can grab your robe and join me, if you want."

He squinted at her. "Where do you plan on stargazing?"

"The gazebo."

Her rapidly reddening cheeks suggested he might very much enjoy stargazing with her. "I'll be right with you." He clambered off the bed. "I have a sudden interest in stars."

"Wait, please," Nadja whispered, wrapping her long legs around Kevin's bottom. Savoring his full length in her heated vagina, she kissed his forehead and tenderly trailed her fingers down his rippling back. "I've never watched the stars with a man inside me like this. And your cock feels wonderful, but let's appreciate the moment."

Kevin propped himself up on his elbows and smiled down at her. Faint light from the patio, filtered by the gazebo screen, gave him a surreal look.

"What will you think of next?" he said, in hushed tones. "You coax me out of the house to this gazebo. You spread a blanket out and spread your thighs, inviting me. And now you want to study the stars!"

"Thought you were a patient man," she teased. "The big dipper is right above us. Look."

Kevin craned his neck back. "I see it. Was the skylight your idea?"

She lifted her hips slightly, making sure he wasn't growing soft. "Uh-huh. Some night I'll show you how to work my telescope. It's not professional quality, but nearly. I've always been fascinated with the stars and planets. That's why there's a skylight."

"But you've not shared this hobby with a man?" He pecked at her nose and laved at a cheek.

"Not until now. Do you suppose there is another couple somewhere in the world in another gazebo, intertwined like this, studying the stars?"

His chest rumbled against hers with a chuckle. "That's hard to imagine, but I guess it's possible."

He flexed his hips, teasing her, reminding her. She closed her eyes and nibbled his shoulder. He settled again. "There is Venus in all her glory," he muttered.

She opened her eyes. "You're not even looking at the sky."

He shook his head. "I wouldn't want to miss *my* Venus. It's hard to believe, but the soft shadows, the scent of flowers, the bright stars make you even more lovely."

Nadja squirmed beneath his weight. If she could, she would preen like a feline. "I didn't realize you were such a romantic."

"Me either. It's difficult not to be, lying here tucked in you like this."

Without disrupting their joining, he shifted back on his knees, lifting himself from her chest.

The skin he'd been covering chilled in the night air. He cradled a breast in his palm, and she smiled her pleasure. He dipped his head and toyed with her swollen nipple. She arched her back, pleading for more.

He chuckled and settled his mouth over her breast, swirling his tongue around the hidden nipple. She raked her fingers across his shoulders and then through his hair. "Heavenly," she murmured to the night, closing her eyes. "I love the way you love my tits. Don't ignore her twin."

He moved off her breast and lapped at the other one. "How," he whispered, "are you going to watch the stars with your eyes closed?"

She curled a finger around his earlobe. "I'm ready to study different kinds of stars." She tapped his butt with a heel. "Stars that only you seem to be able to bring out."

"Ah," he murmured in her ear, "I love to navigate your body. But you're the only star I need to guide me."

She chuckled softly. "No one's ever compared me to the North Star."

She sucked on her lower lip when he pulled halfway out, only to slowly re-enter. She clamped her inner muscles around his cock, gripping him as tight as she could. "How slow can we do this and still orgasm?"

"Slow may not equate with length of time," he cautioned, kissing the corner of her mouth.

"That's okay," she responded, running her tongue the full width of his mouth. "I don't care how long. I just want slow."

Minutes later, Nadja squeezed her eyes tight and dug her nails into Kevin's shoulders. They'd climbed the wall of ecstasy as if it were greased—making progress and then receding. Once her fingers had grasped the top of the wall, but she'd slipped back down into his comforting arms. She was beyond caring about their speed now, though Kevin didn't seem interested in increasing their pace. He hadn't spoken since he'd begun this slow journey to pleasure.

"I'm not sure how much more of this I can take," she whispered, somewhat shrilly. She opened her eyes and saw him gritting his teeth. He was as close as she was.

He nodded and slid a hand between them. His fingers tapped lightly on her clit. Her eyes widened, and her thighs instinctively bucked against his. Closing her eyes again, she clutched his back and held on, knowing that now he'd take her like a whirlwind.

His hips drove him deeper and faster. "Here we go."

"Hurry," she moaned, "do me. Drive us over the edge. Drive us home."

Her muscles burned. Repeatedly, his cock seemed to find a depth she didn't know she had. She felt him erupt—once, twice—she lost count. He churned and churned until she heard him gasping her name.

Her name echoed from his lips across the sky as she soared

across the heavens. From Earth, to Mars, to Venus. Her planet. It would always be her planet, from this night forward.

He rolled them to their sides and trailed soft kisses across her eyelids, her nose, and her lips. She let him chew on her lower lip and claim it for himself, before responding in kind.

"Lovely," she whispered. "Incredibly lovely."

"Me too." He hugged her close. "I never dreamed stargazing could be so sensual."

"I hate to be practical, but fairly soon, we'd better go back inside. I wouldn't want us to fall asleep out here and have the neighbors or Danny find us here in the morning."

Kevin yawned. "You're probably right." He eased out of her and swore, "Damn, the night air is chillier than I thought. This is like moving from an oven to a refrigerator."

"Poor boy," she teased. "Maybe once in the gazebo is enough."

"I didn't say that, woman. But I admit I wouldn't have thought about it."

Nadja didn't respond. She wouldn't have, either, if it hadn't been for Ivett and her own concerns about Danny hearing them if they'd stayed in her bedroom.

"Dad — wake up. Dad!"

Kevin cranked an eye open to see his son still in his superhero pajamas, giving him the Langley glower. Where had he learned that?

"Oh my God!"

He jerked his head in the direction of the shriek to stare at Nadja turning bright red, clutching the sheet around her neck.

He closed his eyes ever so briefly. What a hell of a way to wake up. *Be cool. Be cool.* "What is it, son?" he asked as calmly as he could. "Aren't you supposed to knock before entering a bedroom?"

Danny scowled. "I did, but you didn't hear me. Hi, Nadia." He gave Nadja a bright smile.

That was the way it was. Kevin was the recipient of his son's glower, and Nadja of his smile. But Nadja seemed to have some difficulty taking in this new situation. He'd never seen her speechless. *Welcome aboard. Welcome to the world of small boys.*

"What is it, Danny?" he asked, scratching his head. He'd have to deal with Nadja later.

"I can't find the breakfast food. And it's past seven-thirty." Danny glanced quickly at Nadja. "I thought we were supposed be at the shop by eight."

"Oh my goodness," Nadja gasped, picking up the clock with one hand while holding on tight to the sheet with the other. "I forgot to set the alarm. I *never* forget to set the alarm." She threw a look at Kevin with wide eyes. She stared at Danny, clearly fighting back tears.

"Did I do okay, Nadia? You did want me to wake you, didn't you? You wouldn't want to be late for work."

Kevin held his breath, waiting for Nadja's reply. Danny adored her. If she lashed out at him now, the kid would be crushed.

He saw her breasts heave as she gulped for more air. She shook her head back and forth slowly. "No, I can't be late. That would be terrible. I'm the only one coming in for the morning." She blinked. "Thank you, Danny. But can I ask another favor?"

"Sure." The boy puffed his chest out with pride.

"The next time you want to wake your father or me, would you please knock harder? You can't make too much noise."

"I will," Danny said, coming around the bed to stand at her side. "Nadia, I'm sorry if I scared you."

"That's okay. It looks like I'm going to live."

"So where do you keep the breakfast food?"

Kevin was pleased to see Nadja's smile return.

"My mistake," she said. "I didn't realize you'd be the first one up. Your favorite breakfast food is in one of the upper cupboards. If you leave now, I'll get dressed and come and help you with breakfast."

"Good." He frowned as if undecided about something. "If you store the breakfast food in a lower cupboard, I won't have to bother you and Daddy when I'm hungry."

She nodded, and her cheeks reddened again. "I'll do that. Now scoot. We have to hurry."

Kevin waved at his son as Danny tiptoed toward the door and closed it behind him quietly. He tensed, waiting for Nadja's assault.

He admired her bare back as she sat up and put the clock back on the bed stand. Her shoulders began trembling. Was she that angry? Was she sobbing?

She turned to face him with the sheet only covering her lap. Her lips were curved into a wide smile, and her breasts shook from laughter.

"What is it?" he asked, finally.

"My brain has been in a swirl for several minutes." She stopped laughing. "I wanted to yell at him. I wanted to buy a lock for the door, but I decided against that in case he couldn't wake us in an emergency."

"For a seven-year-old boy, hunger is an emergency. But what's so funny?"

"Now that he's actually seen us in bed together, I guess it's senseless to sneak out to the gazebo again."

"Well, then . . ." His voice husky, he stroked her sheet-covered thigh. "Danny may have done us a bigger service than he realizes—though I will miss watching stars from the gazebo."

"There are cloudy nights. And it storms often in Iowa." She glanced at the closed door. "And it is nice to know we can make love in my bed again once we know Danny is sound asleep." She scowled at him. "He's not a sleepwalker, is he?"

"Not that I know of." He chuckled. "You want to hit the shower first? I don't have an appointment until nine-thirty."

She nodded and hurried toward the bathroom.

Would he ever tire of watching her striding naked before him, like a goddess from his teenage dreams?

CHAPTER TWELVE

"I think you're getting the knack of it, Nadia."

Ignoring the boy, Nadja watched her lure sail and arch over the water. She straightened and smiled at Danny, let the lure settle a few seconds, then began reeling it back in slowly like he'd taught her. "It is getting a little easier," she admitted.

Danny grinned and pumped his fist. "I knew you could do it! Anyone who can dance as easy as you do has to be able to cast a line out."

She brought the lure in slowly and then cast it out again. This time it didn't go as far, but apparently it still met with the approval of her young coach.

Danny nodded at her and picked up his own pole. Seemingly with little effort, he had a lure out beyond hers.

"How long has he been fishing?" she asked Kevin, who sat on the other side of her, where he could handle the motor.

"He's gone out with me since he was four. He graduated from a kids' pole to the one he has over a year ago." Kevin grinned. "He started with worms and a bobber."

She grimaced. She'd heard about people putting worms on hooks.

"We figured fishing with a lure would be easier on you than worms."

"I appreciate your consideration for my feelings. How many more fish do we have to catch?"

"Depends." He shrugged. "These crappies are great eating, but it takes a lot of them to make a meal."

"Are you sure they're called crappies?"

"Absolutely. You don't think I know about fishing?"

"Of course you do. Goodness," she yelped, grabbing on to her pole so it wouldn't jerk overboard.

"You got one!" Danny screeched. "Help her, Dad!"

Nadja moved to the edge of her seat and tried to remember what she'd been told. She must've set the hook instinctively, or the fish wouldn't still be on. She wrapped her fingers tighter around the pole and began to turn the reel. She wet her lips, trying her best to ignore the shouts of the men. Where was the fish?

"Goodness," she exclaimed when she saw the fish leap above the water and splash back in.

"Don't rush him," Kevin shouted in her ear.

She tried not to hurry and braced her feet against the side-wall of the boat, afraid the fish might pull her overboard. Kevin had lost a large fish earlier. She was determined that wouldn't happen to her fish.

"Keep the tension on him. Move your pole to the right some. He's almost in reach."

Out of the corner of her eye, she could see Kevin leaning out over the boat with a net. Maybe he'd go in the water before she did. She tried her best to follow his advice, but the fish didn't seem eager to do the same.

She grunted and tried again. The fish followed her lead until Kevin brought the net up under it.

"Yay!" Danny shouted. "Well done! Right, Dad?"

Kevin chuckled. "You're right." He turned to Nadja. "You look tuckered."

She nodded, gulped in air, and watched Kevin work his fingers into the fish's mouth to retrieve the lure. She couldn't imagine how he'd do that if the fish had teeth. They'd already explained that these large-mouthed bass didn't have teeth, but that if they caught something called a northern, she was to keep her fingers to herself. Those fish apparently had razor-sharp teeth. She had no desire to catch such a fish. This one looked fierce enough.

"Why don't you sit back and rest a while? Danny and I may fish a little longer, but we already have enough for tomorrow's supper. Your fish assures us of a very fine meal."

Nadja set her pole aside and squinted at the fish. Hopefully, she wouldn't recognize it on the supper platter.

She leaned back in the seat, closed her eyes, and let the gentle rocking of the boat lull her like a baby. She hadn't realized how draining fishing would be. Late afternoon sunshine on her thighs and arms warmed her like a soft caress.

Erotic images began to flood her senses. Making love in the gazebo had been surprisingly lovely. Could they make love on a boat? She'd seen houseboats at the marina. Or maybe on a raft? She'd seen a video of a couple doing it on a raft. It had been on one of Ivett's fantasy tapes. The marina rented rafts, too. Had Kevin ever made love on the water?

She squinted at him. He was completely concentrated on his lure. She sighed and chastised herself for thinking about lovemaking with Danny sitting in the boat. She blinked twice, bringing herself alert.

Just in time. Danny's pole bent, and his reel made a whirling noise.

"Set the hook! That's right. Let her play some. Looks like a nice one, son." Kevin reached for the net.

How did Kevin know the gender of fish? He'd called her fish a *he* and this one a *she*. Nadja smiled, appreciating Danny's patience and his strength. He'd screamed when she caught her fish. Now he was silent and entirely focused on the task at hand.

His dad waited, giving a reassuring word now and then. Kevin and Danny really were a team. It amazed her that a seven-year-old knew so much about something she barely understood.

"Here she comes, Dad." Danny's jaw fell open. "It's even bigger than Nadia's."

Nadja leaned forward for a better view. Judging from the excitement between the two males, this was something different from what they'd been catching. Her eyes rounded when she saw the sizeable fish as Kevin hoisted the net out of the water. "That *is* a big one," she blurted out.

"It's a keeper!" Danny shouted. "Right, Dad?"

"It's a keeper, all right. We won't throw this one back. No way! It must weigh a good four pounds. You did a super job of landing it."

A keeper, Nadja mused. Where had she heard . . . oh my! She gripped the edge of her seat tight. Danny had said *she* might be a keeper when she'd told him she'd stocked her refrigerator with his favorite pop and ice cream. She looked wildly about her. She couldn't walk on water — there was no escape.

Kevin and his son remained bent over the *keeper,* rescuing the hook. Neither male seemed at all aware of her distress. Probably neither of them remembered the earlier conversation.

She tugged at the hem of her T-shirt beneath the drab olive life vest and pulled the Cubs ball cap lower over her eyes. She doubted the vest provided much protection from men — though it was more than a little tight across her breasts.

Kevin's shoulders squared as he handed Danny back the lure and then placed the fish in what he called a *live well.* Kevin had been very deft with the net — completely focused on the challenge of landing the fish. And now the unfortunate fish would wait for him to do whatever he did to make it ready for cooking.

Her stomach lurched. *Steady, girl. Steady.*

"You look a little green." Kevin gave her a puzzled look. "Is the water getting to you?"

"I'll be all right." She didn't want to tell him the churn and twisting of her gut had nothing to do with the water. She wasn't convinced it had anything to do with the fish, either.

Keeper. Should she be thrilled, or offended? All because of the offhanded words of a seven-year-old. But hadn't his dad smirked and agreed? Yes, he'd said something like *she just might be a keeper.* Her fingers curled. If he thought she would be landed like some fish, he'd better prepare for a much bigger fight than she'd just witnessed.

She didn't want to be anybody's keeper—and damn if she'd be kept.

Conversation at the supper table had stopped. Nadja tried not to smile at Danny and Kevin as they chewed on crispy pieces of fried fish. Kevin had insisted on frying their catch of the previous afternoon and evening. She had been reluctant to yield her stove to him, but now realized she'd never have done justice to the tasty meal. She'd never eaten fish like this. Flaky pieces nearly melted in her mouth. It was impossible to get that taste from fish sold at the market.

She shivered. Father and son might turn her into a fisher-person yet. *Time to change the subject.* "This is superb." She reached for another small fillet.

"The corn on the cob is excellent, too" Kevin spread a slab of butter over his third ear. "We'll all be overstuffed after this meal, but it'll be worth it."

"Can you go fishing with us again?" Danny wiped his mouth with the back of his hand, and she instinctively handed him a napkin.

She winced—she'd done what most any mother would do. "Probably."

"I'm glad. You make fishing even more fun."

She tilted her head to the side. She couldn't possibly ignore his wide grin. She'd never really enjoyed being teased, but then Danny and his father had somehow raised banter to an art form. "How do I make fishing more fun?"

"You're not like most girls who say *yuck* to fish." He glanced quickly at his father. "We might even get you to bait a hook with a worm."

"Don't count on that." She sat up straighter in the chair.

"It's fun teaching you—isn't it, Dad?"

Kevin made a show of gnawing an ear of corn before answering. When he was ready, he drawled, "It sure is, son. Nadja's a quick learner."

She smiled at Danny and then glared at Kevin. "I had fun, too. Speaking of learning"—she rubbed her tummy—"I may be too full for physical activity tonight." She gave Kevin a meaningful stare. "No dance lessons," she said to Danny, "but maybe we can begin work on some of the other Green Bay Packer dolls."

"All right!"

"After dishes," she added.

"We finished painting the biggest one. It must get harder with the smaller ones—the ones that hide inside." His lips formed a pout. "I'm not sure I'll be able to do the tiny one."

"We'll do it together. You're right—painting the tiny dolls can be quite difficult." She brightened. "But we'll do it together."

He gave her an infectious grin. "It takes a team. Like fishing. It took all three of us to land those bass."

She nodded her agreement. "Something like that."

She couldn't recall actually helping land Danny's fish, but she'd at least been a cheerleader. Apparently, that was good for something.

Glancing quickly from one male to the other, she couldn't help but wonder if this fishing venture hadn't been some sort of test on their way toward deciding if she was a true keeper. She tucked her hands under the table to hide her trembling fingers.

Kevin's voice was soft. "If you think any harder, you may come apart."

She jerked her head toward him. Had she been that obvious? "It's nothing," she murmured. "I was thinking about tomorrow."

"Right. But you're not going to fill me in on that?"

She shook her head and darted her gaze toward Danny.

"Maybe later," Kevin said.

"Maybe." Rising to her feet, she announced, "It looks like it's time for dessert."

"What is it?" Danny squealed. "What is it?"

"Fresh strawberries and vanilla ice cream."

"All right! We sure eat better here than at your place, Dad."

"We sure do," Kevin replied, looking more than a little puzzled. "We surely do."

Tugging with his teeth on the tiny blonde curls guarding Nadja's labia, Kevin grinned at the sight of her flinching away from his mouth and then quickly settling back against it. She wiggled on her knees, sliding her pussy across his lips while she suckled on his engorged cock. Her dangling breasts teased his abs.

He clutched her bottom tighter, holding her in place, and traced the length of her moist pussy with the tip of his tongue. Her groans thrilled him beyond reason. Was she having as much difficulty tracking what each of them was doing as he was?

He received his answer when she dropped his cock from her mouth to lay her cheek against his thigh. Idly, her fingers continued to squeeze him from time to time, but he expected almost all of her sensory awareness had focused on what his tongue was doing to her.

He curved his tongue into her slick portal, and she rocked back and forth against him. She arched her back under his finger as it traced the length of her spine and the shape of her rump.

She mewled against his thigh and clutched his shaft, as if he might take it from her. He had no intention of doing that—instead, he tried to burrow as far as he could into her heat.

"Goodness." She muffled her strains of ecstasy against his thigh.

He smiled—was she trying to remain ladylike? Lady or not, her juices began flowing over his tongue. He lapped at them, making her quiver. When she quieted, he hugged her rump and waited for her breathing to steady.

The crick in his neck caused him to give up his purchase. He settled back and affectionately caressed her ass, and she hummed an inarticulate response.

"Better than strawberries and ice cream." He chortled softly. "I never thought anything in this life would taste as good as you do."

Her fingers around his cock slackened. Her words came to him like an echo from a distant land. He frowned and then grinned. Did she say what he thought she had? He'd swear her garbled message was *Maybe I am a keeper.*

He doubted he'd ask for clarification even after she awoke. She probably had no idea what she'd said as she sank into slumber. He fondled her butt cheeks affectionately before closing his eyes and smiling to himself. They never had gotten around to discussing what a *keeper* meant. She'd obviously picked up more on their little fishing excursion than some basic fishing skills.

What did she make of the idea of being a keeper? Hell, what did *he* make of that notion?

He grazed his cheek against her inner thigh. Would he ever get his fill of her? His eyes sprang open, admiring the sight of her vulva and anus remaining open and available to him. Was it even possible to get enough of Nadja?

Two days later, Kevin sat next to Nadja and watched Danny playing with a couple neighbor kids. Danny's adaptability often amazed him. He led his new friends, a boy and a girl, around Nadja's backyard as if it was his own.

He smiled when Danny ushered his companions into the gazebo, then glanced quickly at Nadja. "We should try out the gazebo again before I have to go back."

"Umm," she responded. "Is that why you've been brooding all day?"

"The gazebo?" he teased.

"Going back. You knew what I meant."

"That's part of it, I suppose." He slouched lower in his chair. "I can't stay down here forever. I can hardly stay any longer. I can propose three alternative sites to Java Beans. One here in Jefferson City, one between here and Lakeside, and one in Lakeside."

Nadja caught her breath. "When will Java Beans make a decision?"

"They'll consider what I've come up with, but I doubt if a final decision will be made until we know more about what's going on with the threats to you and the Cappuccino."

"Maybe those people have given up. It's been nearly two weeks since anything has happened."

She didn't sound totally convinced, and he wasn't about to mislead her. "May not mean much. Who knows how they think? They may be waiting for us to drop our guard."

"You mean me and Ivett, don't you?"

Turning, he caught a glimpse of her pained eyes and winced. He hesitated. What was she looking for? What did she want him to say? He shook his head.

"Of course I meant you and Ivett." He glanced out at the

gazebo. "I guess I thought I was sort of part of the *we,* too."

"Because Java Beans's reputation has been questioned?"

He nodded. "And maybe because I like being part of the *we.*"

"I see," she muttered.

He didn't think so. Shouldn't she be exuding more warmth? Seemed like he was taking all the risks for both of them.

"What happens to this *we* after you go back to the Cities?"

He slipped his hand under the table and settled it in her lap. She quickly placed it back on his thigh and then folded her hands on the table, striking a prim and proper pose that irritated him.

"Do you think this is the time to discuss this?" he groused. "With Danny and his friends in the gazebo?"

"Perfect time and place," she replied coolly, without taking her focus off the gazebo. "If we were anywhere else, you'd be talking with your hands."

"And you'd let me."

Unsmiling, she turned to face him. "Probably."

He twisted his neck and raked fingers of both hands through his hair. "I don't know what to do with you. I didn't expect to find you. I didn't want to find you."

Nadja's eyes rounded into small balls.

Why had he rambled on so? He was moving too quickly for her, and for himself. "Let me be clear." He gave her a half-smile. "I'm glad I did find you. And I definitely don't know what to do with you."

"Seems like you've found a lot of things to do with me."

He frowned. Was she being coy, or was she avoiding? *She* was the one who'd asked where they were going. He would've been fine without the question ever being raised, but now it was on the table—whether she wanted to withdraw it or not.

"Danny will go back to his mother's on Monday. We're only about two hours apart. I can certainly pop down on weekends easily enough—sometimes Danny will be along."

She nodded but gave no indication of her thoughts.

"When my business takes me south, I could stop over on the way down and back."

Again she made no comment. His heart pumped. Was she preparing to brush him off? "You've never been to my place. You could come up and stay as long as you want. I have loads of vacation time. Hell, we could get away entirely."

He peered at her misting eyes. "If you want. I don't want to end this," he insisted. "Unless you do. What do you want, Nadja? You've sat there and let me rattle on. What do you want?"

She wet her lips and swallowed. "I don't know what I want." She crossed her arms under her breasts. "But I don't want to go back to where I was before you came along."

"Good." He smirked at her. "And you're not ready to find my replacement."

To his relief, she shook her head slowly. "I would like to see your place."

"Great! How about next weekend? I'll check out what's happening at the Guthrie and some of the other theaters. You'll love the Cities, Nadja. It's a cultural festival."

She flinched and stared out toward the gazebo. "I'm not sure I want to love the Cities."

"Ah." He squeezed her thigh, and this time she didn't remove his hand. "Let's take this one small step at a time. I can't see beyond the horizon." He interlaced his fingers with hers. "But I'm happy we're walking toward it hand in hand."

"Don't make me cry." She sighed, and her fingernails dug into his palm. "Perhaps the horizon is merely a mirage."

"That's a risk I'm willing to take. How about you?"

Her mouth bowed into a grin. "If the children weren't in

the gazebo, I would take you there now and make wild love with you."

"In broad daylight?"

She laughed. "That's right—you've only been out there in the dark. You probably didn't notice the sunshades that allow me to enclose the gazebo entirely." She drew the tip of her tongue across her lips. "Maybe another time."

He blew her a kiss. "You do know how to keep a man coming back."

"Not just any man," she murmured, bringing his fingers to her lips.

Saturday morning, Nadja knelt and hugged the brown-haired boy tight. He had his arms locked around her neck. She glanced up at Danny's father, who was focused on checking out a cardinal in a nearby tree. She'd learned Kevin was a softy when it came to mushy goodbyes.

She unwrapped Danny's arms from her neck. "It's been fun having you here."

"You're so tall. I can't even see over your head when you're kneeling."

Nadja laughed and rose to her feet. Maybe Danny wasn't quite as easy with his feelings as she'd thought. Maybe he modeled himself after his father too much. Was that how men learned to hide their feelings so well? She grimaced. Where had *she* learned to perfect that skill?

"Are you for sure coming up next weekend?" Danny bounced from foot to foot. "Will I see you? I have so much to show you."

"Your mother has a camping trip planned for next weekend."

"Oh, right." Seldom did Danny look so crestfallen.

"You'll be back again," she said, trying to reassure the boy.

"You'll have a great time camping."

"I know. I love sleeping outside in a tent. Do you, Nadia? Maybe you can come with my dad and me when we go camping."

"I don't know about that." She looked quickly to Kevin for help. He stared at them as if he hadn't heard Danny. "We'll have to wait and see."

"I don't like waiting. Adults always say that when they don't want to answer."

"I thought you were so good waiting on those fish the other day."

"That's different," Danny argued, without providing more explanation.

Kevin checked his watch. "Okay, we've got to hit the road, son. Hop in." He opened the passenger door, and Danny clambered in. Nadja double-checked his seat belt.

Once Danny was safely buckled in, Kevin turned her about and drew her into his arms. Their lips met as if it were the most natural thing to do. He hugged her close. "Remember, you can always call," he said, breaking away from her. "See you next Saturday. If you have questions about the directions, call me."

She nodded, not trusting her voice.

He opened his door and smiled at her. "Maybe I'll call you. Those directions may need clarification."

"Please do," she said through blurred vision. "They did look rather confusing."

Danny waved as Kevin backed the car out the driveway. Kevin waved before pulling out, and she waved back. Both of them knew she could find driving directions easily by checking out the web.

But she already missed the sound of his enticing voice. The week ahead promised to be long. She hoped it would also be uneventful.

Nadja wandered back toward the house. She bypassed the main entrance and opened the gate to the backyard. She ambled toward the gazebo. It had so often been the place where she could think most clearly, where she went when she was elated or sad.

She climbed up the three short stairs and entered. Once inside, she hugged herself. What a pleasant place, filled with so many rich memories — of solitude, writing, warm sunshine, rain pounding on the roof, moon and stars visible through the skylight — she tasted her lips — and lovemaking. Oh, such precious, fulfilling lovemaking. She could hardly wait until Kevin came back. With a little effort, she could turn the gazebo into their private love nest.

Nadja took a deep breath. Wouldn't it be pleasing to make love as the birds called to the rising sun and the scent of garden flowers wafted on soft breezes? That would be like making love in her favorite meadow.

She twirled around happily. Unlike the meadow, the gazebo was private; it was her space. Space she'd shared intimately with Kevin and eagerly looked forward to sharing again.

She left the gazebo and headed for the house. She'd grab a pad of paper and begin sketching some emerging ideas for redecorating the gazebo. Apart from dancing and developing the Cappuccino, she most enjoyed decorating. The image of her body intertwined with Kevin's flitted across her mind. Maybe she'd have to revise her list of joys.

She heard the phone ringing before she reached the house. She dashed into the kitchen and grabbed the phone. Kevin hadn't been gone more than a half an hour. Had he missed her already?

"Hi," she purred into the phone.

"Bitch!" The male voice shouting at her was definitely not Kevin's.

"Don't hang up, bitch," the voice snarled. "I think you're going to want to hear what I have to say."

Nadja said nothing. Her heart thumped fast and bile inched its way up her throat, but she listened in terror.

"Now that lover boy is gone, you're much more vulnerable."

Nadja closed her eyes and slumped against the kitchen counter. Someone had been spying on them.

"We want your building. We'll get it one way or another. It would've been simpler if you had sold to Java Beans. Now that you have Langley pussy-whipped . . ." There was harsh laughter. "That's not going to happen. I've been told Russian women are not only sexy but clever. So be it. Now listen, and listen good. You and your aunt will put the Henderson building up for sale. There will be only one lucky bidder.

"I can hear your wheels spinning, bitch. If you don't cooperate, I can't vouch for your safety or that of others you seem to hold dear. Accidents happen — even to little boys."

She gasped audibly.

"Thought that might get your attention. Nobody's going to get hurt if you do what we say. Do you understand?"

"Yes," she whimpered.

"Think about it, if you must. But don't take too long. We're not saying you have to leave. Our people have enough strings that we could get you deported. We want that building. We don't care if you set up a half-dozen other shops, but that Henderson building will be ours. Got it?"

"I understand," she said, more calmly than she felt.

The shrill dial tone brought some relief. She set the phone in its cradle, slid to the kitchen floor, and wrapped her arms around her knees.

She shook so hard she couldn't think. She pressed her fingers to her temples; she had to think.

She sobbed. Only minutes ago, she'd been almost giddy.

And now her world was in danger of being crushed.

Should she call Kevin? No. He might rush back, putting both him and Danny at risk.

She'd have to sort this out. She had to talk to Ivett. Together they'd work something out. Would it be that bad to sell and move their stores to another location?

CHAPTER THIRTEEN

"You're not seriously considering caving in to these gorillas?" Ivett sat ramrod straight at her kitchen table, and Steve squirmed in a chair next to her.

Nadja felt her shoulders sag and air escape from her lungs. Her aunt had her heels dug in. Nadja was trapped on all sides by her aunt, by Kevin and Danny, by an unseen man with a harsh voice. Her own ambition, pride and stubbornness didn't help. There had to be a way out of this morass.

She heaved a sigh. "I don't know if I'm even thinking straight."

"I can answer that," Ivett huffed. "You're not. We're not back under the Soviet heel. That's how business was done then. Corruption was normal. That's not how it's done here. We won't be intimidated. Do you hear me?"

Nadja raised her hand to forestall Ivett. "You don't have to yell." She shook her head and glanced at Steve, who looked nearly as distressed as she felt. "I don't want to sell any more than you do. You know that. But there are others to consider here."

Ivett's features softened slightly. "I understand, but if we give in to these people now, what will stop them from coming after us wherever we might set up shop? This is my home, Nadja. I'm not moving from Jefferson City."

"I don't want you to," she wailed. "I don't want to leave either."

"We don't know that they would actually try to harm any of us," Ivett continued.

"I wouldn't count on them not to," Steve grunted.

"And what makes you say that?" Ivett glared at her husband.

He reddened and shrugged. "Clearly they've been watching Nadja."

"So?" Ivett spat. "Maybe the creep is a Peeping Tom, trying to catch Nadja and Kevin in the act."

"Ivett!" Nadja felt her skin warm. It might not be so farfetched that they'd been spied on.

They had spent much of one night in the gazebo. And she couldn't remember if she'd drawn the curtains every time they'd made love. She loved experiencing the first rays of sunshine each morning. But she wasn't about to concede the possibility of such a spy to her aunt.

"I'll talk to Kevin tonight. We were planning on me going to visit him next weekend. There was no specific plan for Danny to come back here."

"That's good." Ivett frowned and then reached over to squeeze her fingers. "I'm glad you're going to take a weekend off and spend time in the Cities. You haven't done that in ages. And it should be good for you to get out of here for a while. Did this creep who talked to you this morning say anything about a deadline?"

"No, he didn't." She ran a hand through her hair, trying to remember. "No, I'm sure of that. He wanted us to move, but he gave no timeframe, no sense of urgency."

"You have any thoughts on that?" Ivett asked Steve.

"They were prepared to wait a fair length of time if Java Beans had bought you out—probably a year or more."

Nadja raised her eyebrows. "You don't think they'll wait that long now?"

Steve shook his head. "They might not be in a rush. Maybe they'd prefer to scare you out without having to escalate their tactics too much. But I don't see why they'd want to wait that long unless there was a third party like Java Beans involved."

"You're the realtor," Ivett said sharply. "What's your best guess?"

"None of us knows what they want to do with the building." He squinted at Nadja. "My guess is they'll want to take over either this fall or next spring. Winter's not a good time for renovating, if that's what they have in mind."

Nadja flexed her fingers. "It's doubtful they're going through all of this to run a coffee shop and an antique store." She shuddered. "They'll probably gut the place, or heaven forbid, tear it down. If that were to happen, I'm not sure I'd want to live here any longer."

"Whoa, let's not jump too far ahead," Ivett interjected. "We don't want to take any knee-jerk actions. Let's slow down. You talk to Kevin. He needs to know about the call, and he may have some useful ideas. I'll get back to my friend in the police department. I'm not sure at what point we make a formal complaint. So far the department only sees us as victims of vandalism and possibly harassment."

"Personal accidents," Nadja pointed out, "won't be harassment."

"I know." Ivett brushed a strand of hair out of her eyes. "If we have to"—she glanced quickly at Steve—"we can list the building with Steve and see who comes out of their holes to claim interest."

Steve nodded his agreement. "That's part of what I don't understand. If you list the place on the market, these people aren't going to be able to prevent other bidders."

"But they could flush them out like they planned to do with Java Beans."

"Like they're trying to do with us," Nadja huffed. "Won't they approach us one day with a check or something?"

"Doubtful." Steve shook his head. "Even if they had someone front for them, that would be too easily traceable." His eyebrows arched upward. "Upfront money is not a problem for these guys. If there is some sort of bidding war for the Henderson building, they could easily outbid all comers. They'd then purchase the property aboveboard without drawing any attention to what they have planned for the building or the land. If I'm right, the key for them is getting you to put the property on the open market, now that Java Beans has made it clear they won't be buying you out."

"That's plausible," Ivett concurred. "But let's not move too quickly. Even if we list the place with no intention of selling, it will take a lot of our time to deal with potential buyers, and it may have negative consequences for our businesses."

Nadja saw Ivett's humor return as she cast a tiny smile to her husband. "If we do list, it will be with you."

"I should hope so," he replied, rather tightly.

"At least we could count on you keeping our secret that we have no real intention of selling."

"Of course." He pushed his chair away from the table. "If that does it, I have an appointment to get to."

Ivett nodded at Steve without commenting.

The sudden sadness in her aunt's eyes made Nadja wince. Had she noticed Steve's trembling fingers when he'd responded to her?

Ivett remained perfectly still until Steve closed the door to the garage. "I wish I didn't have this feeling he knows more about all of this than he's telling us."

Nadja saw no need to try to explain away his behavior. "Maybe he's waiting for the right moment."

Ivett gave her a quizzical glare. "And this wasn't the right moment?"

"Apparently not." Nadja rose to leave. "I'll let you know what Kevin has to say tomorrow."

Clearly still focused on her husband, Ivett nodded absently. "Maybe we'd better have future discussions at the store or at your house."

Nadja shrugged. "I'm sorry you can't trust him."

Ivett grimaced. "Yeah, this is beginning to feel too much like the old days — never knowing who you could trust. Even your family."

Later that evening, Nadja sat in her bedroom Queen Anne chair and rotated her head to one side and the other, working tension from her neck muscles while she listened to Kevin grappling with her latest news. One moment he cussed, and the next he overflowed with concern.

"Are you sure you're okay?" he asked. "I can be there in two to three hours."

"I'm fine," she reassured him. "Really. I think Ivett and Steve are right. Nothing too bad will happen right away. I expect more threats, but if that becomes too extreme, then we'll list the building and see what happens."

"I don't like this. None of this. I had no idea what I would unlock when I stepped into the Cappuccino the first time."

"We know now these threats against us would've happened even if you hadn't come into my shop." She paused, welcoming the tingle of her nipples. "And some of the things you've unlocked have been quite pleasurable."

"Are you trying to distract me?"

"No."

"Well, you're doing a good job of it." His sigh was audible. "I may be overreacting some. You've had all day to process this news. You could've called earlier."

"That's true, but I didn't." Did she sound as smug as she thought she did? "I wanted to be more relaxed when I talked to you. We don't think this is an immediate crisis."

"And what if you're wrong?"

Her flesh chilled. "I don't think you should bring Danny down here until we can figure more of this out."

"You don't think the bad guys can reach this far?"

She shook her head, glad he couldn't see the fright in her eyes. She tried to respond evenly. "I think my caller was using scare tactics."

"Probably, but . . ."

"Maybe we should just sell." She nearly bit her tongue. Was she testing him? She had no intention of selling. Ivett wouldn't even talk about that option.

Another heavy sigh kept her waiting. "No. There's no guarantee these people wouldn't continue to harass you at another location. They claim their interest is only the building, but there's too much ethnic slurring going on. Maybe even some sexual overtones."

Remembering the card she'd received, she said softly, "Yes, I've wondered about that."

"I really think I should drive down there tonight."

"No, please. I'll see you this weekend." She slipped into her sultry voice. "If you want, I could probably get away a day early. Barb will fill in for me if I ask."

"I'm asking."

She appreciated his husky tone. "I'll come up Friday morning."

"Why not Thursday night after work?"

"Okay." She realized he was trying to reduce the number of nights she'd have to be in her house alone. "I can probably do that."

"I may come back with you. I'll talk with my bosses about taking vacation time."

"You don't have to do that."

"I want to. If I do come down, will you have room for me?"

She giggled. "My bed hasn't shrunk since you left."

"Are you wearing your white robe with nothing on under it?"

"Of course."

She heard him clear his throat. "I'm too out of sorts to even talk you through an orgasm."

"That's okay," she soothed. "I'm not sure I could get up for that."

"Know you're being hugged."

Nadja smiled and warmed. "I can feel you hugging me. Thank you. Talk with you tomorrow. Bye."

She set the phone aside, crossed her ankles, and squeezed her body inward. Kevin's desire and his concern had caused dampness to form at the apex of her thighs. She hesitated. It would be so easy to take herself the rest of the way, with or without her magic wand.

She shook her head and stood. She could wait. She *would* wait. She'd wait for the weekend, or maybe she'd encourage him to help her the next time they talked.

It amazed her how sexy his voice sounded over the phone. If anything, it was even sexier on the phone than when he sat next to her. Maybe because with so many miles separating them, she only had his voice to cling to. She stretched — that, and her muscle memories. She did have some pleasantly aching muscles. Things could be worse. Much worse.

At moments it seemed like the days dragged by, and at other moments time seemed to fly. Nadja completed a few finishing touches on the gazebo Wednesday evening. She'd leave for the Cities tomorrow after work, so this was her last opportunity to freshen up her love sanctuary.

Kevin had insisted he'd come back with her Sunday evening. When he was ready to go back, either she'd drive him, he'd rent a car, or he'd fly.

She smiled at the new daybed. Its wood matched her desk. How many hours had she spent at that desk writing poetry, short stories, or sketching out plans for the Cappuccino?

She'd also installed Levolor blinds more inviting than the

ratty shades Kevin had failed to notice the one night they'd been in the gazebo. And she'd placed several fat scented candles judiciously around the interior. She wouldn't succumb to the temptation some of her neighbors had to install electricity in their gazebos.

She wanted privacy out here, but she didn't require modern conveniences. Her laptop had plenty of battery life when she wanted to work at the gazebo desk. She glanced around the large yard once again, thankful for her mother's insistence on spaciousness and privacy—something she'd known little of in her lifetime.

Why had this little space become so important? It had been so from the time she and her mother had moved in. She hated to admit it even now, but it had provided a kind of sanctuary from her mother. There had been times when she just had to get away, even for a few minutes. In her last two years, her mother had rarely been able to venture off the patio.

On some days right after her mother's death, she'd nearly become a recluse in her private sanctuary. And then it had become a place for dreaming. And now—she hugged herself—it had become a place for loving.

What an amazing transformation. The place felt so cozy, so magical.

Kevin leaned back against the pillows of his bed, held the phone to his ear, and reveled in the sounds of Nadja chirping away. He grinned. She probably wouldn't appreciate his characterization of her, but when she was happy, she chirped.

And she sounded happy. He hoped it wasn't a false happiness. He firmly hoped she hadn't underestimated the danger she was in, that perhaps they were all in.

But she'd be in his arms tomorrow night. He hoped that had something to do with her happiness. He'd breathed easier once he'd discovered no more threats had occurred since they last talked.

"I can hardly wait to see you," she purred into his ear.

He smiled at the picture he had of her on his bedstand. She didn't even know he had it. Danny always wanted pictures of the fish he caught, and Kevin had snapped several of Nadja when they were in the boat. She hadn't been paying much attention at the time, perhaps because she'd focused so much on her fishing rod or on Danny.

"You don't have to wait. I can help you take the edge off."

"Kevin."

"I'm not kidding. I wouldn't want you so ravenous tomorrow that you drive off the road in a rush to get here."

He smiled when she didn't respond. "You must be terribly hot, Nadja. At least open your robe and let your body cool down."

After what seemed like an eternity, he heard her voice. "I don't think that's working. I'm only getting hotter. I keep imagining your fingers on me."

Kevin swallowed hard. Who was teasing whom? "Wouldn't want you to die of heatstroke. Do you own a vibrator?"

"No," she said softly. "Did your wife?"

"Yes. Damn, we'll have to do without."

"I do have a crystal wand."

His brow furrowed. "What?"

"Ivett gave it to me. She called it a dildo."

Laughter began deep in his belly and bubbled from his mouth. "That's precious. You are familiar with using this wand?"

"Yes."

"Have you used it while imagining me?"

A brief pause followed before he heard a plaintive *yes*.

"Nice. You'll need to introduce your wand to me; I already

feel like we're partners. Is it handy?"

"I'm holding it. I got it out of the drawer once I decided to let you know I have it. And I now have you on the speaker phone. My hands are free."

"Damn. So how far ahead of me are you?"

"Not far," she said, her voice rising slightly. "My nipples are swollen and on fire, and the wand is working its magic along my belly button and abs."

"Jesus. What an enticing image."

"I want you to join me. Is my favorite cock hard?"

"Absolutely. I love the way you pronounce that word—so authoritative. We'll join you a little, but I don't want to waste anything before tomorrow night. At these times I'm envious of women—you can come and come with little concern for recovery."

"Sorry I wear you out so."

"Don't be. I'm not. I assume you've stayed busy while we've talked."

"Of course. The crystal wand has traveled up and down both my thighs."

"But it hasn't said *hi* to your fluffy curls."

"I didn't want to get that far ahead of you, but I can't wait much longer."

"Don't. Tell me what you're doing."

"Okay. I'm bringing the crystal to my mouth to wet it."

Kevin agonized for what seemed like minutes before he heard her voice again.

"That should do it. That was nice, but I would prefer wetting your cock . . .its entire length."

"Me too. Tomorrow night. We'll count on that. You have such a warm mouth. What are you doing now?"

"I'm running the smooth tip of the wand up and down the crease of my pussy. Oh!"

"Must be pretty good."

"Uh-huh. Oh, Kevin. I wish you were here." She gasped. "I'm pushing the wand in my cunt. Oh, wow! It just slipped in. I am so open for you."

Kevin didn't trust himself to speak. Apparently she needed no coaching. He couldn't tell whether he was hearing squishy sounds or if that was his overwrought imagination.

"I'm working it . . .in circles."

"Jesus," he mumbled. "Don't forget your clit."

"I'm not," she giggled. "I forgot to tell you. I'm trying to strum it like you do. There. You know you are superb at that. Oh goodness! I'm coming. Wait for me. It's a good one. Wish you were here. Yes. Yes. Oh!"

Kevin struggled for breath as he imagined Nadja pulling her knees to her chest to nurse her orgasm along. He waited patiently.

"I'm back," she said, moments later. "Are you still there?"

"I'm here," he said with effort. "You are a rare find. The most precious woman I've ever known."

It was probably just as well he couldn't see her. It was certainly good she couldn't see him. He'd never be able to take those words back. Would he ever want to?.

He detected her yawn. "I've never even thought of doing this—what do they call it? *Phone sex?*"

"Good," he said cheerfully. "We will have many firsts."

"We already have." He heard another yawn. "But I'm afraid I'm going to fall asleep on you now."

"I wish you were here to actually fall asleep on me. Tomorrow night. Drive carefully. Sweet dreams."

"I will. You, too."

With some effort, he managed to set the phone aside. He flicked off the light and hugged a pillow to his chest. He'd nearly blown everything.

Her combination of innocence and daring had nearly done him in. He'd almost said *I love you.* He'd have to keep himself in better check than that. Would she flip out if he told her what he really felt about her?

And was he certain? He'd never been more certain — but he already had one ex. He hardly wanted to risk having another.

And Nadja would no doubt want her own children. He couldn't go through another birthing process. He'd nearly lost Danny twice now. He wasn't willing to set himself up for that kind of pain again.

"You didn't," Ivett said, bug-eyed. "You brought yourself off while he listened in?"

"Of course. That's what I just said." She flipped several switches on her coffeepots before turning back to her aunt. "That's why I'm thanking you again for the gift of the crystal wand."

Ivett nearly bounced from foot to foot. "Sometimes you amaze me. So did Kevin enjoy it?"

"It sounded like it. Why should this surprise you so much? It was fun. One of those fantasy tapes showed a couple having phone sex. Haven't you done that with Steve when he's away at a conference?"

"Yes, but that's me. We're talking about you."

"Ah." Nadja began scrubbing the counter. "Good old reliable, reserved Nadja."

"Something like that, I suppose. I'm sorry," Ivett said earnestly. "You're so full of surprises these days. It takes some getting used to. But I am so pleased for you. It's like someone has found a hidden grotto of pleasure in you that you didn't even know existed."

Nadja looked up from her work and grinned at her aunt. "You may be right." She sobered. "But will I be able to close the door when I must?"

"Maybe" — Ivett leaned closer — "you won't have to close

the door."

Nadja straightened. "I'm not *that* naïve." Her lips trembled slightly. "I'll throw the key away once I've closed the door this time."

"Don't be rash—even in your thinking. If this doesn't work out with Kevin, there are other guys. He should at least have opened your eyes to that reality. You are an attractive, engaging woman. Many men would love to share themselves with you."

Nadja returned to her coffee pots. She heard her aunt's footsteps as she left. At least Ivett had taken the hint.

She leaned back against the counter. She didn't want any other guy. She wasn't completely certain she wanted Kevin, but she knew she didn't want to replace him.

Her thoughts drifted again to her aunt's shocked reaction, and she smiled. It felt good, for a change, to be able to shock Ivett.

She inhaled deeply. And it had been immensely satisfying to listen to Kevin's breathing grow more haggard as she gave him a verbal tour of what she was doing with her body while he listened long distance. She was pleased he hadn't tried to take over by telling her what to do. Where had this inner seductress been all her life?

Wherever she'd come from, she wasn't ready to give her up yet.

Nadja raised her chin. There would be more surprises for Kevin. She wet her lips—maybe he'd have a few more for her, too.

Chapter Fourteen

Feeling awkward, Nadja tried not to stare at Amy Jacobson sitting in a booth across from her and Kevin in the small St. Paul restaurant. She hadn't planned on having brunch with a private investigator.

Kevin had sprung that surprise on her after they'd made love earlier in the morning. She'd hardly had time to explore his house before he whisked her away. Admittedly, she enjoyed many of his surprises. But this was not one of them.

He shouldn't have hired a private investigator to look into her troubles without talking to her first. And why couldn't he have found a male private investigator? And why did he have to choose a former lover?

She scowled. How former was Amy?

Kevin had shared that piece of information in an offhanded manner as they drove to the restaurant. At least he'd told her.

When they'd settled into the booth, Kevin had made the necessary introductions, the waitress had quickly taken their orders, and they'd chatted about matters that could hardly hold her concentration. She hoped her fury wasn't obvious.

How was she supposed to sit across from this sprite of a woman and talk about her troubles at the Cappuccino without imagining her and Kevin in bed? Had they been good together? As good as she and Kevin were? Why had they broken up? Was Kevin on the rebound? Were they finished?

They behaved like good friends with an acceptable level of friendliness and banter. They certainly looked much more comfortable than she was.

Amy gazed at her strangely. "It'll be a while before our food arrives. Nadja, why don't you and I go freshen up a bit?"

Trapped. She was trapped. She looked quickly at Kevin. How could he help? She didn't want to be alone with his former lover. But neither could she refuse such an innocent request.

She nodded and slid out of the bench seat when Kevin stood to let her pass. She straightened her shoulders. Maybe she did have a question or two to ask the redhead.

When they reached the outer area of the women's room, Amy motioned to a chair. "Why don't we sit for minute or two? It appears we have some matters to discuss without Kevin's ears."

Nadja settled in a chair next to Amy's. "Maybe we do."

"I'll go first," Amy said with a half-smile. "I assume from the look in your eyes that you know Kevin and I were once lovers."

"He did manage to say that on the way to the restaurant."

Amy chuckled. "Men are seldom comfortable talking about past relationships."

Nadja arched an eyebrow.

"And while we remain friends and work together at times, we are no longer lovers—haven't been for a long time."

"Why not?" Nadja frowned. "Why aren't you still lovers?"

"The chemistry wasn't right. We always seemed a little out of step, whether in bed or out. You, on the other hand, seem to have a very satisfying chemistry with Kevin."

"What do you mean by that?"

"He can hardly keep his eyes and hands off of you. And even though you're probably pissed as hell at him at the moment, you still indulge him with a self-conscious lover's smile. You'll forgive him for hiring me. He knows that. And you know that. Did he tell you I'm his boss's sister?"

"No." Nadja folded her hands in her lap. "That could be a

problem."

"It was — for both of us. My sister meant well. Kevin and I were coming off of rough experiences. She was only trying to help."

"But it didn't."

Amy's mouth curved into a smile. "I'm not going to tell you I didn't enjoy being with Kevin. I don't think you want me to lie to you."

"Please don't."

"There's a small part of me that's probably jealous of you. I wanted to make it work with Kevin, but it didn't. We both knew that — and we moved on."

"But you remain friends."

Amy nodded. "We're comfortable together. We don't often work together, but when we do, we seldom get in each other's way. Maybe you can think of us as cousins."

Nadja couldn't withhold a chuckle. "I've heard of kissing cousins."

"That'll work. A hug. A peck on the cheek. That's all. And . . ." Amy sobered. "A deep respect for each other. I wish him only the best, and I know the feeling is mutual. I hope, as you and I get to know each other better, that we'll be able to forge a bond of friendship, too."

"That takes time. I don't know how long I'll be around."

"Fair enough. But from what I've observed and heard, I'd wager you'll be around for quite a while." Amy got to her feet, and Nadja followed her lead.

Something clicked in Nadja's memory. "That's where I've seen you. You've stopped in the Cappuccino a couple times."

"I wanted to find out what all the fuss was about without letting you know why I was there. I hope you'll overlook that, but PIs are deceptive people."

"But now you are working for me?"

Amy scowled and glanced at her feet. "I'm working on

your behalf."

"Who is paying you?"

A flicker of dismay flashed across Amy's face.

"Be honest with me. Who is paying you?"

Amy shrugged. "Java Beans is paying half, and Kevin is paying the rest."

"His own money!" Nadja froze.

Amy nodded.

"We pay our own way."

"You'll have to be stubborn with Kevin," Amy quipped. "I just spend the money. I'm not particular about who pays me."

Nadja ground her fists against her thighs. She really had no reason to be angry with Amy. She should save her ire for Kevin. But she wasn't about to let him pay for her security. It wasn't that she hadn't thought about hiring a private investigator—but she'd had no knowledge of how to go about doing that. "How much?" she asked.

Amy took a half-step backward. "I'm on a retainer—a five thousand dollar retainer that can go up or down."

It was Nadja's turn to flush. Five thousand dollars! It wasn't like she and Ivett didn't have the money, but it wasn't sitting around in cash.

Amy stepped closer and grabbed her by the hand. "May I give you a little advice?"

Nadja scowled.

"You don't have to take it." Amy squeezed her fingers.

"Okay. What is it?"

"I think I understand how you must feel about some of this. Kevin isn't attempting to buy you."

"He isn't?"

Amy shook her head. "He would never have told you. I'm only telling you because you asked. And if I'm going to continue working on this case, I don't want you out of the loop any longer. You need to know what is happening. This entire situation can blow up in our faces at any moment."

Amy paused for breath. "So. I'd suggest you might consider splitting my fees three ways. Java Beans has a stake in all of this and will do most anything legal to preserve its reputation. Kevin feels responsible, rightly or wrongly. And I doubt you'll be able to talk him out of taking on a share of the costs. And of course you and your aunt are most directly affected by these threats and, at least from my point of view, have a right to know what's going on with the investigation and to pay your share." She smiled pertly. "I expect your money spends as well as Java Beans's and Kevin's"

Nadja mulled over Amy's suggestion and nodded her agreement. "Kevin won't be happy."

Amy laughed lightly. "I imagine you know more than one way to keep Kevin happy. We'd better head back to the booth before he storms the ladies' room."

"Thought you two got lost," Kevin groused as he stood to let her back into the booth. "You okay?" he asked softly, looking directly at her.

"I'm fine," she said, reaching for her purse. She grabbed her checkbook, wrote a check, and handed it to Kevin.

He glared at it. "What's this?"

"Ivett's and my share for Amy's retainer. You are taking one-third, Java Beans one-third. We have the other third."

Kevin blanched and then reddened. She gave him credit for not immediately ripping the check into tiny pieces. He shrugged at Amy. "I suppose this is your doing?"

"Nadja asked. I did suggest thirds might be an equitable solution." She narrowed her eyes at him. "Then no one feels bought or particularly obligated."

"I see." He sighed. "Sounds like a done deal. We'll talk about this later. For now, I want to hear what you've found out. Seems like you're getting paid, no matter what."

"Of course I am. I don't guarantee results, only work."

"And?"

"At least five different holding companies own properties adjacent to the Cappuccino." She must've seen Nadja's puzzled look. "Holding companies, at least in this case, are corporations who have ownership of land and buildings—but they make it very difficult to discover who actually owns the holding companies."

"Oh, I see. Secret landlords."

"That's right. We have managed to get behind three of the holding companies. Rick Adams is involved in each of them."

"That's progress," Kevin said eagerly. "Are there other names in common?"

Amy smiled easily. "You're getting ahead of me. I'm the sleuth, but then I forgot you enjoying sleuthing too."

Nadja frowned. What did Amy mean by that comment? She tried to listen carefully. When Amy got excited, she spoke very rapidly. Nadja feared she was losing some things in translation.

"We do have a couple overlapping names—none appears on every corporation. But the overlapping names are aliases of known Chicago mob members."

Nadja froze. Kevin clutched her hand in his. She knew about mobsters. She'd watched too many old movies not to. And her country had such ruthless men also. "Why?" she squeaked. "Why would mobsters want the Cappuccino?"

Amy shook her head in dismay. "We still don't have an answer for that, though it does seem clear that someone wants to own all the property in your block. We just don't know why. We'll find out. Sometimes this kind of work takes a lot of time. We're dealing with people who don't want to be discovered."

"What about the threatening call Nadja received last weekend?" Kevin asked.

"I have some questions for Nadja about that. It will help to talk with her directly." She scowled at Kevin. "Now that we're not trying to protect her from her own fears."

Nadja thrust out her jaw at Kevin. "You and I will want to talk about that later, too. I don't need or want that kind of protection. What questions do you have for me?" She shoved aside her half-eaten omelet. Was it her imagination, or had she seldom eaten an entire meal when Kevin was around?

"I take it from Kevin they've given up on Java Beans buying you out."

"Yes, that's what the man said."

"And he wants you to list the property on the open market."

"That's right."

"They're really into covering their tracks." She glanced at Kevin. "And they seem quite confident they will be the highest bidder. They could try to win by force, but that's really hard to do if there are a number of interested parties." She shrugged. "Maybe they're confident their scheme is such a moneymaker they can afford to outbid anyone—though they will need inside information from a realtor to know what the other bids are."

Nadja arched an eyebrow at Kevin.

He nodded at her. "You must know he's up to his neck in this somehow."

She sighed heavily. "Even Ivett suspects. I don't understand Steve. He loves Ivett so very much. It doesn't make sense that he'd do anything to tear her down."

Nadja didn't go after the pained look on Amy's face. She waited as patiently as she could for more questions. She was nearly exhausted from this morning's adventure.

"This man's threats," Amy asked. "How specific were they?"

"He said accidents can happen"—she bit her trembling

lip—"even to little boys."

Amy curled her fingers and flexed them before responding. "He's probably trying to get an emotional response out of you. If these folks don't want to show themselves as potential bidders for the property, they're not going to want to be identified with personal violence. Vandalism and harassment are quite different from causing bodily harm."

"So what do we do?" Kevin asked, showing some impatience.

"There may be more calls." She peered at Nadja. "We could tap your phone."

Nadja squeezed Kevin's thigh, and his hand settled over hers. She shook her head. "No, I won't have that. This is America."

"Thought that might be your response. Okay for now. But if this escalates much more, I will ask you to reconsider. Okay?"

"Okay," Nadja whispered.

"I want you to call me immediately if anything happens." She ripped a piece of paper from a pad. "Here is my cell phone and my home phone. Call me at any time of the day or night."

Nadja nodded. "I hope I won't have to."

"Me, too. Now, I've taken enough of your Saturday morning. New lovers shouldn't have to put up with private investigators—or," she added with a smile, "former lovers for longer than an hour or so at a time."

Nadja smiled warmly at her. She couldn't pinpoint when she'd decided to trust her, but she had. And she even felt at ease with Amy teasing about her prior relationship with Kevin. That was a huge step, but at least no one was trying to hide or pretend the relationship hadn't happened or didn't matter.

With Nadja's arm tucked through his, Kevin pulled her off the walking path to stand on a small deck overlooking the lake. He slung an arm around her waist and tugged her close.

She leaned into him as if it were the most natural thing to do. "I can't get over how beautiful it is here. And this spot is right in the middle of the city."

"That's right. There are lots of lakes within the boundaries of St. Paul and Minneapolis. People here pride themselves on maintaining at least a touch of the country in their midst."

"The water could be cleaner, but the sounds are delightful. Look"—she pointed skyward—"a pair of geese. Don't they look majestic?"

He watched them extending their wings to brake for a landing. If he had wings, he'd do the same thing. Nadja had hardly mentioned their brunch with Amy, and he hadn't been eager to bring the subject up either. But they'd better talk about it soon, or it would fester. The two geese paddled their way toward where he and Nadja stood, probably looking for a handout. "I forgot to bring bread," he said as the geese turned away.

"Seeds would be better," Nadja said. "Bread is not part of a normal goose diet."

"I didn't know you were an expert on goose diet."

She turned in his arms to look directly at him. "Are you angry with me?"

"Not yet." He glanced away. "Maybe a little frustrated. Why aren't you grilling me about Amy, about brunch, about hiring a private investigator?"

She giggled and grazed her lips across his neck. "Because I like to watch you stew. And I very much like to keep you guessing."

"You don't have to work very hard at that." He stuffed his hands in his pockets.

"So why did you go behind my back and hire a private investigator?"

"My boss came up with the idea first."

"But you agreed. And you chose to say nothing to me."

He exhaled. "That's right. I thought maybe it would blow over quick."

"And you didn't think I'd like the idea of someone snooping around my business."

"Um." He'd often found the best strategy with women was to impart as little information as possible.

"Did you really think I wouldn't learn about Amy at some point?"

He shrugged. "You know now."

"Only because things have gotten worse."

"If you must know, Amy insisted. She needs to have direct access to you."

"Good for Amy!" Nadja reached out and cradled his chin. "Amy thinks I'll forgive you for not telling me you hired her — and for not telling me you and she were lovers."

"I did," he said reflexively.

"About thirty seconds before I met Amy. Thankfully, for you, I like Amy. She wants to be above board and honest with me. I appreciate that very much."

He scrunched his mouth. "Yeah, well she could keep her mouth shut more often. So are you going to forgive me?"

She reached around him, tucked a hand in each of his jeans pockets, and pulled him close. His arousal was swift and hard. "What do you think?"

"I'm not sure I like that sudden gleam in your eye."

"Ivett is the churchgoer, but I do know that forgiveness for a good Russian Orthodox — and I assume for a Roman Catholic — is not expected without due penance."

He relaxed a trifle and cupped her rear in his palms. "And what sort of penance do you have in mind? And how much?"

She shook her pretty head, and her eyes filled with humor. "I haven't decided yet. But I will. I've been considering that question for hours. I'll let you know when I've chosen."

"I don't suppose I have a say in this matter of penance?"

"Of course not. What a ridiculous thought."

"Maybe tonight?"

"Maybe. Maybe not. We will have to wait and see."

"For someone who doesn't like secrets, you can be damn coy when you want to be."

"A woman can be veiled without being secretive."

"Is that Ukrainian folk wisdom?"

"Perhaps."

"Ah—so you won't even disclose the source of your wisdom."

She raised her lips to his, and he met them greedily. She even tasted wise. He slipped off her mouth and nibbled at her earlobe; her moans soothed him. "You know, a veiled woman can be very seductive."

She pressed her lips against his forehead. "I certainly hope so. I fully intend on seducing you. Maybe I should wear a veil the next time we make love."

"Thank you for taking me to the symphony. It was splendid." Nadja tapped her wine glass against Kevin's, and he nodded smugly. She'd known better than to suggest splitting the expenses. After all, he was courting her.

She wasn't exactly sure how to feel about that. But he'd made it clear they were dating, unless she wanted out. She didn't want out. Strange, though—in her country, couples typically dated *before* having sex, not the other way around. Though she wouldn't have taken back anything they'd shared. Odd that Amy hadn't found him more satisfying in bed. It was difficult to imagine a more satisfying partner.

She settled back against the couch, appreciating the feel of his thigh pressed against hers, and glanced around his oak-paneled living room. It was a masculine room. In fact, the entire house was masculine—lean, but rather stark. He'd told her he had a housekeeper come in once a week. Even his furniture was typically dark and heavy. He apparently didn't have a broad range of tastes when it came to home decorating. Her place looked like an artist's palette compared to this.

She curled her toes in the thick carpet and peeked over at Kevin, who eyed her with no effort to mask his hunger. Would he ever be sated? She rotated her head slowly. That was a fair question for her, too. Her answer was *no*. What was his answer? "Was she good in bed?"

Kevin jerked as if he'd been prodded with a sharp stick. "What?"

Apparently he hadn't anticipated her question. "Amy," she said, with a half-smile. "Was she good in bed?"

"Have I asked you about any of your men?"

"No, but then you didn't know any of them, either. And if you did ask, I would tell you. I'm not expecting step-by-step details."

"Well, at least that's something." He reached across the small space separating them and cupped a silk-covered breast with his palm. "She was good. We were good together. But bells didn't go off. We never quite meshed. But Amy is history. Why should you wonder?"

"Because the two of you have achieved something most couples don't. You've remained friends."

"And that threatens you?"

She shook her head. "Should it?"

"Of course not."

"So how are *we* different?"

"Ah, the real question, at last." Sliding a finger along her nose and tapping its tip, Kevin chuckled. "You are creative and innovative. Innocent, yet daring. You make me feel like I'm a hundred feet tall, and then you can slice me down to the size of peanut."

Nadja glanced at his crotch and snickered. "You don't look like a peanut now."

He tried calmly to straighten his cock, which she'd noticed had grown considerably in the last minute or two. "With you, I sometimes can't stop the chimes ringing in my head."

He folded her hands in his. "Seriously, Nadja, I've never felt more at one with a woman than I have with you. I can't explain it. It simply is."

She wet her lips and lightly grazed his erection — she'd also become more than a little aroused. Her wetness attested to that simple fact. "I know. You don't have to explain. Being with you is very special for me, too."

"I like being with you, Nadja. And I'm not only talking about in bed."

She tried to breathe. "I know," she muttered. "Me, too."

This was definitely one of those moments when she hated depending upon a second language; not that she'd be very clear in her native tongue, either. What was Kevin trying to say?

"I know it's too soon for us to talk about anything permanent."

Was it? Maybe he was right. At least she could breathe again. And she didn't have to seriously consider things she'd only just begun to fantasize about. "Yes, it is too soon for that."

"Then you have thought about it?"

Trapped. Why did she feel so trapped lately? She took in a sharp breath and let it out slowly. "Yes. I've never been involved with a man for this length of time."

"Really?" He leaned back and admired her. "I find that hard to believe. But then you can be a fairly testy woman."

She swallowed and let out a breath. "Did you find out what you wanted to?"

"Yes. I didn't want to be the only one agonizing about possibilities."

"You're not the only one."

"Good. Then I would like to present you with a token of possibilities."

She flinched when he withdrew a small box from the sofa cushion.

"You are a proud woman, Nadja. You probably don't accept gifts easily."

She shook her head and held her breath.

"We are lovers," he said, softly. "I think we've established that. And we are dating—perhaps it's called courting in your country."

"Oh, my gosh." Involuntarily, her hand flew to cover her mouth.

He nodded. "I thought as much."

She watched his fingers pry open the lid of the box and hand it to her. A sparkling blue sapphire winked at her, set on a delicate gold chain. "My goodness. For me?" Her voice squeaked, and she couldn't hold back tears. "No man has ever . . ."

"I'm not just any man."

"I know. I know. But this is too much. I can't."

"Nadja, Nadja," he chastised. "We just agreed we are lovers and that I'm courting you. This is what lovers do." He stared at her for what seemed like much too long. "I don't know how this will end up, but I'm going to risk sharing my heart with you. I've only used these words with one other woman."

He flinched. "That might not inspire confidence. Anyway, I love you, Nadja. I can't tell you exactly why, and I sure don't know where we're headed. But I do know I love you very,

very much. Sometimes, so much I'm in danger of bursting."

"Oh, Kevin," Nadja blubbered. "I've never been in love before, but I think I love you. I doubt if my feelings are wise, but I won't deny them."

She slid easily into his arms and let him kiss her tears away, gulping and gasping for breath. She'd never dared think about actually saying those words—and here she'd gone and blurted them out. Now what?

"May I put this pendant on you?"

She nodded, trying to focus on Kevin. Sometimes there seemed to be more than one of him.

He began unbuttoning her blouse. She arched an eyebrow at him.

"For days I've imagined this sapphire nestled between your beautiful naked breasts. If you don't have an objection, I'm going to find out if reality matches my imagination."

She grinned. "I have no objection to you satisfying your strange curiosity."

She shrugged out of her blouse and let him unsnap her bra. Together they slid it aside; his eyes gleamed as he looked at her. She was surprised, if not disappointed, that he failed to touch or fondle her tits. Instead he placed the pendant chain around her neck and clasped it. And then he settled the jewel between her breasts.

He bent back and smiled broadly. "Better than my imagination. Much better. You are stunning." Finally he cradled a breast in each palm, swirling a thumb around each nipple.

Nadja moaned her appreciation.

He lifted one breast to his mouth and kissed its protruding nipple, then did the same to the other. He lifted the jewel and brought it to his lips, and then to hers. "May you wear this close to your heart and remember the love it symbolizes."

"I will," she whispered. "Believe me, I will."

Kevin held her gaze. "I want to make love to you. Right

here. Right now."

She intertwined her fingers behind his head. "I want you to make love to me. I want us to make love to each other. Right here. Right now."

"Would you stand?"

She rose to her feet and stood in front of him. He reached for the zipper on the side of her skirt. He eased it down until it pooled at her feet, and she kicked it aside.

He knelt and lapped at her silk panties; she clutched his head and writhed against his open mouth. "Sweet," she crooned. "I'm already creaming."

"I know," he whispered. "And I love that you are so responsive."

He kneaded her butt. She squirmed—she didn't even want silk to come between them. Hooking her thumbs over the panties, she worked them lower. He gave up his perch only long enough to tug her panties over her thighs and down her legs.

She kicked them aside and widened her stance, welcoming Kevin's probing. He plundered her as if he'd never tasted her before. Fingers and tongue moved in and out and around her until she lost track of where he was. She only knew the wellspring of emotion coiling beyond his probing.

She stood on her toes and swayed against him. Moist fingers slid the length of the crease of her buttocks. One tapped on her rosebud. "So exquisite," she mewed.

She cried out his name and chanted silently *love, love, love.* Her inner world crashed in waves. His sipping became swallowing as his large hands kneaded her buttocks, demanding more. She rocked against his mouth, and his finger slipped into her ass. She threw her head back and wailed as her juices released in wave after wave. Clenching Kevin's head between her thighs, she feared he might leave her prematurely. She had so much more to give him.

He didn't disappoint. He stayed with her. His tongue sought more and more of her. Her legs shook against him as she came again and again. At last he guided her back to the couch, where she curled up in his arms and let herself cherish the aftershocks of love.

Savoring her taste, Kevin held Nadja close and settled back against the sofa. He loved it when she lost control and simply gave herself to him. Now, if she needed to nap, that was fine with him. They had all night. They might have a lifetime. Wasn't that the implication of their words?

Would she insist on marriage? They lived in a fairly tolerant society. And he'd heard that many Europeans considered the blessings of the church somewhat incidental.

He kissed her brow and lightly rubbed her shoulders. Would she insist on living in Jefferson City? He could probably handle that, though it would likely mean more traveling. And he was tiring of always being en route to someplace else.

Half-asleep, she snuggled closer, and he cupped her bottom. Even with his eyes closed, he knew the topology of her body like the back of his own hand. Would she insist on children? He tried not to choke. What if she did? Danny's birth had nearly been disastrous. Could he do that again? Could he risk losing Nadja? Did she have any idea about the overwhelming responsibility of raising a child? He shuddered, remembering Danny lying in the hospital bed in a coma, hooked up to machines that both provided and monitored life.

"Umm," she whispered in his ear, "that was spectacular. I will miss this. You don't have to come back with me."

Kevin gave his lover a piercing look. "I thought we'd finished that debate. We'll go back together, and that's final."

Nadja giggled. "You look so male when your nostrils flare

like that."

"Guess that happens when I'm angry."

She batted her eyelashes. "They also flare just before you climax."

"You must be quite observant."

"I've had to learn to be." She clutched her sapphire in her hand. "Especially when it comes to men."

He steadied his breathing and watched her trace the length of his arousal through his trousers with her index finger, her gaze focused on her finger. Was she mesmerized by his erection, by her finger, or by the reaction she incited? His cock strained against her touch, and she giggled softly.

"I think someone wants to come out and play," she said, tugging at his zipper.

He helped her by undoing his buckle. She dipped her fingers under his boxers and drew out his length; he groaned as she lowered her mouth to wet his crown.

She peeked back up at him and slid to the floor, pulling his trousers down with her. With some effort, she disentangled them and tossed them aside. With his trousers no longer impeding her progress, she spread his knees wide and settled between them.

Both of her hands curled around him and she smiled brightly. "I want to taste you like you tasted me. Don't try and stop me this time."

Alarms rattled in his brain as she awaited his assent. "Are you sure?"

She nodded. "Positive. Never more so. I want you to come in my mouth."

He licked his lips and managed to perceptibly raise and lower his chin. She gave him a devilish grin in return and flicked her tongue to graze the tip of his cock. He tried to relax. This wasn't going to be quick. Where had Nadja learned about erotic torture? He grinned to himself—maybe from him.

He kept his eyes open, not wanting to miss any of her efforts at teasing and torture. She licked him from base to tip, focusing on her work, and then on his eyes. His shaft weaved back and forth.

"I believe your cock is looking for a warm home." She chuckled. "Should I put him out of his misery?"

"He is feeling loved," Kevin grunted, "but a little lost. A warm moist home might be just what he needs."

Nadja pursed her lips and placed them around his cock-head.

Kevin sighed deeply. The warmth of her mouth infused heat throughout his body. "Ah," he moaned. "Home at last."

He heard her muffled giggle as she took more of him into her mouth. She closed her eyes, no longer paying attention to anything but what she was doing to him and for him. He rested his hands on her shoulders. He had to touch her, to feel her quivering flesh, but he held her gently in case she changed her mind.

He watched her blonde head slowly rise and lower. She cradled his balls as if she were painting one of her precious dolls. He inched forward, his toes curling in the carpet.

Her bobbing quickened. The sapphire hanging from her neck behaved like a pendulum. He dug his fingernails into her shoulders. There was no turning back now, and they both knew it. One of her fingers found that sensitive spot between balls and asshole, and he was gone.

His hips bucked beneath her. Instead of backing off, she seemed spurred into a frenzy by his response. His hamstrings burned. Could she sense him expanding? Could she sense him nearing?

"Good God," he shouted, "you've got me, woman. All of me." She didn't flinch at his warning. "Oh, hell."

He flexed his hips, matching her stroke for stroke. His

release came in spurts. He watched her throat muscles working rapidly to keep up with him.

At last he brushed at his eyes as she slowed her efforts but continued to pump him steadily. Would she ever stop? Would he ever stop coming? He clutched her head between his hands and helped her slow and steady herself. His cock softened, and she lifted her head and greeted him with a broad, triumphant smile.

"Beyond my wildest dreams," she purred, licking her lips. "You taste fabulous. And there was so much of you." With obvious effort, she climbed up beside him.

He kissed her cheek, her nose, and her lips. Whatever he did, Nadja couldn't stop grinning. "Amazing. You must be the eighth wonder of the world. I may not recover for days."

She chuckled against his neck. "I'm glad I could do that for you, for us." She leaned away from him, so obviously comfortable with their nakedness, and cradled her pendant. "I will cherish this moment and this sapphire always."

With his heart soaring, Kevin couldn't form words. He reached for Nadja and hugged her against his chest as close as he possibly could. He wished he could keep her with him in St. Paul, where she would be safe. But that wasn't possible. They would drive back to Jefferson City tomorrow.

CHAPTER FIFTEEN

"Oh my God! Who would do such a thing?" Nadja wailed, dashing across her patio. Numb, she came to a halt at the edge of the pile of rubble that was all that remained of her wonderful gazebo.

She heard Kevin's feet pounding behind her. His arms surrounded her, and she shuddered against his chest. So many dreams shattered. So much work for nothing. Would she feel more violated if she'd been battered?

"Why?" she muttered.

"To frighten you." He held her tighter.

"I don't know what is worse — that the gazebo is destroyed, or that it was torn apart so methodically. There must not be a nail or a screw left in place."

"This took some time to do, but I imagine whoever did it was much less likely to be noticed than if they'd been loudly smashing it to bits. Or if they had been noticed, they might've been mistaken for a construction worker. Perhaps even had a story prepared that you wanted the gazebo replaced while you were away."

"There's not even a message."

He gripped her tighter. "There's a message, all right. We only have to fill in the blanks."

"Sell or else?"

"Something like that."

"Should we call the police?"

"Probably, though it's not likely any fingerprints were left behind."

"No, I don't suppose so. And if we call the police, this will get in the paper again. I don't want that. Amy will want to know what happened."

"I'll let her know." Kevin left her to sift through the debris. "Do you want to salvage any of this? I can find out how we rent a dumpster, if you want."

She nodded. "It doesn't look like much to save. And I don't think I could ever be comfortable in it again, knowing that someone dismantled it this way."

"Maybe after all this crap is settled, you'll want to erect another one."

"Maybe."

"We might want to do some more stargazing."

She smiled through tears. "I had planned on that. I was looking forward to it." She frowned. "My telescope. Do you see it? Is it in pieces, too?"

"I'll look further."

She watched Kevin carefully lift board after board. Even her desk had been taken apart piece by piece. She gasped when he uncovered the new daybed, its frame busted and its cushions ripped. There was nothing of value left.

"I see it," he called out, straddling a pile that included the Levolor blinds. He held up the telescope and beamed. "It appears to be in one piece."

Her legs shook terribly, but she made her way to where he stood and accepted the fine old instrument he handed to her. "Why?" she struggled to say. "Why would anyone save this, given the total devastation of everything else?"

"Who knows?" Kevin dislodged himself from the rubble and coming to stand beside her. "Maybe the creep forgot to get back to it. It must've been one of the first items he disposed of, given how deeply buried it was."

"Maybe he did forget. Maybe the rubble protected it." Her lips curved slightly. "Maybe there is a God. I have owned this since I was a child. It was a gift from my father before he went off to war."

"I'm glad it was saved. At least you have this treasure."

"And," she whispered, "my memories."

Grimly, Kevin glanced about the Chambers's neighborhood before ringing the doorbell. He'd had a busy morning since Nadja left for the shop. He'd called Amy to inform her about the gazebo, then located a company that would deliver a dumpster that morning, and now he was ready to confront a man he should've challenged earlier.

Shortly after he pressed the buzzer, Steve Chambers cracked open the door.

It looked like he hadn't shaved yet. Maybe he was a late sleeper. "I've got to talk with you."

Steve hesitated and then opened the door wider. "I don't have much time. I'm showing a property in an hour."

"I won't keep you long," Kevin replied, wedging the door open with his shoulder. He stood in the foyer. Steve couldn't hold his stare. "I need a favor."

The man visibly relaxed some. "Sure. How can I help you? I thought you were done looking at properties."

"I am." He fixed his gaze on Steve's. "I need to borrow one of those guns you had out at the gravel pit."

"What!" Steve stumbled backward as if he'd been slapped.

Kevin tried to ignore the wave of relief he felt at Steve's shock. It seemed unlikely Ivett's husband knew about the gazebo. "Someone methodically dismantled Nadja's gazebo over the weekend."

"Jesus." Steve wiped his mouth with the back of his hand. "Methodically. What do you mean?"

"It wasn't the work of your typical vandal. Every piece was taken apart, as if the guy was a surgeon."

"Damn."

"I'd like that Colt of yours, if you don't mind." Steve nodded. "I should've brought my own, but I didn't. I don't want to be away from Nadja long enough to run back to the Cities to get it. And I doubt I'll be able to buy one locally very quickly, given that I'm not a resident."

"No problem," Steve stammered. "I'll go get it. Why don't you wait in the kitchen? The coffee is fairly fresh."

Kevin strolled into the kitchen and poured himself a cup of coffee. He swallowed and smiled. He'd recognize Nadja's coffee anywhere.

He didn't have to wait long before Steve reappeared with the Colt and a box of shells. Without a word, he set them down on the table next to Kevin, then grabbed a mug and refilled it.

He came back and drew up a chair opposite him. "I know you know how to use that—better than I do. But I hope you won't have to."

"I hope I won't either. I saw enough gunshot wounds in Bosnia to last a lifetime."

"Oh."

"Are you ready to tell me how you're involved in all of this?"

Steve glanced at the gun.

"Don't worry, damn it, I'm not going to shoot you." He paused long enough to notice Steve squirm. "At least not yet. Let me help you. I know about your strained relationship with Rick." He watched fear flicker across Steve's face. "I know about the co-ed, Steve."

Steve turned ashen. "What? How could you?"

"You'd be amazed at what a good private investigator can find when she puts her nose to the ground."

"You hired a private investigator." He gasped. "A woman."

"I don't know how trustworthy the local cops are going to be if this involves one of their long-time residents, like it seems to."

"The chief is beyond reach."

"Even Rick's?"

Steve nodded. "Even Rick's. Maybe especially his. Their relationship soured years ago."

"What about other cops?"

"It's not a small force." Steve shrugged. "It's hard to imagine Rick doesn't have someone in his pocket."

"That's what I thought. I take it your old college roommate provided you with an airtight alibi when you needed it. And he's still holding that favor over your head."

"Something like that." Kevin watched Steve's fingers clench. "But you have to believe me—I did not kill Mary Beth."

"If I didn't believe that, you and I wouldn't be having this conversation.

Steve's brows flew up.

"That seems to surprise you. I could be wrong, but I've learned to rely on my gut when things really get bad. Did it ever occur to you that you may have been set up to take a murder rap?"

"Not at the time." He reached for the coffee mug, but his fingers trembled too much to lift it. He gave up. "That possibility occurred to me years later."

"And who might've been in a position to set you up?"

Steve only glared.

Kevin broke the silence. "Rick Adams."

"Yes, if I was set up. But I don't know why he would do such a thing, or how. And someone killed her. He didn't do it, if that's what you're thinking. His alibi was better than mine."

"Perhaps. Perhaps he lied to you. In any case, he might've

planned the murder."

"That's possible, I guess. But the police never considered him a suspect."

"Do you know that for a fact? Have you seen the police files?"

"No, but . . ."

"Ah, hell," Kevin said in frustration. "Why are we wasting time talking about the past? The real question is, what are you going to do now? I assume from the way you've been behaving that Ivett doesn't know about any of this history."

"That's right."

"You're going to have to tell her."

"Because you know?"

"Because a private investigator knows, and because I know. And because I'm going to tell Nadja. I won't keep this from her. She has a right to know how she has become a pawn in a much larger game. You can tell your wife, or she will find out from your niece."

"What choice do I have? I'll tell her tonight. I'd appreciate it if you don't tell Nadja until tomorrow."

"I'll give you until tomorrow at noon. So, how involved are you in this larger game to get a hold of the Henderson building?"

Steve's shoulders slumped. "I agreed to take you to undesirable properties. I think Rick hasn't trusted me beyond that."

"Maybe he's smarter than I thought," Kevin grunted. "Do you know why he wants that building so badly?"

Steve shook his head. "He won't say. I do know he's not alone in this."

"Yeah, looks like he has some Chicago friends."

"They're not real friendly types. I've met a couple of his *friends* over the years."

"I'm sure my PI will want to talk with you about that. I

assume you're willing to talk to her?"

"Do we have to do it here?"

"No. I'll check with her, but I'm sure she'll meet you in Minnesota." He smiled grimly. "Perhaps that gravel pit will do."

"Rick claims to own most of the property in the Henderson block. I've never attempted to verify that. It would take a lot of effort."

"Doesn't appear he's bragging. His fingerprints or those of his friends seem to be on most of the land and buildings in that block. Has he made personal threats against Nadja or Ivett?"

"Nothing more than that he's pissed as hell and won't let Nadja stand in his way. Rick can be a lot of hot air at times."

"But not all the time."

"That's right."

Kevin stood and picked up the Colt and cartridges. "Thanks for the coffee. I'll see that this gets back to you. And you have until noon tomorrow before I bring Nadja up to date on your past misadventures."

Trying not to be obvious, Kevin glanced at the clock on the mantle again. He peeked at Nadja, who sat across from him, focused intently on a pattern she was sketching for another of her eggs. She'd told him that doing such intricate work often relaxed her.

Given what he knew — or at least, hoped — was taking place at her aunt's house, he didn't expect Nadja would have much of an opportunity for relaxing.

The phone rang. Nadja set aside her work and headed for the kitchen. "Who could be calling this late? It's nearly ten."

She wasn't gone more than a few minutes. When she reentered the living room, she appeared nearly as shell-shocked as she had when they'd first spied the destroyed gazebo.

"That was Ivett," she announced in a hushed tone. "She and Steve are coming over."

He stood and reached for her. Instead of folding into his embrace, she pounded his chest with her fists. "You didn't tell me!" she snapped. "I knew Amy wanted to say more, but you wouldn't let her. Why? Why do you keep doing this to me?"

Kevin grabbed both of her wrists, an attempt at self-preservation as well as an effort to calm her. "I wanted Steve to tell his wife and you himself. I figured I owed him that opportunity. If he hadn't said anything by tomorrow noon, I would've told you. Believe me, Nadja, I didn't enjoy keeping this from you. But it seemed best that Steve have the chance to come clean with you and your aunt."

She squinted at him through tears. "You're not lying? You would've told me tomorrow?"

"Ask Steve. I gave him a little more than twenty-four hours to make up for years of deceit. And apparently he has talked to Ivett."

"Yes. She gave me the short version." She looked away and then back at him. "I can't believe he killed that girl."

"I can't either. If I did, I probably would have told you sooner without talking to Steve first. If I believed he was a threat to you or your aunt, I would've taken the initiative."

She nodded and wiped at her eyes. "I do think it was important for him to be the one to tell Ivett. But you still should've told me."

"And you wouldn't have immediately gone to tell your aunt?"

"I would've. You know I would've." She molded her body into his, and he folded his arms around her. "That would've been terrible. Ivett is having a hard enough time. If I had learned about Steve first, she would never have forgiven you, and maybe not me."

"Does this mean I'm back in your good graces?"

She nodded against his shirt. She leaned back and looked at him, and he brushed away the tears still clinging to her cheeks.

She gave him a wobbly grin. "This is one more deception I'll have to take into consideration as I plot your penance."

He kissed her forehead. Puckering her lips in invitation, she tilted her head. He grazed her lips, then nipped at the corners of her mouth. They held each other for a long moment. Too bad they couldn't simply spend the rest of the night clinging to each other, but that wasn't going to happen — not with Ivett and her husband on the way.

Glancing at the others sitting at her kitchen table, Nadja couldn't remember ever crying so much. Nor had she ever witnessed so many tears. Ivett cried every five minutes or so. Steve had been a basket case, crying and cussing at his lack of confidence in his wife and pleading for her love.

Nadja squeezed Kevin's hand in her lap. She'd been gripping his hand so hard for so long, he might want it back to stretch some muscles. Even Kevin's eyes had misted several times.

Was he questioning his involvement with her and her family? If so, he didn't show any outward signs. So far, he'd been her rock ever since they'd discovered the gazebo. She'd never thought she needed a rock. But she was discovering it was good, now and then, to know that someone else had more strength in the moment than she did. There was no question she was prepared to provide him with the same kind of support if he needed it.

"Where do we go from here?" Kevin asked quietly.

Both Ivett and Steve stiffened and avoided looking at each other. Nadja knew Kevin had asked the right question. If someone hadn't asked that question soon, they might've sat at that table until the sun came up.

Steve turned to his wife and cleared his throat. "I'll leave, if you want me to. I'll understand."

Ivett's eyes begged her for intervention or wisdom or something, but Nadja held her tongue. Ivett had to work this part out.

After what seemed like minutes, Ivett turned to face her husband. "I should kick you out on your lying ass." Her brow furrowed. "I know you didn't actually lie to me, but how was I supposed to know to ask if you'd ever been a murder suspect?"

Steve closed his eyes and reopened them. "You didn't have a crystal ball."

"No, and I still don't," she huffed. She heaved a huge sigh. "No, I don't want you to move out. We've had too many good times for that. And I do believe you didn't kill that girl."

"That's something." Steve's voice was nearly inaudible.

"But believe me," Ivett glared hard at her husband, "you will be paying me back for this for the rest of your life — since I've decided not to kill you first."

"Whatever you want."

"You two are my witnesses. Whatever I want. That may very well be an endless list."

Kevin's fingers tightened around Nadja's. "You Ukrainian women do seem to have a penchant for enjoying wielding control over your men."

Ivett ignored Kevin's comment. "You can sleep on the couch until I decide if and when I want to share my body with you."

Steve nodded. "I understand. However long it takes."

Nadja smiled when she saw her aunt bat an eyelash. "That may depend on how long my batteries last."

Again, Steve nodded.

"Your batteries?" Kevin blurted out.

"Shh," Nadja whispered in his ear. "She's talking about her sex toy batteries."

Kevin blushed, and Nadja couldn't help smiling. She knew he wanted to ask why Ivett didn't go out and buy more batteries. She might try to explain that answer to him later.

"I do wish you had trusted me." Ivett looked sadly at Steve. "I still love you and I know you love me, but how am I going to be able to trust you?"

If Steve sank any further, he'd be under the table.

"Perhaps" — Nadja flinched at the sound of her own voice — "perhaps Steve can begin earning that trust back by being straightforward with us about his dealings with Rick and our building."

Ivett nodded and glared at her husband.

Steve held his palms up. "As I've told Kevin, Rick doesn't tell me much about his plans. I don't know why he wants the building. I don't know how he's planning on getting it — but I do know he won't give up easily. The guy has a long memory."

"Maybe we need to clarify whether you're on our team or his," Kevin pressed on. "What are you going to do if Rick comes to you with another scheme?"

"Listen. And let you all know."

"That's a start," Ivett said. "I suppose."

"And you'll cooperate with the private investigator?"

Steve scowled at Kevin. "I told you I would."

"I just want the women to be part of this. No more secrets."

Steve snorted. "Bet you didn't tell Nadja you borrowed one of my revolvers."

Nadja turned sharply to Kevin.

"I hadn't gotten around to it yet." He scrunched his mouth. "Do I have to tell you everything I do?"

She grinned. "Only when it affects me. I assume this gun is in the house now."

"Yes."

A choirboy would not have looked more contrite. "Then it affects me. I appreciate knowing, even if you weren't forth-coming about it." She eyed him evenly. "Why didn't you ask to borrow my gun?"

"Your gun?" Kevin nearly bolted out of his chair. "Your gun?" he repeated.

"I'm a woman used to living alone. I own a pistol." She narrowed her eyes at him. "And I guarantee I know how to use it."

"Shit! Asking you for a gun never occurred to me."

"That and a few other things. Be that as it may"—she glanced at Ivett—"if we have our overly protective men back on track, we may want to call it a night." She glanced at the kitchen clock. "Or an early morning. We do have to be at the shops to open."

"We've come a long way." Ivett nodded. "Looks like we both need to keep closer tabs on our guys."

Nadja stood. "You take care of yours. I have plans for mine."

She did her best not to look at Kevin. She did wonder if he was grinning or scowling—but she didn't want him to know she was curious.

Unable to sleep, Kevin cradled Nadja in his arms, pondering for the umpteenth time what he'd gotten himself into and whether he should get out. He squeezed his eyes shut. It was too late to get out. Why was he even kidding himself with that question? He was hooked—solidly.

Where had that asshole Steve Chambers come up with the idea of telling the women he'd borrowed one of his guns? He peeked at Nadja, who was breathing evenly. And why would a beautiful woman like her own a gun, and on top of that, know how to use it? Cripes. She was beyond his capacity for reason.

And wasn't that part of what he loved about her? She was different from any woman he'd ever known. Maybe part of that could be explained by her having been raised in a different culture, or by her accent. But he seriously believed whatever mold was used to create her had been shattered into a million pieces; she had to be one in a million.

He laid his lips on her temple, and she moaned softly. They'd both been too exhausted to even attempt making love. They didn't have to — it had been enough simply to hold each other.

His eyes popped open. They couldn't go on simply hugging each other and ignoring the world around them. In the morning, he'd call Amy and fill her in. Maybe it was time to begin thinking about ways to flush Rick and his partners out of their holes.

He lay back against the pillows and closed his eyes. He'd let Nadja know when there was something to tell her. He never promised he'd tell her everything he was thinking about. She wouldn't like it, but somehow, he figured he'd enjoy whatever penance she might devise to pay him back.

"This may be the break that'll take some heat off the Henderson building," Amy Jacobson said, handing Kevin a sheaf of papers.

They sat in Amy's car in a Jefferson City shopping center parking lot. Kevin scanned the top sheet and smiled at the internal memo of the Iowa State Gaming Commission. "How did you get this? It says *to be released tomorrow*."

"My business, like most, works on contacts." She cocked her head to the side. "Let's leave it at that. It looks like the Commission was under a fair amount of pressure to consider inviting a casino proposal from Jefferson City. We may not

243

have proof that Rick's Chicago contacts were involved, given the smell of dollars that such a casino would've generated. But this is a no-go. The Commission is going to approve a casino twenty miles away. No way can this area support two casinos."

"How did Rick ever think he could get this community to support a casino—and downtown, of all places?"

"Hubris. From what I can tell, he suffers from an inflated ego and believes he can move mountains."

"But not this time."

"It looks like he was trying to use Duluth as a model. They have a downtown casino that seems to blend in well enough."

"This town would've been torn apart by such a move."

"Granted. But if Rick's group had prevailed, his power within the community would've soared."

Kevin glanced at a car slowing and then turning in the opposite direction. "Do you really think this is it? No more threats to Nadja and her aunt?"

Amy shrugged. "Depends on how Rick handles defeat. I'd be surprised if the Chicago connection will be a factor anymore. They're not going to get involved in this unless there are big dollars to be made or laundered. Assuming we're right, and their interest had to do with establishing a casino, then I'd say they're back on the sidelines. It's hard to figure anything else here that would attract their willingness to take risks. And believe me, they are constantly weighing risks and rewards."

"Still," he groused, "seems like a lot of assumptions to me."

"Sorry, that's all I have. We'll have to wait a while for this to play out. Rick remains a question mark. All I'm saying is that this memo probably means we don't have to worry any more about heavy hitters from Chicago."

"At least that's something."

"That's huge. I've agreed to meet with Ivett's detective

friend in an hour. Then I expect to head back to the Cities." Amy reached in her purse and pulled out her keys. "Let me know if anything happens. It won't take me long to get back here, if I'm needed."

"I appreciate that, and all you're doing." He grinned. "I know we are all paying you well."

"Damn right."

Kevin stretched his tired muscles. "I do hope this is the end."

"Do you? Really?"

"Of course I do." Kevin scowled at his one-time lover. He had never appreciated this smug side of her. "Why wouldn't I?"

"Don't get your back up," Amy said, reaching across to squeeze his arm. "I know you want Nadja out of danger, but once this threat to her shop is finished, then you'll have to deal with Nadja."

Kevin gasped. She might as well have kicked him in the stomach. Amy had a way of carving away the fat. He didn't want to admit it, but she was right. The troubles with Nadja's shop provided them with a buffer, of sorts. They could play at romance while protected from having to make decisions that might otherwise be more pressing.

He shrugged and nodded at Amy. "We can only take one step at a time."

"And I wish you the best, both of you, and you know that." Her lips curved up into a bow. "Don't blow this one, Langley. I doubt you've ever been loved more than Nadja loves you. And you seem quite taken with her. Does she know about your fears?"

He frowned at her raised eyebrow. She knew him too damn well. He shook his head.

"She looks like the mothering type to me."

"I know," he grunted. "Maybe Danny will be enough."

"Maybe." Amy checked her watch. "I've got to run. Keep me informed." Kevin watched her hesitate—something he'd seldom seen her do. "Trust her, Kevin. I think she's a good listener."

Kevin pulled on the door handle and lurched out into the parking lot. He didn't bother waiting for Amy to pull away. What did she know about anything? There was a time when he'd thought *she* was a good listener.

"You think the Gaming Commission's decision will be in tomorrow's paper?" On break, Nadja sat next to Kevin at a corner table in the Cappuccino while Barbara and Max handled customers. Business was brisk. The live country band helped draw in new patrons. She smiled. It paid to offer a wide range of musical tastes.

"If not tomorrow, then the next day."

"And I have news to share with you." She rested her hands on the table. "Mrs. Pickens dropped by before the evening crowd began to gather. She's the head of the Arts Council and also a member of the Chamber. She informed me she and several others are working to move quickly to get this building on the historical register."

"That is news."

"That'll mean no matter what, no one will be able to tear this building down."

They both applauded when the band finished a number and announced they were taking a break. Nadja beamed at the customers using the opportunity to get refills. "Do you really believe this is the end of it?" she asked, not liking the anxiety in her voice.

"Too soon to tell, but Amy thinks we don't have to worry about the mob any longer."

"That's something." Nadja studied the bottom of her cup.

"I guess."

"We won't let our guard down yet."

Nadja felt her pulse quicken. Not too long ago, she would've challenged him for using words like "we" and "our," but now it seemed perfectly normal.

She shivered. Good grief, what would they do if her troubles were over? She glanced quickly at Kevin and then away. Would that only be the beginning of bigger troubles?

Kevin traced the back of her hand with an index finger. "Let's try not to outthink ourselves. Danger still exists."

She nodded and pursed her lips. The status quo was quite fine with her. She clutched the sapphire in her fingers. She had tonight. That was something. She couldn't see beyond tomorrow, and she'd have to learn to live with that.

She glanced up in time to see Ivett bouncing their way. Apparently Steve had told her about Amy's discovery. It had been thoughtful of Kevin to tell Steve, so he could be the one to inform Ivett. No doubt that would help Steve get back into her good graces. Kevin was much more of a romantic than he wanted her to believe.

"So how are our lovebirds doing?" Ivett said, pulling up a chair.

Nadja felt her cheeks warm. She wasn't accustomed to being called a lovebird—and Ivett wasn't known for keeping her voice down. Nadja looked around the room and glanced quickly away from several grinning stares. She never had liked others knowing her business. It wasn't that she was ashamed of having an affair with Kevin. But she didn't want to raise expectations—hers, or those of curious observers.

If they broke up, then she'd have to deal with embarrassment in her own shop. Her eyes widened as she peeked over at Kevin. She'd always thought about *when* they'd break up. How had *when* changed to *if?* She was sinking—slowly, but surely.

"Looks like Steve told you about the Gaming Commission," Nadja said, ignoring her aunt's lovebird comment.

"Yes, that's great news!" She looked at Kevin. "Thanks for letting Steve tell me. That was good for him." She smiled happily. "And for me. We're going to get it back together," she added, directing her attention at Nadja. "So maybe we all can get back to living."

"I'm happy for you," Nadja said, finding Ivett's enthusiasm infectious. She sobered. "But we don't really know that this is done."

"I know, but I can hope, can't I?" Ivett's eyes crinkled. "Will you ever learn that sometimes that's all we have to go on—hope?"

Nadja groaned. She knew her aunt was talking more about Kevin than about their recent troubles. But this was not the time or place for such a discussion.

Nadja stood. "When will you learn that my faith is not as strong as yours?" She glanced over her shoulder at the line of customers. "I'd better get back to work. At least I'm quite hopeful about good results in the cash register this evening."

Kevin watched the sway of Nadja's rump as she weaved through the tables to her position behind the counter. Turning to Ivett, he said, "You two seem to have a language all of your own—and I'm not speaking of Ukrainian."

"I suppose you're right." Ivett sipped her latte and set it back on the table. "Don't most people who know each other very well?"

"Probably. Can't say I've thought about it much."

"That's a beautiful sapphire you gave Nadja. You have exquisite taste."

"Thanks."

"I understand you're courting her."

He narrowed his eyes. "That's right. Does that bother you?"

"Not in the least."

He watched her lips thin — was that a smile or a sneer?

"And what are you courting her for?"

He winced and sat straighter. "What do you mean by that?"

"Oh, I think you're familiar with the possibilities: the occasional but reliable lover, the live-in partner, the wife, the mother of your children."

"This seems like a discussion I should be having with Nadja down the road, not with her aunt."

"Ah. You're probably right, but maybe it's harder for me to shake the ways of the old country than I thought." She eyed him levelly. "Don't hurt her."

"I'll try not to. But didn't you once imply that she could hurt me?"

"She can. And she will if she has to." Ivett sat pensively for several moments. "I'll say this much. You should know that Nadja takes very seriously her responsibility for carrying on our line. She won't be interested in a casual affair that never goes anywhere."

"Is that Nadja's concern, or her aunt's?"

"It's a shared concern." Ivett's eyes filled with pain. "Unfortunately, I've not been able to have children."

"I'm sorry. Nadja's never mentioned a desire for children to me. And she hasn't seemed overly eager to link up with men. That is the way a woman becomes a mother."

"I can see I've rubbed a sensitive spot." She nodded again, as if debating how far she should take this subject. "You're right. Nadja won't settle for just any man." She snickered. "I'm not even positive she'll settle for you. But she has talked about looking into the possibility of a donor before she gets too much older."

"Donor!" Kevin rose halfway out of his chair. "You're kidding!"

"I don't kid about such matters. But I've probably meddled too much already. Here comes the band back." She pushed her chair away from the table. "Customers are returning to their tables. Nadja will rejoin you in a few minutes. Let her know I've gone home to attend to my husband's needs."

She leaned over and grazed his cheek with her lips. "Thanks for including Steve today. And I do wish you well with Nadja. She will make some lucky guy a fantastic wife. And she will be a neat mother. Bye."

Kevin blinked and brushed his cheek where Ivett's lips had so recently been. Lucky. Why did he have the nagging feeling his luck was running out?

CHAPTER SIXTEEN

Steve didn't have to look at the newspaper Rick flung on his desk. He'd read both stories enough to nearly have them memorized. He should've gone straight home after showing a client property on the South side, but he'd wanted to pick up some specs for the next morning. Damn, it was already late.

He'd never seen Rick in such a rage. Clearly, he'd been drinking—heavily, judging from his disheveled appearance. Apparently he hadn't liked the Gaming Commission's decision, and he probably wasn't pleased with the citizens' group seeking to fast-track the Henderson building for historical status.

"Did you," Rick bellowed, "have anything to do with these articles?"

"Not me," Steve replied innocently. "Looks like you got two strikes on one day. If they get historical status for the Henderson building, you can kiss it goodbye."

It gave him great pleasure to watch his old college buddy turning purple.

Rick sneered at him as if he'd said the dumbest thing possible. "Using your metaphor, buddy, I have one more strike left. And I expect to hit a home run, not strike out. That bitch has far too much luck."

"Who?" Steve scowled. "Ivett? Nadja?"

"If she'd played along with me when she first got here," Rick continued, as if not hearing his question, "none of this would've happened. She owes me. Big time."

Steve watched Rick's eyes glaze over. Was that rage, or lust? He didn't even flinch, not wanting to disturb Rick's rant.

"She's got a rack on her that begs to be manhandled. Yet she ignored me as if I didn't exist."

Rick paced back and forth in front of Steve's desk, stopping only long enough to catch a breath. "And now she's letting this Java Beans bastard bang her. I even tried to support her business when she first opened her shop. She took my money all right but she wouldn't do more than grunt a thanks at me. She treated me like shit!"

Rick placed both palms on Steve's desk and fought for control. Steve said nothing. Neither did he look away.

"The gloves are coming off, buddy. That bitch of a niece of yours isn't going to squash me like I'm some bug."

"I doubt she was even aware of your overtures, Rick." Steve's voice sounded hoarse even to him. "She's not the easiest person for anyone to talk to. And she's not all that experienced with men."

"Bullshit! All of those Russian women ooze sex. You should know that."

Steve watched Rick push away from his desk.

Rick nodded as if they'd just reached a deal. "Hell," he snorted, "I'm going to hit a grand slam. I'll get that building, and I'm sure as hell going to fuck that bitch until she's begging for more. Experience. She'll be experienced when I'm finished with her."

Steve leaned back in his swivel chair as the echo of the door slamming shut reverberated around his office. He exhaled and drew in a sharp breath.

He'd better call Kevin. He glanced at the clock on his desk. It was already past ten o'clock. He'd call first thing in the morning.

He didn't want to interrupt his niece and her lover. It stretched his imagination to think that Rick thought he'd ever get into Nadja's panties. No wonder the guy was so pissed.

He straightened his shoulders. He'd better get on home. With any luck, he might have his own sexy woman waiting for him.

"Remove your robe," Nadja ordered. "I want to see how much you want me."

Kevin stood briefly to do as she requested and sat back down on the straight backed chair she'd provided him when they entered her dance studio. Her image reflected from mirror to mirror around the room until he was surrounded by her. This was his penance.

If this was her idea of penance, he'd be her supplicant any day. Entirely naked except for her sapphire and a light orange veil she'd used as an added visual tease, she'd been twirling and dancing for several minutes before she came to stop and told him to remove his robe. This was better. Even the robe had been too restrictive.

He skimmed his stiff shaft with his right hand.

"Don't," she commanded. "Unless I tell you to." She gave him a tiny smile. "Which I doubt I will. I want to see him seeking me without your assistance. He is seeking me, isn't he?"

Resting his hands on the chair seat, Kevin watched his cock weave about. "Yes. Can't you tell? He wants your heat."

"Good. Maybe this will teach you to trust me more in the future."

"Will you still put on a show like this for me if I do?"

She ignored him and let the veil drop to the floor. Without looking at him, she walked to a line of crates on one wall and began tossing out pillows, mats, and throw rugs. He watched her move about without any display of self-consciousness until she'd arranged a bed of sorts in front of his chair.

He swallowed hard when he saw her lie down on her back and spread her thighs before him. Penance had all of a sudden gotten a bit edgy. She tucked a bolster under her butt, providing him with an even more pronounced view of her alluring orifices.

She reached for a small knit bag that he hadn't seen and unzipped it. Then she pulled out a long crystal object and held it up for him to see.

"You," she cooed, "wanted to meet my crystal wand."

He tried to breathe.

She placed the wand in her mouth and made a show of sucking it in and out. "Right?"

"Absolutely," he croaked.

"You may watch, but don't touch — me, or yourself."

"My penance?"

He watched her swirl the crystal slowly around one nipple while she pulled on the other one.

"Nice," he murmured.

"For me, too." She groaned, closing and opening her thighs. Her pussy glistened with moisture. She closed and opened her eyes too, and he waited for them to refocus.

She gazed at him as if from a distance. "I wasn't aware of how much I'd be turned on myself, doing this for you."

"I'm pleased to hear that, though I imagine you have much more penance in store for me than that."

She propped herself up farther on the pillows. She slid one hand downward and separated her pussy lips. Electrical shocks coursed through him as he peered at her pinkness, and she lowered the crystal wand to give him a better view. "Tell me what you see."

"Jesus, Nadja. I see you. Your luscious pussy, your swollen clit, your delicate asshole." He licked his lips. "What do you want me to say?"

"What would you like to do right now?"

"Have wild sex with you."

She gave him an innocent look, and her mouth opened

slightly. "But you're not going to, because I told you not to touch me."

"That's right."

"You're being such a good boy, after being so naughty." She stretched her thighs wider still.

She gave him a soft smile and eased the crystal shaft into her vagina, and his heart stopped. She leaned forward and moved it deftly in small concentric circles. She smacked her lips, and her eyes grew huge. More of the crystal object disappeared, until Nadja gasped. Her breasts heaved and then quieted.

"There," she murmured, "all tucked into my cunt. Are you enjoying yourself?"

"Yes," he muttered, reaching for his cock.

"No! Sit on your hands, Kevin. I don't want you disobeying. This is your penance."

He obeyed, which only caused his pole to jut out farther.

She laughed.

"Are you going to show any mercy for him?"

"I haven't decided yet. Maybe for your cock, but not for you." She withdrew the crystal dildo until only the tip remained in her. The crystal glistened with her juices.

He ground his butt against his hands, keeping them where they were.

"That's right," she said. "You only get to watch me play." She pushed the wand back in. "Are you envious of my wand?"

There was no need for reply. He nodded, unsure if he could utter a coherent sound.

She brought her fingers to her mouth and wet them.

He expected she'd tease him next by playing with her clitoris. He watched her fingers trail over a breast and graze her bud, then travel lower.

Her eyes full of smoky innocence, she traced the narrow

path between her vulva and her anus.

Kevin's eyes watered from the strain of staring.

She chewed on her bottom lip. "Are you watching closely?"

He bobbed his head in disbelief as he watched a finger gradually disappear into her asshole. She groaned and closed her eyes. He couldn't close his eyes if he wanted to—and besides, he had no desire to do so.

Her eyes opened, and she winked at him conspiratorially. "Surprised?" she murmured.

"Very," he managed to say. "Awed, actually."

"I like surprising you." She took a moment to enjoy the dildo and her finger. And he tried to breathe.

"Do you wish this was your cock in my ass?"

"Yes," he grunted. Was she going to relent and let him participate in this little play?

"Don't move," she warned. "I may let you try that sometime. I haven't decided whether to let you or not. I've enjoyed your finger and your thumb. And of course as, you can see, I enjoy my finger. Do you think your cock would really enjoy fucking my ass?"

He nodded, groaning his frustration.

"Penance, remember. You're doing penance. Watch me."

How could he not?

Almost imperceptibly, her hips began to undulate. "Oh," she purred. "I am doing just fine. Watch carefully while I work a second finger into my ass. I do think you'll fit if I decide to let you."

Her hips moved more rapidly until they were bucking against the dildo and her fingers. A strained smile spread across her lips. He could tell she was trying really hard to keep her eyes open, but he doubted she could even focus on him at this point.

"There!" she cried. Her hands stilled. Juices flowed around

the crystal dildo. Her jaw slackened. Her thighs squeezed tight, and she rolled to her side, where she curled into a ball. He heard her call his name, but he knew better than to go to her.

She would come to him when she was ready. He glanced down at his straining cock. *He* was way beyond ready.

He waited, taking the opportunity to mentally check his pulse rate and breathe once again.

Minutes later she stood and handed him his robe.

"I thought you were going to take care of him," he said, rather hurt by her oversight.

She laughed. "I think he and his master can wait a few more minutes." She glanced about the studio and then gave him a mischievous smile. "That was so good that I think I want to save this studio for your penance room. Why don't you come with me upstairs to our bed and make wild love with me? This time I want to be fucked."

He grabbed her outstretched hand and let her lead the way. They had nearly reached the door before he brought her up short. "What if *I* need *you* to do penance?"

She nodded and smiled brilliantly. "I was hoping you might ask. Yes, this room will work for both of us; but right now, let's not talk about what might be. Let's go upstairs so I can feel you in me."

Kevin stood still and watched her bare rump swivel as she left the studio. He blinked. What the hell was he doing, standing there like some fool? He followed her with as much grace as he could manage, which was hardly any at all, given his straining cock.

Nearly two hours later, Nadja pressed her ass against Kevin's groin. She couldn't remember ever feeling more loved and so well fucked. She smiled to herself. Fucked. Not a word she would've used before watching all those tapes. Now it seemed both natural and naughty. It was one of the tapes that had helped her come up with penance ideas.

Had the penance session been that powerful for him? It had been incredibly fantastic for her, but she hadn't expected Kevin to accept the voyeur role so easily.

She smiled to herself. He'd certainly made up for that once they'd finally managed to climb the stairs. They hadn't even reached the bed before he'd emptied himself into her while she writhed beneath him on the carpet. As she'd hoped, he'd mounted her without more foreplay. Their lovemaking had bordered on the savage. She'd begged to be fucked. And that was what he'd done.

And then, perhaps somewhat chagrined by his aggressiveness, he'd led her to the bed, where he'd proceeded to give her a tongue bath. He'd left nothing unexplored in his striving to wash her. Her body still hummed from his adoration. Then without a word, he'd turned her and entered her from behind.

She flexed against his half-hard cock, and his lips caressed her shoulder. They'd been doing this now for over an hour. Neither of them seemed eager to climax again. It was simply enough to touch each other intimately.

She hugged her tits. She'd been surprised he hadn't claimed her ass after all the teasing she'd done downstairs, but that was something they could still look forward to. She certainly was.

Maybe they'd have to explore more penance sessions. That probably wasn't what the church had in mind when it talked about penance; but this had been much more delicious than any other penance she could remember experiencing.

Her back shivered against Kevin's chest. Was he lying there, enfolding her in his arms, devising a penance game for her? Maybe she did allow herself to hope more than she'd let on to her aunt.

Kevin couldn't trust himself even to open his eyes and look at Nadja in the soft moonshine filtering into the bedroom. They had to talk. He heaved a sigh. Wasn't that supposed to be what the *woman* wanted?

But they really did have to talk. He was hooked — completely. He'd hate to lose her, but if he had to, then better sooner than later. The elation on her face when he'd told her the mob was no longer interested in her shop could have lighted the entire city of St. Paul. And he was convinced her happiness hadn't just been about the shop.

She expected more from him now. And he expected more from her. But they had to talk. They had to talk about children. If Ivett was right, then — he shuddered — he and Nadja were headed for the proverbial train wreck.

But she'd never mentioned wanting kids. Maybe that was because she assumed he'd be willing to have more. Or maybe she wasn't really considering that what they had could lead to marriage.

He couldn't decide which explanation he disliked most.

Nadja struggled for air. Was she drowning? Kevin's arms held her, held her down. She had to get away.

Using all the strength she could muster while weighed down by sleep, Nadja broke away from Kevin's grasp to grab the ringing phone.

"Hello," she groaned.

"Nadja Petrov."

"Yes, who is it?"

"This is Officer Harris of the Jefferson City Police Department, Ms. Petrov. Sorry to disturb you at such an hour, but I figured you'd want to know right away. There's been a fire at your store."

"Oh, my God!" Nadja bolted straight up, vaguely aware of Kevin looked anxiously at her.

"How bad?"

"Could be much worse. Looks like it started in the dumpster. Fortunately, a passerby saw flames before the fire was able to really get going."

"We'll be right there."

"Ms. Petrov. While the building looks like it is in good shape, there has been considerable smoke and water damage. That can't be helped when we're fighting fires."

"I understand," she said automatically. *How much damage,* she wanted to scream. She had to get to her shop and find out for herself.

She hung up the phone and only then realized that Kevin was nearly dressed and had tucked his gun in his waistband. She blinked and scrambled out of bed.

"It's not over," she said, welcoming his arms circling around her.

"We didn't think it was."

"I guess I'm good at fooling myself."

"You're no fool." He kissed her forehead. "You just wanted it done. The police are involved now. Maybe all of this is coming to a head."

She started throwing on clothes. "I sure hope so. I'm getting awfully tired of somebody trying to mess up my life." She reached into a dresser door, pulled out her small Beretta, and tucked it in her purse.

"Jesus." Kevin took a step toward her and halted. "Don't suppose I can talk you into leaving that gun behind?"

She glared at him before taking long strides toward the door. "Don't even try!" she snapped over her shoulder.

The acrid smell of heavy, damp smoke assaulted Nadja's

nostrils as soon as she stepped out of the passenger door. Not waiting for Kevin, she ran toward her shop.

A burly fireman stepped in her path. "We can't let you go in yet, Nadja."

She looked at the man and realized it was Jim Edwards, one of her regular customers. Several firemen routinely stopped in to pick up coffee.

She fought back tears and nodded, trying to focus on the building. There were no flames evident, just gray smoke and men carrying things out of the shop. *Her* things. "How bad?" she stammered.

"We'll do our best to clean up, but there's going to be quite a mess. You do have insurance?"

She nodded.

"That'll help. You'll be back up and running soon."

"What about Ivett? The antique store?"

The man removed his hat and wiped soot from his forehead. "Strange. The fire never reached her store. There's smoke damage, but there shouldn't be nearly as much water damage. We were able to contain the fire to the Cappuccino.

"Nadja, it may not be much comfort." The man gave her one of the saddest looks she'd ever seen. "But if we'd arrived five minutes later, this entire building might've been lost."

She nodded, taking in the import of his words. "I thank you. Ivett and I both thank all of you." She smiled at him through her tears. "Once I'm back in business, coffee will be free for firefighters."

He nodded and managed a tiny smile. "Thank you. We might accept a cup or two, but we want your business to survive. We'll pay our way. Now, you and your man can watch from here, if you want. But it will probably be another half hour or so before we can let you in the store."

"That's okay," she said, squeezing Kevin's fingers. "We'll wait."

She let Kevin cuddle her close. His warmth provided some comfort.

"There you are!"

Nadja turned in the direction of her aunt's voice. Ivett's grim face was matched by Steve's. "We're here," she mumbled, taking her aunt into her arms.

Ivett's body heaved with sobs. Nadja rubbed her back — both of them were crying for more than their shops. Someone had managed to shatter their dreams of what it would be like to live free in America. The cold reality was that evil people existed all around the world.

If only she knew for sure who had done this. She studied the smoke, which at least was diminishing. Was this, as Kevin and Steve seemed to believe, really the work of Rick Adams? She hardly knew the man. He'd been a regular customer for the first month or so after she opened the Cappuccino, and then she'd seen him only rarely at civic functions.

She'd hardly given him a thought until recently.

"We'll refurbish," her aunt insisted. "We won't let them drive us out. We can't."

"We won't," Nadja said through clenched teeth. "We will fight. We have no other choice."

"I'll call Amy as soon as the sun is up," Kevin said, putting his arm around her shoulders.

"With the police involved, will Amy still be able to help?" Nadja brushed hair from her face. "I don't want her to waste her time."

"Let's let her decide that. She may be following a different lead. She never did think the withdrawal of the mob was enough to bring this to an end."

Nadja turned toward her uncle when Steve cleared his throat. Even in the poor light, she could see him turning red. "What is it?" she asked.

Steve hesitated. "I was going to call first thing in the

morning. Rick dropped by the office late last night. He was drunk and irate. He blames you for more than the building, Nadja."

"What? I hardly know the man."

"I know. Rick thinks you treated him poorly when he made advances."

"Poorly? Advances?"

"You mean," Ivett yelled, "that bastard was interested in Nadja?"

"Apparently. But I told him Nadja probably didn't even notice." He coughed. "He was so drunk last night, he claimed he was going to not only get the building, but also get Nadja."

Nadja felt Kevin's grip tighten around her waist.

"What did he mean, get Nadja?" Kevin sounded alarmed.

"You know." Steve glanced around as if afraid someone was listening. "Have his way with her. He's also very jealous of you."

Nadja's mouth went dry, and Kevin's voice rose, "Why the hell didn't you call last night?"

"Why didn't you tell *me* last night?" Ivett squealed, punching her husband's shoulder.

Steve slumped. "I thought the morning would be soon enough. I didn't think . . ."

Nadja stepped away from Kevin until she was nose to nose with her uncle. "You weren't going to call me, were you? You were waiting until I left for the shop so you two macho men could decide how to best take care of me. Weren't you?"

"Not exactly like that."

"Right. You're not a very good liar. Both of you should be locked in a room with the key thrown away until all of this crap is resolved. I don't know which is worse—figuring out who's trying to destroy me or figuring out what you two are trying to hide from me."

"What?" Kevin said hoarsely. "I didn't even know about

this. Why am I being blamed for Steve's actions?"

She whirled on him. "Can you stand there and tell me that if none of this had happened tonight and Steve had called you in the morning with this little update of his, you would've told me?"

She needed nothing more than his hesitation to confirm her suspicion. She bit back her retort when a fireman approached.

"It's safe enough for you to go in the store, Nadja." He doffed his hat. "Again, I'm sorry for all the water damage."

"I know," she said, exasperated. "It couldn't be helped. Seems like that's becoming a popular refrain in my life."

She peered at a very chagrined Kevin, shook her head at him, and grabbed his hand. "You might as well come along. One of these days I should toss you back in the water."

Birds calling back and forth across the meadow cast an eerie calm over the conversation as Nadja, Kevin, and Amy strode along the nature trail. They'd wanted privacy, and this setting provided that. Nadja spied what little remained of a rabbit carcass that had likely fallen prey to a hawk or owl— so much for nature providing calm for the soul.

"Neither Detective Jarvis nor Chief Fillmore seemed particularly surprised by our suspicions regarding Rick Adams," Amy said. "Sounds like he's been in and out of the shadows most of his life. He and his family were never fully accepted in the inner circle of Jefferson City—though not from lack of trying or spreading money around."

Amy bent down and picked up a stick, tossing it toward the woods. "They weren't pleased to hear about the dummy holding companies and how much property he's actually been able to get his fingers on. They'd had no cause to do much poking into his affairs. Until now. And they still don't have enough to justify much more than routine surveillance."

"At least that's a beginning," Kevin acknowledged.

"And" — he chuckled sarcastically — "if any of us disappear, they may know where to begin searching."

"Kevin." Nadja jabbed him in the side. "You don't really think he's going to come after us?"

She wasn't pleased that he glanced at Amy before answering. "I don't like the way he threatened you when he talked with Steve. And then the fire happened the same night."

"But he was drinking. We've hardly exchanged more than a few dozen words since I've moved here."

"Don't underestimate the man," Amy cautioned. "He can always get his hands on booze. And you remember the card you received? It most likely came from Rick."

"Yes." Nadja began to tremble. "How could I forget?"

"I don't mean to frighten you any more than you already are." Amy hesitated. "But I don't think this guy is screwed together right."

Nadja caught the look of caution on Amy's face. "Tell me. I'll be more frightened if you don't."

Amy stopped in the middle of the path and reached out to clutch Nadja's hands. "You were depicted on the card with huge breasts and no vagina. Right?"

She nodded.

"Your gazebo was taken apart methodically, piece by piece, as if it was being stripped rather than demolished at the hands of a vandal, and arson often has sexual overtones." Amy squeezed her fingers tight. "It may be that you have been the principle target all along. It may be that the building — even the mob — were ways of retaliating or trapping you in an even more sinister web."

"Cripes, Amy," Kevin gasped, "don't you hold anything back?"

"I don't want her to hold anything back," Nadja snapped, darting a look at him. "Remember, that's your problem, not mine."

"Sorry." He stared off toward the woods. "This just makes me feel so damn helpless."

"We're all doing what we can," Amy said evenly. "We must acknowledge the dangers openly — then we must be vigilant. All of us. That includes you, Kevin, and Nadja, and me — even your aunt and uncle, Nadja. Though I expect all of this has much more to do with you than with them."

Nadja nodded her agreement. "We'll keep them informed."

"How long will you stay here?" Kevin asked as Amy started walking again.

"I'm not sure. As long as I can, but there's no telling when he'll try something again."

Nadja braced herself. "I noticed you didn't say *if* he tries something again."

Amy shook her head. "If I'm right, it isn't a matter of if. It's a matter of when."

"But this time we'll be ready," Nadja said, mustering her confidence.

"We're all counting on that," Amy agreed. "And we have an element of surprise."

"What's that?" Nadja squeaked.

"He doesn't seem to have a clue that we suspect him. He'll slip up. He'll make a mistake. These guys always do."

Nadja nodded and tried to keep her stride short enough so Amy wouldn't have to run to keep up. Amy hadn't mentioned that many mistakes made by criminals often occurred after a crime, rather than before.

CHAPTER SEVENTEEN

Feeling Kevin's gaze on her, Nadja stopped scrubbing the crud-covered floor tiles in front of her Cappuccino counter. They'd been working since early morning. She didn't need a clock to know it was past eight p.m. Meals had consisted of fast food. They should quit soon. Ivett and Steve had left an hour earlier.

She grinned on seeing the hunger so evident in Kevin's eyes. They did have to take time to rest, but she and Kevin were driven to reopen the Cappuccino as soon as possible.

She didn't get off her hands and knees. "I don't know how you can find me attractive after I've scrubbed my fingers to the bone all day."

Kevin gasped. "You must be kidding. Barefoot. Worn pale blue shorts that only highlight your incredible ass. And that yellow blouse knotted below your breasts. I've hardly been able to keep my eyes off of you all day. Even that yellow scarf makes you fetching. I seldom see a woman in a scarf anymore."

He set aside the broom he'd been using to shove debris into a pile. His grin had an edge to it. "Maybe we should make love with you wearing only your scarf and your sapphire. You'd be my peasant woman."

She chuckled at him. "The scarf might fit the traditional image of the European peasant woman, but I don't think many peasant women owned sapphires."

"I'm glad *you* do."

"Me, too." She settled back on her heels. "Maybe I should

dump this dirty water and head home. We can't stay at this twenty-four hours a day."

Kevin looked around the store. "We've made good progress the last couple days. Clean-up might take another day or two, and then we'll be ready for the more creative part of this job."

"I am looking forward to that." Nadja groaned, rising to her feet with the bucket of dirty water in one hand. "This is dreary work, but I have been considering some ideas for brightening the place. I've lost at least half of the books I owned. I haven't decided whether to continue with the books or to do something else."

"This fire has been wrenching, but I'm glad to see you turn a tragedy into an opportunity."

"Isn't that the nature of tragedy?"

"I couldn't agree with you more," thundered a deep male voice from behind her.

She whirled to see Rick Adams standing in the doorway between her shop and Ivett's. Water from her bucket splashed on her legs, and her eyes rounded at the sight of the pistol Adams was gripping with both hands. As she watched in horror, he leveled it first at her, then at Kevin, then back to her.

Her gun! It was useless, tucked in her purse on the other side of the counter.

She caught movement coming from behind her.

"Keep your hands in front of you," Rick shouted at Kevin, "unless you want this little tragedy to begin earlier than I've planned." Although his words were slurred, he didn't seem drunk enough to be easily foiled.

She turned slightly so she could see both men. "Don't do anything stupid," she muttered to Kevin.

"She's right, Mr. Businessman. Turn around so I can see what you were reaching for."

Kevin lifted his arms and turned around.

"Our hero," Adams said sarcastically. "Nadja, lift that gun with two fingers, put it on the floor, and slide it over here. Any false move, and your lover is going to be deader than dead."

She nodded and did exactly as she'd been ordered. She was surprised to see that her fingers didn't shake. She shoved the gun across the floor. If they were going to get out of this alive, it wouldn't be because they had superior firepower.

Rick stepped farther into the Cappuccino. His gun wavered only slightly, and his eyes shone a kind of lust she'd only witnessed once before. That had been years ago. Earlier, had she subconsciously detected the similarity between Rick and her former dance coach?

Her body chilled. She entered a kind of calm she'd rarely encountered, even through yoga and dance. She was prepared. She didn't know how Kevin was doing. But this wasn't about him — this was about her. With any luck, that would be her assailant's downfall.

Kevin stepped up beside her. She could hear him breathing heavily.

Rick shook his head. "Take a couple steps to your left, Langley." Rick's laugh rumbled from his lips. "I want you to be a little over one arm's length from her shoulder. Got it? Do what Simon says."

Kevin shuffled away from her.

"That's right. Not so far away that I can't watch both of you at the same time, but not close enough to get in the way."

Rick swiveled his head quickly about, checking the area. "You two really have been busy. This damn place would've burned to the ground if it wasn't for some damn busybody passerby."

"What do you want, Adams?" Kevin barked. "It's not too late for us to work out a deal."

Rick sneered at Kevin. "You shut up. This is between me

and her," he said, nodding directly at Nadja. "I'm not stupid. The only deal we're going to make will be made with this gun.

"Remember, I'm only going to say this once more. Any move out of you, Langley, and you are dead meat. That includes your mouth. I don't have a hell of a lot to lose. You think I don't know the cops are sniffing around me? And I'd sure like to have ten minutes alone with that red-headed private investigator you hired. Banging her would be worth the effort."

"You think you could last a full ten minutes?" Nadja was surprised by the iciness of her voice.

"You," Rick said, stepping closer, "think you're a tough bitch, don't you?"

She could only think of one way to distract him. If she kept him busy long enough, maybe he would make a mistake, or maybe she or Kevin would be able to overpower him. "Tough enough," she said, thrusting her jaw out at him.

"We'll see about that." He sneered at Kevin. "Is she as stacked as she looks?"

Kevin didn't say a word. His cheek muscle twitched, but he kept his mouth shut. She was grateful for that.

"Untie that blouse. I've waited years for this."

Never flinching, she raised her hands slowly to the knot that held her blouse in place. "Don't interfere," she said softly to Kevin. "It's only my body. It's not my soul. It's not our lives."

"My, my, she is a woman of wisdom. Hurry it up, Nadja. We don't have all night."

"I thought you would want to last the whole night." She shrugged out of the blouse.

Rick wet his lips. "Now the bra."

She unsnapped the front clasp and let the bra slide down her arms. Rick's eyes seemed to grow twice their normal size.

"Jesus," he mumbled, grabbing his crotch. The gun in his

right hand remained steady. "I've seen smaller melons than those. Look at those nipples. They're getting larger by the second. Because of me."

She doubted that. Didn't he know lust and fear were often interchangeable?

He took a half step forward.

She stood her ground.

He raised his arm but didn't come close enough to touch her.

She knew he was weighing his risks. He had to do something with Kevin before he could force himself on her. It was her turn to take the initiative before he could reach a decision about Kevin. Looking directly at Adams, she cupped her breasts and twisted her nipples.

Adams let out a harsh breath, and his gun lowered ever so slightly. "I knew you were a tease. Play with those tits for me. They may be your lifeline."

She forced a smile to her lips and lifted a breast until her mouth closed around a taut nipple. Rick's weight shifted from foot to foot. He clawed at his crotch. Was he going to jerk off, or try to rape her? In any case, she had him unsettled.

She flicked her tongue at her nipple, and it swelled even more. She made a show of sucking on it.

Awkwardly, Rick undid his belt and slid his free hand inside his pants. "I've got something much, much bigger here for you to suck on."

She shook her head and lowered her hands to the snap of her shorts. "I thought you weren't in a rush. Don't you want to see what else I have to offer a patient man?" She wiggled her hips.

"Do it," he snarled, grinding his teeth.

She inched the zipper downward and kept her gaze trained on his, which was glued on her crotch. She peeled the tight shorts down her thighs and legs, careful not to touch her bikini panties. She straightened.

Rick stood transfixed. She slid her fingers inside her panties and flexed her fingers. He looked like he would lunge at the slightest provocation, and that was precisely what she wanted him to do. It was their only chance.

"Like what you see?" she purred, widening her stance and tilting her hips provocatively. She wiggled her fingers against her hidden pussy. She swore she saw something snap behind his eyes. He was on the verge of losing control.

His laugh was maniacal. "I know what you're trying to do, bitch. You want to be in charge when I fuck you. I've only known one other woman as brazen as you. She was a temptress, too." His voice turned shrill. "And Mary Beth's dead, too!"

"Mary Beth." Without thinking, Nadja withdrew her hand from her panties. "Steve's Mary Beth?"

"The bitch! She was giving me plenty on the side, until she decided she'd be better off marrying my old buddy." Rick had a faraway look about him. "Hell, I would've been fine fucking the shit out of her even then. But no . . .she said she was turning over a new leaf. The whore." His laughter grated on Nadja. "She turned up a few leaves, all right."

"But you provided Steve with an alibi."

"And he's paid me back in a hundred ways." He sneered. "That's the way you keep friends loyal."

She watched Rick sober a little. Did he regret what he'd just said? If she'd had any question about his plans for her and Kevin, there was no doubt left.

"Now where were we?" Rick asked, his lips curling into a wolfish grimace. "I believe you had more you wanted to show me. It's show and tell. You show me your cunt, and then I'll show you my cock. And then I'll have another game or two for us to play. How does suck and fuck sound to you?"

He stared hard at Kevin. "Don't think I've forgotten you. I

won't kill you until you've had the pleasure of watching me fuck your whore."

Rick gave her a sugary smile. "Get on with it, bitch. I wouldn't want you to have to wait much longer. If you're really good, I might change my mind about killing you. I have a pleasure palace in Brazil that you might decorate quite nicely. Your fair skin would look quite fetching against the two local women who take care of the place. Your cunt will make a tasty morsel for them as well as for me. Once I'm bored with you, you'll bring a pretty penny at one of the local brothels. I'll shop around to get the best price I can for you. Still better than being dead, right?

"Perhaps you should do your best to convince me how much you crave my hard cock. He's more than ready for you. You must be soaking for me. Get rid of the panties. I want to see my prize. Do it!"

The guy was crazier than she'd thought. Brazil? That'd explain his long absences from Iowa. She gave him a slight nod and hooked her thumbs in her panties.

"No!" Kevin shouted, hurling himself toward Rick.

The shot deafened her ears. She couldn't hear her own screams as Kevin fell face down to the floor, blood quickly soaking his right shoulder. She dropped to her knees beside him, ignoring Rick's shouts to stay away from him.

She grabbed her blouse from the floor to stanch his wound and only then noticed that her thighs were blood-splattered.

"Get back up, bitch," Rick yelled at the top of his lungs. "Or I'll kill you, too."

Nadja tried to focus on him. His gun weaved back and forth. He was going to kill her anyway. What difference did a few minutes make? She fell across Kevin's back, shielding him. She sobbed into his hair.

Shouts penetrated her daze.

"Drop the gun! Police!"

She looked up in time to see Rick spin around and direct his gun at Detective Jarvis and Amy, who crouched on either side of the door between her shop and Ivett's.

Shots rang out nearly in unison, and Nadja gagged as more blood flew in her direction. Only this time it wasn't Kevin's. It was Rick's. He collapsed in a heap only feet away from her. Nadja clamped her hands over her ears, but the shots continued to reverberate through her head.

Detective Jarvis cautiously approached Rick, and Amy ran to where Nadja knelt over Kevin. Amy took over trying to stanch the flow of Kevin's blood, while Nadja rocked back on her heels and stared, wide-eyed.

It was over.

She looked at the inert form of her lover. It couldn't be over. She wanted to wail, but the bile in her throat made sound impossible.

Detective Jarvis knelt beside her and offered her one of the gunny sacks that had so recently hung on the Cappuccino wall. "Use this to cover up. A backup team and ambulance are right behind us. We called them before we entered the building."

The detective glanced at Amy. "I'll call for another ambulance for Rick. They won't have to hurry. Where he's going, ambulances are of little help."

Amy nodded. "He didn't give us a choice."

The detective shrugged. "Sounds like he never was into giving women choices."

Hunkered down on a squishy hospital chair, Nadja clutched Kevin's hand. She rubbed its back and caressed his fingers. Numbed by the patter of machines monitoring the essence of life, she did her best to will life back into Kevin's flesh.

The doctor had told her it might be some time before he

awakened, but given the ordeal they'd been through, it might help Kevin when he awoke to see her and know that she'd survived. He'd also said Kevin would likely move in and out of consciousness and not to be frightened if his speech was impeded by the tubes.

She tugged at the jacket Steve had loaned her before he and Ivett had gone home. Amy had been determined to wait for her in the lounge. Nadja had reluctantly agreed to the plan Amy and Ivett had concocted. Amy would go home with Nadja when she was ready and stay in a spare bedroom.

Nadja squeezed her eyes tight. She hadn't resisted very hard. She did want to go back to the house long enough for a shower and a change of clothes. And Amy had a car.

She appreciated that Amy understood she needed to be alone with Kevin. She sighed. The Cappuccino would survive. She tried to blink away the memory of Rick lying in a pool of blood on her shop floor. Would she ever go into her store again without that image hovering over her?

She opened one eye and gave Kevin a twisted smile. Now it was just the two of them. She was ready to get on with the rest of their lives. She believed he was, too. The doctor had said he'd heal completely. Fortunately, he'd taken the bullet in the right shoulder, where there were no critical organs.

She shuddered. He'd been trying to save her life—but then, she'd been prepared to use her body to save his. She whimpered. And where did that leave them?

She lowered her eyelids. She drifted. Then she popped her eyes open. She couldn't have dozed for more than a moment or two. Kevin was studying her through partially open eyes. A tiny smile crossed his lips when he saw her awaken.

"Hi," she said softly. "I can't tell you how sweet it is to see you awake."

"Hi," he mouthed. His fingers grazed hers.

She fought back tears. There was no reason to cry any

more. "You're going to be fine," she assured him. "The bullet didn't hit anything vital."

His lips formed a single word with no sound: *you?*

"I'm fine. Really. I'll be better when you can come home with me."

His grin widened slightly.

She read his lips: *Rick?* She shook her head. "Dead." How soon after his injury had Kevin slipped into unconsciousness? "Amy and Detective Jarvis shot him shortly after he shot you."

Kevin's brow furrowed into a question.

"He never had a chance to touch me."

Kevin visibly relaxed, and Nadja continued. "You were a fool to try to take down a man holding a gun."

He tilted his head slightly and gave her a fierce look.

"Maybe I was a fool for provoking him. But together we bought enough time. That's all that matters now."

She watched his eyelids close. Was he drifting back to sleep? "You'll need to get all the rest you can. I'll go home and shower and come back later." She squeezed his fingers. "I want you well soon. I want us to make a baby."

His eyes shot wide open. The look of horror on his face shattered whatever fantasy about them she'd been holding onto. She wet her lips and didn't try to hold back the warm tears. "I see," she mumbled. "I'm sorry I said that."

His fingernails dug into her palm, but she removed his hand from hers and stood. "I'll check with Amy. We'll notify your son and ex-wife. I don't know how long the doctors expect you to be in the hospital." She sniffled. "Perhaps they can have you transferred to a hospital in St. Paul." She ignored his widening eyes. "Bye. I loved you."

After she'd showered the following morning and changed into fresh clothes, Nadja made her way downstairs to the kitchen, where Amy sat with two coffee mugs.

"Sit," the redhead ordered. "You've hardly said a word since we left the hospital last night. I've dug up a number for Kevin's ex. I figured you'd want to make the call."

Nadja shook her head and looked away from Amy's steady gaze. Would Amy leave if she asked her to? She just wanted to be alone, to drown in her sorrow. She didn't need comfort, she didn't need to be rescued, and she surely didn't need to talk with Kevin's ex-wife or his son.

Danny. She'd never see him again, either. Life could be grossly unfair.

"Something happened in that hospital room between you and Kevin."

Nadja glowered at Amy, but the woman didn't flinch.

"Given how elated you were about waiting for him to awake, I'm going to take a wild guess that you've learned about Kevin's greatest fear — having more children."

"He didn't have to tell me. He couldn't speak. He was horrified when I mentioned making a baby." Nadja held herself together with tiny threads. "That's okay. Better to find out now than later. We had some good times."

"Good times, shit. The two of you are madly in love, and one of you had better do something about that before it's too late."

Nadja scowled, wrapped her fingers around her coffee mug, and did her best to ignore the woman.

"Has Kevin ever talked to you about Danny's birth?"

Nadja shook her head and wished she could as easily close her ears. "Danny?" she murmured.

"He almost didn't make it."

Nadja gasped and blinked. "Kevin never said . . ."

"It's not something he likes talking about. The baby's heartbeat was irregular. And Kevin's wife's kidneys were shutting down. They told him to call his pastor if he had one.

It looked like they weren't going to be able to save both mother and child. Within an hour of having to decide whether to save the child or the mother, somehow her kidneys began working. Shortly thereafter, he held his son in his arms. If you can get him to talk about it, he'll tell you that was the worst and best day of his life."

"But their marriage didn't survive."

Amy shook her head. "No, their marriage was on shaky ground before the birth. Both Elizabeth and Kevin worked at keeping it together, and then it was over. I don't know anything more about that. Here is her number if you want to call her."

Amy stood. "I'm going to go back to my hotel. Looks like you have a lot to sort through." She smiled wanly. "You shouldn't have to deal with more than one ex at a time."

Nadja rose and accepted Amy's hug. "Thank you," she mumbled. "For telling me. And for being there — at the shop." She leaned back and wiped tears from her eyes. "I would like to know how you managed to be there when we needed you most."

"I was wondering if you'd ever ask. I'd been pretty much tailing you since the fire. Anna was putting in extra hours to help keep track of Rick. We converged on Ivett's store about five minutes after Rick entered."

Nadja's cheeks warmed. "How long were you in the store?"

"Ten minutes, maybe fifteen. We didn't want to do anything to set Rick off. We were waiting for him to get distracted enough by your gutsy little strip show so we could make a move. Unfortunately, Kevin was one step ahead of us."

They stepped into her entryway, and Amy turned to face her. With a wry smile, she said, "Good luck with Kevin." She stood on her tiptoes and brushed her lips across Nadja's cheek. "Bye."

When she entered Kevin's hospital room that afternoon, Nadja had given up on guarding her heart or her pride. But she wouldn't let him slide out of her life like some sneaky weasel. They'd talk about children. Then he could run from her if he had to. She could live with that. But they'd talk first.

She smiled to herself at the sight of him propped up against a couple pillows. The tubes were out of his throat, but he still had an IV attached. He was her captive audience. She couldn't ask for more than that. Yet.

"You're back," he said, his voice rasping.

"I'm back. According to a mutual friend, we have some more business to talk about. Babies."

He shut his eyes and opened them quickly, as if she might leave before he could defend himself. "Sounds like you've been talking to Amy."

"Listening, actually. Something I expect you to do until I've said my piece."

"But . . ."

She held up her palm to keep him quiet. "I was very sorry to hear about the agony you and Danny's mother went through at his birth. And I know it was harrowing for you when Danny had his bicycle accident."

She took a deep breath, a little surprised he wasn't trying to take advantage of this brief pause; but he lay still, providing not a single clue of what he might be thinking. "That's part of who you are. It's not my experience in the same way as it is yours. Just as I've had some harrowing experiences that you can only listen to."

She blinked a couple times. "You've helped me overcome some of my worst fears. You've helped me learn that I have to move on from my past. Not to do that allows the pain to wear us down over time. Don't you see? If I hadn't found ways to be open to you, to enjoy having sex with you, then that coach would've still controlled me after all these years."

She did the best she could to hold back the tears that wanted to flow. "I love you. I've never loved another man. I think you love me. But I do want to at least try to have children. That desire is as much a part of me as my blood and my heartbeat. I can't deny that. I won't deny it.

"I love Danny already, and I believe that together, you and I could make some incredible kids, and that our love will carry us through the tragedies as well as the joys. And there would be both. But I won't walk away from joy for fear of tragedy. Maybe you will."

Her chatter came to an abrupt halt as she struggled for breath.

"Are you quite finished?" Kevin asked, reaching for her fingers.

She nodded.

"Yes, I love you very, very much." His eyebrows shot upwards. "You caught me at a disadvantage last night. I couldn't exactly speak. And I'm sorry you saw my initial shock about making a baby."

"In my culture," she sniffled, "there's no greater way for a woman to tell a man she loves him."

"Ssh, woman. Let me speak. Nadja, I've spent most of the time since you left thinking about many of the same things you just spoke about. Hell, we just survived a maniac who wanted to kill us both. I doubt there's anything that life can deal us that we won't be able to survive. I know there are no guarantees. Believe me, I do know that."

Nadja swiped at tears until she could see his easy smile. "What are you saying?"

"I'm saying that I want to make babies with you."

"Oh my." She clutched the sapphire he'd given her in one palm and gripped his fingers with the other. Her heart raced wildly. She straightened and squared her shoulders. "In my country, a couple is expected to be married before they try to make babies."

"That's a custom I'm familiar with." He winked at her. "What day of the week is it?"

"Wednesday."

"Do you have plans for Saturday?"

She frowned. "Probably more cleaning at the Cappuccino."

He shook his head. "I was thinking of something a little more celebrative than that. How about a wedding?"

Her mouth fell open.

"You and me."

"That quick?" she squealed.

"They're going to release me in the morning. Figured I'll be ready to start making babies by Saturday night. Of course, if you don't want to . . ."

"No, no." She laughed and bobbed her head. "Saturday will work fine. I never wanted a large wedding anyway. Oh, I didn't tell you. I'm meeting your ex-wife after work this evening halfway between here and the Cities to pick up Danny."

"Super. He can be part of the wedding." Kevin frowned, apparently having second thoughts. "But what do we do with him for the honeymoon?"

Nadja smiled broadly. "We don't have to go away for a honeymoon. We'll have a lifetime for that. Danny can stay with us and help us build a new gazebo."

"Oh, I like how you think. I do love you, Nadja. I hope that's not a secret."

She nodded and leaned over to graze his bruised lips. "It's not. Thankfully. And I love you so very much."

"We're going to make this work."

"Of course we will."

"And I'm really looking forward to making babies with you."

His hand slipped inside her blouse and covered a breast. She inhaled deeply and then removed his hand. Straightening, she shook her head. "Not till Saturday night. There's so much to do before then."

"I trust you'll be ready by Saturday night."

"I know I will." She batted her eyelashes. "Get your rest, husband-to-be. You're going to need all the strength you can muster once nurse Nadja takes over your healing."

The End

ABOUT THE AUTHOR

When it's Time to Heat Things Up: Award winning author Adriana Kraft is a married couple writing Sizzling Romantic Suspense and Erotic Romance for Two, Three, or More. Whether readers open our romantic suspense or our erotic romance, they can expect characters they care about, hot sex scenes, and a compelling story. Our suspense stories deliver one man, one woman, danger and intrigue. Our erotic romance is edgier and nearly always includes ménage or polyamory, sometimes with two women and a man, sometimes with two (or more) couples. We write our Erotic Romance stories to entertain, of course, but most of all we write them because we believe in happy endings for all who fall in love, whatever their gender, sexual orientation or numerical combination.

www.ingramcontent.com/pod-product-compliance
Lightning Source LLC
Chambersburg PA
CBHW061548170626
46811CB00001B/131